AN OBJECT OF
BEAUTY

Also by Steve Martin

NOVELS
The Pleasure of My Company
Shopgirl

PLAYS
Picasso at the Lapin Agile
WASP

NONFICTION
Born Standing Up
Pure Drivel
Cruel Shoes

SCREENPLAYS
Shopgirl
Bowfinger
L.A. Story
Roxanne
The Jerk (coauthor)

AN OBJECT OF BEAUTY

A Novel

STEVE MARTIN

GRAND CENTRAL
PUBLISHING

NEW YORK   BOSTON

Grand Central Publishing
Hachette Book Group
237 Park Avenue
New York, NY 10017

www.HachetteBookGroup.com

Printed in the United States of America

First Edition: November 2010
10 9 8 7 6 5 4 3 2 1

Grand Central Publishing is a division of Hachette Book Group, Inc.
The Grand Central Publishing name and logo is a trademark of Hachette Book Group, Inc.

Library of Congress Cataloging-in-Publication Data
Martin, Steve, 1945–
An object of beauty / Steve Martin.—1st ed.
p. cm.
Summary: "Steve Martin's latest novel examines the glamour and the subterfuge of the fine art world in New York City"—Provided by publisher.
ISBN 978-0-446-57364-1 (regular ed.)—ISBN 978-0-446-57374-0 (large print ed.) 1. Art—New York (State)—New York—Fiction. 2. Art auctions—Fiction. 3. New York (N.Y.)—Social life and customs—Fiction. I. Title.
PS3563.A7293O35 2010
813'.54—dc22
2010007885

AN OBJECT OF
BEAUTY

PART

I

1.

I AM TIRED, so very tired of thinking about Lacey Yeager, yet I worry that unless I write her story down, and see it bound and tidy on my bookshelf, I will be unable to ever write about anything else.

My last name is Franks. Once, in college, Lacey grabbed my wallet and read my driver's license aloud, discovering that my forenames are Daniel Chester French, after the sculptor who created the Abraham Lincoln memorial. I am from Stockbridge, Massachusetts, where Daniel Chester French lived and worked, and my parents, being parochial Americans, didn't realize that the name Daniel Chester French Franks read funny. Lacey told me she was related to the arts by blood, too, but declined to tell me the full story, saying, "Too long. Later I'll tell you, French Fries." We were twenty.

I left Stockbridge, a town set under the glow of its even more famous citizen, the painter of glad America, Norman Rockwell. It is a town that is comfortable with art, although uncomplicated art, not the kind that is taught in educational institutions after high school. My goal, once I discovered that my artistic aspirations were not accompanied by artistic talent, was to learn to write about art with effortless clarity. This is not as easy as it sounds: whenever I attempted it, I found myself in a convoluted rhetorical tangle from which there was no exit.

After high school, I went south to Davidson College in North

Carolina, while Lacey drove north from Atlanta, and there, Lacey and I studied art history and had sex together exactly once.

Even at the age of twenty, Lacey's entry into the classroom had the pizzazz of a Broadway star. Our eyes followed her down the aisle, where she would settle into her seat with a practiced hair-flip. When she left a room, there was a moment of deflation while we all returned to normal life. It was apparent to everyone that Lacey was headed somewhere, though her path often left blood in the water.

If one of her girlfriends was in a crisis, Lacey would rush in, offering tidal waves of concern. She could soothe or incite in the name of support: "Honey, get over it," or, conversely, "Honey, get even." Either bit of advice was inspiring. The emotions of men, however, were of a different order. They were pesky annoyances, small dust devils at her feet. Her knack for causing heartbreak was innate, but her vitality often made people forgive her romantic misdeeds. Now, however, she is nearing forty and not so easily forgiven as when her skin bloomed like roses.

I slept with her in our second year. I was on the rebound and managed to avoid devastation by reconnecting with my girlfriend days—or was it hours—later, and Lacey's tentacles never had time to attach. But her sense of fun enchanted me, and once I had sufficiently armored myself against her allure by viewing her as a science project, I was able to enjoy the best parts of her without becoming ensnared.

I will tell you her story from my own recollections, from conversations I conducted with those around her, and, alas, from gossip: thank God the page is not a courtroom. If you occasionally wonder how I know about some of the events I describe in this book, I don't. I have found that—just as in real life—imagination sometimes has to stand in for experience.

2.

LACEY'S LIFE AND MINE have paralleled each other for a long while. When we were twenty-three, our interest in art as a profession landed us both in New York City at a time when the art world was building offshore like a developing hurricane. Our periodic lunches caught me up with her exploits. Sometimes she showed up at a Manhattan café with a new boyfriend who was required to tolerate my unexplained presence, and when she excused herself to the restroom, the boyfriend and I would struggle for conversation while he tried to discover if I was an ex-lover, as he soon would be.

In August 1993, she showed up at one of these lunches in a summer dress so transparent that when she passed between me and a bay window hot with sunlight, the dress seemed to incinerate like flash paper. Her hair was clipped back with a polka-dot plastic barrette, which knocked about five years off her age.

"Ask me where I was," she said.

"And if I don't?"

She made a small fist and held it near my face. "Then socko."

"Okay," I said. "Where were you?"

"At the Guggenheim. A furniture show."

The Guggenheim Museum is Frank Lloyd Wright's questionable masterpiece that corkscrews into Fifth Avenue. Questionable because it forces every viewer to stand at a slant.

" 'The Italian Metamorphosis,' " I said. "I wrote about it. Too late to get into a magazine. What did you think?"

"I'd rather fuck an Italian than sit on his furniture," she said.

"You didn't like it?"

"I guess I was unclear. No."

"How come?"

"Taste?" she said, then added, "Only one thing could have made it better."

"What's that?"

"Roller skates."

Lacey talked on, oblivious to the salivations that her dress was causing. She had to know of its effect, but it was as though she'd put it on in the morning, calculated what it would do, then forgot about it as it cast its spell. Her eyes and attention never strayed from me, which was part of her style.

Lacey made men feel that she was interested only in that special, unique conflation of DNA that was *you*, and that at any moment she was, just because *you* were so fascinating, going to sleep with *you*. She would even take time to let one of your jokes sweep over her, as though she needed a moment to absorb its brilliance, then laugh with her face falling forward and give you a look of quizzical admiration, as if to say, "You are much more complicated and interesting than I ever supposed."

"Come with me," she said after coffee.

"Where to?"

"I'm buying a dress. I'm interviewing at Sotheby's tomorrow and I have to look like a class act."

The New York heat baked us till we found the inside of a moderately cooler downtown dress shop that featured recycled class-act clothing. Music blared as Lacey zeroed in on a dark blue tight skirt and matching jacket. She winced at the price, but it did not deter her. She pulled the

6

curtain of the changing room, and I could hear the rustle of clothes. I pictured the skirt being pulled on and zipped up. She emerged wearing the jacket loosely opened, with nothing on underneath—which created a sideways cleavage—and started buttoning it up in front of the mirror, surveying herself. "I've got a blouse at home I can wear with this," she muttered to me. She straightened up and pulled the barrette from her hair, causing the blond mix of yellows and browns to fall to her shoulders, and she instantly matured.

"They're going to love you," I said.

"They goddamn better because I'm broke. I'm down to seven thousand."

"Last week you said you had three thousand."

"Well, if I've got three, I'm fucked. So let's call it seven."

Lacey turned from the mirror for the first time and struck a pose in the preowned Donna Karan.

"You look great. A lot of people our age don't know how to go in and apply for a job," I said.

Lacey stared at me and said, "I don't go in and apply for a job. I go in and *get* a job."

And so Lacey joined the spice rack of girls at Sotheby's.

Sotheby's and Christie's, the two premier auction houses in New York, drew young, crisp talent from Harvard and its look-alikes. Majors in art history were welcomed over majors in art making, and pretty was preferred in either sex. The houses wanted the staff to look swell as they crisscrossed the busy galleries on exhibition days, holding in their arms files, faxes, and transparencies. Because the pay was low, the young staff was generally financed from home. Parents thought well of it because their children were at respectable firms, working in a glamorous business, with money of all nations charging the atmosphere. The auction houses seemed not as dull as their financial counterparts on Wall Street, where parents of daughters imagined glass ceilings and bottom patting.

Sotheby's was an institution that implied European accents and grand thoughts about art and aesthetics coexisting with old and new money in sharp suits and silk ties. This was a fresh and clean New York, where you dressed nicely every day and worked in a soaring, smoke-free, drug-less architectural building filled with busts, bronzes, and billionaires. What the parents forgot about were the weekends and evenings when their children left the Cézannes and Matisses and crept underground, traveling back to shared downtown spaces where they did exactly the same things they would have done if they had joined a rock band.

Lacey's first assignment was in the bins, cataloging and measuring nineteenth-century pictures in a dim basement that was largely unpopulated. Her Donna Karan was wasted on the shippers and craters, but she kept her wardrobe keen for her occasional pop-ups to the fourth-floor offices. An ivy-embraced college may have been her education in the high ground of art, but Sotheby's basement was her education in the fundamentals. She hoisted pictures onto a carpet-covered table, stretched her tape measure over their backs, and wrote down everything she could. She flipped them over and noted signatures and monograms, trying to decipher artists' illegible scrawls, and she scratched around in the cumbersome reference dictionaries, Myers and Benezit, to find listings of obscure artists so she could report a successful attribution to her superiors. During her first year, she saw the fronts and backs of thousands of paintings. She learned to precisely tap a painting with the back of her finger: a hard, stiff canvas indicated the picture had been relined, usually a warning sign about a painting's poor condition. She was taught to identify varnished prints that were trying to pass themselves off as paintings—a magnifying glass would reveal printer's dots (to the disappointment of excited sellers who believed they owned an original). She learned to distinguish etchings from lithographs by raking the print in a hard light, looking for telling shadows in the groove of the etched line.

The paintings in the basement were generally dogs; the finer works remained upstairs, hung over a director's desk or in a private room until their grand display in one of the large galleries. The masterpieces were examined by conservators bearing loupes and black lights, while Lacey toiled downstairs in the antique dust like Sneezy the Dwarf. The subject matter she faced every day was not the apples of Cézanne, but the kitsch of the nineteenth century: monks tippling, waifs selling flowers, cardinals laughing, cows in landscapes, Venetian gondoliers, baby chicks in farmyards, mischievous shoeshine boys, and still lifes painted so badly that objects seemed to levitate over the tabletop on which they were supposed to be gravitationally attached. On her rare visits upstairs, she found serenity in the sight of the occasional Seurat or Monet and, sometimes, Rembrandt. However, through the drudgery downstairs, Lacey was developing an instinct that would burrow inside her and stay forever: a capacity to know a good painting from a bad one.

Her walk-on role at Sotheby's stood in contrast with her starring role in the East Village bars and cafés. After her practiced and perfected subway ride home, which was timed like a ballet—her foot forward, the subway car doors opening just in time to catch her—she knew the bar lights were coming on, voices were raised, music edging out onto the sidewalks. She felt like the one bright light, the spotlit girl scattering fairy dust, as she walked the few blocks to her walk-up. Once inside, she slumped sideways on her bed, cocked the phone against her head, and sipped Scotch while she phoned Angela or Sharon, or sometimes, me.

"Hey…God, I miss you! Where are you? Meet me at Raku for sushi. Goddamn it! Sorry, I sloshed Scotch on me. Meet me now… No, *now.*"

Raku was the mystery restaurant of the Lower East Side. Large portions, low prices, and never more than four customers no matter what time of the day it was. Tables waited for Lacey like kennel puppies hoping to be picked. She rolled in at seven p.m. and sat down in solitude.

Lacey was just as happy alone as with company. When she was alone, she was potential; with others she was realized. Alone, she was self-contained, her tightly spinning magnetic energy oscillating around her. When in company, she had invisible tethers to everyone in the room: as they moved away, she pulled them in. She knew who was doing better than she was, what man she would care to seduce just to prove she could. She was a naval commander knowing the location of all her boats.

The East Village mixed the fast life with the slow life, and the two were sometimes indistinguishable. Actors huddled and chatted in crappy bars, while old-timers to whom the neon beer sign was not a kitschy collectible but simply a neon beer sign sat on stools and remained unaware that they would be, this year or next, pushed out of the increasingly younger neighborhood. Sometimes the newer crowd would clumsily light up cigarettes, and Lacey occasionally joined them.

The contemporary art scene was the left bank suburb to Lacey's right bank, uptown art world. Her connection to it was the numerous young hyphenates that would drift across the barroom floors: artist–house painter, artist–art mover, artist-musician. One of her favorites, Jonah Marsh, had a rarer label, artist-deejay. He could be a good artist but made paintings that no matter how much he changed them or developed them still looked derivative of someone better. However, as a deejay, he was very, very cute. One night at a bar, he was circling around Lacey, trying to appear smart, funny, impetuous, raucous, pathetic, anything to get her in bed, that night, now. Lacey, giving in, said to him, "Look, I just want to get off." They went to her place and afterward he conveniently said, "I have to get up early," and left, to Lacey's relief.

3.

ONE TUESDAY, near starvation caused Lacey to finally splurge in the Sotheby's lunchroom, a smartly done, packaged-sandwich place with Formica tables and uptown prices. Here, the staff mingled with the department heads and Lacey could easily discern one class from the other based on thread count. The department heads were usually less alluring than the staff, since they were hired on expertise, not glamour, and they were usually less haggard than the tireless employees who were sent running from floor to floor. At one table was Cherry Finch, head of American Paintings, while at another was Heath Acosta, head of European Paintings and natty in a gray suit and tie, sitting with an obvious client. Obvious because of his black hair that hung in short ringlets and was laden with *product*. His Mediterranean skin and open silk shirt said clearly that he was not an employee. He was mid-thirties, foreign, and handsome enough that Lacey's inner critic did not object to his playboy rags.

With regularity, the client's eyes strayed to Lacey. Lacey ate more and more slowly, trying to stop the clock before she had no further excuse to stay. Eventually, when their check was paid, Acosta and the client made a deliberate move to her table.

"Hello, I've seen you, but we haven't met. I'm Heath Acosta, from European Paintings."

"Well then, you're like everyone in the company: my superior. I'm Lacey Yeager. I work down in Hades."

"Ah, the bins."

"Hence my lack of tan."

The client lurched in: "Better than leather skin at forty. Hello, I'm Patrice Claire." His face was a bottle bronze, and his French accent surprised Lacey; she was expecting Middle Eastern. "Do you enjoy European painting?"

"I'm sure I will one day," Lacey said.

"Maybe you haven't seen the right ones," said Patrice. Then to Acosta, "It's unfair that you separate the Impressionists into their own group. Aren't they Europeans?"

Acosta replied, "Impressionists aren't tidy enough for our European collectors."

"Well then, they wouldn't like me, either," said Lacey. Patrice's face signaled the opposite.

"Have you been to an auction yet?" said Acosta.

"I didn't know if I was allowed . . ."

"Come to the European sale next week," he said. "Ten a.m. Thursday. We can excuse you from Hades that day."

"Do I need to get there early for a seat?" said Lacey.

"Heavens, no, not for European. The recession has seen to that."

Acosta turned to go, and Patrice added, "Be sure not to cough, sneeze, or scratch."

She had no doubt that the visit to the table was at Patrice's request, to make contact and take a closer look. Lacey gave him a look back that said she was fuckable, but not without a bit of work.

4.

THURSDAY MORNING, Lacey slipped into one of the folding chairs at the European sale. The hall was half-full, and the rumored excitement of a live auction was belied with every tired raise of a paddle, followed by bidders' early exits. The art market had collapsed a few years ago and was still sputtering. By 1990 the boom had withered, but before that date, carloads of inferior French paintings had been sold to the Japanese and then hurriedly crated and shipped overseas before the buyers realized that perhaps their eye for Impressionism had not been fully developed. Sotheby's, Christie's, and dealers along Madison Avenue had found a repository for their second- and third-best pictures, and they all feared the moment when the Japanese would decide to sell the gray Pissarros and the fluffy, puffy Renoirs—proudly hung in Japanese department stores to impress their customers—and recognize that they had been had. Thankfully, an art market crash gave the dealers an excuse to avoid urgent pleas for buybacks when the Japanese would discover just how bad were the pictures they had been sold: "Oh, the economy has just collapsed!"

Lacey watched the auction unfold and wondered how people could afford twenty thousand dollars to buy a sketch by an unfamiliar Spaniard with three names. She watched Heath Acosta on the sideline, beaming, but she couldn't figure out what he was beaming about. Every other picture remained unsold. He was probably trying to put a brave face on the crashing sale. She watched as pictures she had grown fond of downstairs stiffed in front of the sullen crowd, meaning they would be returned downstairs, where they would wait for their disappointed owners to claim them.

Next up was James Jacques Joseph Tissot's picture of a theater lobby filling up just after the curtain call. Men in opera hats steer their young femmes toward the exit; the women wear lavish dresses, sport hats that cost as much as carriages, and swim under billows of fur. Tissot was the master of a small subject—the rich—and he swathed the women in yards of fabric and painted them midflounce as they

La Mondaine, James Tissot, 1883–1885
58.3 × 40.5 in.

disembarked from boats, lounged in parks, or sat on window seats overlooking the sea.

The estimate on the Tissot was five hundred thousand to seven hundred thousand. There was a small stir when the rotating display brought it into view; it looked good. If it stalled, it would be hard for Acosta to maintain his plastered beam. The picture started off at three hundred fifty thousand, and no paddles were raised. Acosta seemed unfazed. He scanned the room, then nodded, and the auctioneer called out, "I have three hundred fifty thousand." Soon, four hundred thousand. Then, four hundred fifty thousand. Then the auctioneer took a leap: no more fifty-thousand-dollar increments. Six hundred thousand. Seven hundred thousand. The picture crossed a million, then a million five, and then once again in fifty-thousand-dollar increments, finally selling at two million dollars.

Was this a one-off, or was the art recession loosening? Was Acosta smiling because he had known of secret bids aimed at the Tissot? Auctioneers often knew in advance what someone was willing to bid. Lacey noticed that as the pace of the bids picked up, she felt a concomitant quickening of her pulse, as though she had been incised by an aphrodisiacal ray.

That evening she called Jonah Marsh, the cute deejay, and met him late night at MoMA. They walked around and looked at paintings until she had recharged the morning's ardor, finally taking him home with her. After sexual due process—an outbreak of inhibition, contortion, flying words, and sweat with fair exchanges on both sides—Jonah groggily left, again relieving Lacey of the burden of postcoital chat. She sipped port and stared out her window, a window still grimy with the residue of winter, and relived the auction earlier that day. One million, one million five…two million. Someone had just cashed in grandly, unexpectedly. It made her wonder: Could she make money in art, Tissot money?

At Sotheby's, she started to look at paintings differently. She became an efficient computer of values. The endless stream of pictures that passed through the auction house helped her develop a calculus of worth. Auction records were available in the Sotheby's library, and when a picture of note came in, she diligently searched the Art Price Index to see if it had auction history. She factored in condition, size, and subject matter. A Renoir of a young girl, she had witnessed, was worth more than one of an old woman. An American western picture with five tepees was worth more than a painting with one tepee. If a picture had been on the market recently without a sale, she knew it would be less desirable. A deserted painting scared buyers. Why did no one want it? In the trade, it was known as being "burned." Once a picture was burned, the owner had to either drastically reduce the price or sit on it for another seven years until it faded from memory. When Lacey began these computations, her toe crossed ground from which it is difficult to return: she started converting objects of beauty into objects of value.

5.

LACEY KNEW I was coming uptown and insisted I stop by Sotheby's for lunch. She had something to show me, she said. I met her at the Sotheby's sandwich bar, and we snagged a sunny corner table.

"Do you want to see a picture of my grandmother?" asked Lacey.

"Is this a trick question?" I said.

She reached into her wide-mouth purse and withdrew a very used art book covered with library acetate and bearing a small, rectangular label with what looked like a Dewey Decimal System number and a second label that clearly, seriously said, "Property of Sotheby's." She handled the book so freely in the lunchroom that I knew it had been legitimately checked out of the library and did not represent a heist.

"Remember when I told you I was related to the arts?"

"Well, no, but go on."

"My grandmother is Kitty Owen."

Lacey laid the book on the table and spun its face toward me. On the cover was a painting by Maxfield Parrish. I knew a bit about him. In the twenties, he was America's most famous artist. His pictures featured young girls lounging by lakes or sitting naked on tree swings in fanciful arcadias. These delicately painted pictures also sold tires and magazines. Logos were emblazoned across reproductions on calendars and posters, sometimes painted into the work itself. Parrish hovered between being an illustrator and an artist.

Daybreak, Maxfield Parrish, 1922
26.5 × 45.5 in.

Lacey poked her finger down on the cover.

"That's my grandmother," she said. "She was eighteen when she took off all her clothes for him and posed. See, you're not the only one with wise-ass art credentials."

"Is she..." Alive, I was going to say.

"She's ninety-two. She still has that skin, but the red hair is phfft." I looked at the slender, pale girl on the cover of the book, who looked like a faun standing over an idyllic pool trimmed in iridescent tiles.

"She owns a print with her in it. He gave it to her. I checked the Sotheby's records to see how much it was worth. Not much. Two hundred bucks. It's our only artistic heirloom. It's got a nice story with it.

"Kitty, Gram, had posed for a painting. She was nude, lying on a rock. Parrish had prints made. There was a stack of them on a table, and he told Kitty he wanted to give her something. Then he reached from behind the table and gave her one in a very expensive frame and under glass. Very special."

"You think there was...involvement?" I said.

"No, Parrish went for another model. He and his wife and the model lived happily/horribly ever after. The picture has hung in our house for as long as I can remember, and sometimes, when the house was empty, I would take off all my clothes and lie on the floor and look up at the picture, dreaming that I was like her, in the most beautiful forest, stretched long, arching up, and facing the twilight. I pretended that I was in heaven."

6.

A YEAR AND A HALF passed well. I had reviewed a small show for the *Village Voice* and received a complimentary note from Peter Schjeldahl, who was the main critic there at the time. Lacey was moving up at Sotheby's, literally. Frequent paperwork kept her upstairs, and she found that newcomers, mostly young white girls just off a collegiate slave boat, were being sent down the mine shaft to replace her, staggering out of the elevator hours later with dilated eyes, happy once again to see the sun. She was kept from a significant raise on the premise that new employees were really interns learning the business, and during one of our increasingly rare lunches, she told me this: "Guess what I figured out: Sotheby's is my yacht. *It's a money pit.* I'm losing money just to work there. I can last another year and then I'm headed for whore town, which could be kind of good, depending on the outfits."

Upstairs, information passed more freely. It came in overheard slices and tidbits, and in facial expressions, too. A sneer or sigh directed at a Picasso by one of the experts meant something, and she started to grasp why one Picasso warranted a snub while another one elicited awe. Her clothes meant more, too. Like a teen at Catholic school, she knew how to tweak the prescribed outfit with sultry modifications, the outline of her black bra under white silk, an embroidered cuff, an offbeat shoe. So, while fitting in, she was like a wicked detail standing out against a placid background.

In the glamorous world of the fourth floor, the artworks she had cataloged downstairs—the minor works of art by well-known names and the major works by unknown names—became like old high school friends: she had moved on, but they hadn't. Oh yes, she still liked them, but when two handlers with white gloves brought in a 1914 Schiele drawing of a nude and handled it like something precious and valuable, it made the basement seem like playschool. The special treatment it received made her look closer, too. After the conservative, unimaginative dabs downstairs, Schiele's daring teen nudes, contorted and imaginatively foreshortened, were shocking. These were not cows in a landscape. She imagined his boudoir in Vienna with its swinging door of stoned young girls spreading their legs while Schiele drew them in.

The fourth floor brought an annoyance into Lacey's life. Tanya Ross was one year older than Lacey, had been at her job a year longer than Lacey, and had already steamed ahead in her career at Sotheby's. She bustled around with confidence, and she always seemed to be in Lacey's view no matter how often Lacey twisted in her chair. She was taller than Lacey; she was prettier than Lacey: a deep brunette whose trademark was efficiency. This last quality made her perfect for dealing with serious clients who expected no nonsense. Certain dour customers asked for her by name, which gave Tanya a splendid position as an up-and-comer in the company.

Lacey had a keen eye for rivals, and at one of our lunches only a week after the elevator promotion, she pronounced Tanya an "up-talking Canadian. She touts Art History 101 like it's a PhD, but she also knows that cleavage works." I checkmarked this comment, since Lacey was capable of an equally manipulative display of cleavage at the right time, for the right person, for the right ends.

"Maybe you have to get to know her," I mistakenly said.

"There's nothing there to know," she rasped, and held up her fist as if to punch me. "They brought up a Picasso the other day, and I saw her look at the label on the back to find out who painted it. *She had to look at the label.* Plus she's financed. I think her last name is Wham-o or something. Tanya Wham-o. When someone less capable is ahead of me, I am *not pleased*. It makes me insane."

"Makes you insane? You already are," I said. Then, "What if someone more capable is ahead of you?"

"That's even worse," she said.

This being a cool spring, Lacey's clothes were less revealing than in the torrid summer, and she relied on fashion quirks to make up for the lost power. She buttoned up her blouse neck high, over which she had donned a child's sweater, a size large but still too small, which clung to her and rode up three inches above her waist. The food came.

"I'm thinking of getting a dog," she said.

"What kind?" I asked.

"One that's near death."

"Why?"

"Less of a commitment," she answered.

This was Saturday. Lacey would return to work and process a few midrange pictures that were being delivered. She liked the Saturday deliveries because they were special arrangements always brought in by clients, since the art handlers only worked weekdays. Sotheby's wasn't a pawnshop, so the sellers usually weren't desperate; they were just sellers. They might be a New Jersey couple who had heard about a successful sale of an artist they owned, or people with inherited pictures, or a young man helping his elderly relatives through the hoops of a Sotheby's contract. Pictures from Connecticut were generally overframed decorator concoctions surrounding dubiously attributed horse paintings. But pictures from New Jersey were usually the genuine article, purchased years ago from galleries or even from the artists themselves. The pictures typically bore ugly frames created by local framers who used gold paint rather than gold leaf or slathered them in a dull green or off-white substance reminiscent of caulk. One elderly couple hobbled in carting a small but sensational Milton Avery in a frame so ghastly that Cherry Finch looked at the painting with her fingers squared so as to screen it out. When Cherry told the couple the picture would be estimated at sixty to eighty thousand, the gentleman's phantom suspenders almost popped. They had paid three hundred dollars for it in 1946, the year it was painted, and the price was still stuck to the back.

Milton Avery was an isolated figure in American painting, not falling neatly into any category. He would reduce figures and landscapes to a few broad patches of color: a big swath of black would be the sea, a big swath of yellow would be the sand, a big swath of blue would be the sky, and that would be it. His pictures were always polite, but they were polite in the way that a man with a gun might be polite: there was plenty to back up his request for attention. Though his style changed only slightly during his career, he was not formulaic, indicated by the

Nude Bathers, Milton Avery, 1946
25.5 × 35.5 in.

existence of as many paintings that worked as ones that didn't. The painting that Cherry was looking at was one that did.

When the couple left, Cherry turned to Lacey and asked her what she thought the picture would bring. Lacey knew this was a test and decided to make a calculated but extravagant guess. She thought it might be better to have her guess remembered than forgotten. She considered the picture to be a small gem that could easily snare a strong bid, so she said, "Probably one hundred seventy thousand." Cherry smiled at the poor, innocent child.

Lacey ran down the interior escalators. The Avery couple were on their way out of the building when Lacey caught up with them. "Do you mind if we reframe the picture?" she asked. "It might help."

Not quite understanding why—it had been framed the same way for fifty years—they consented at Lacey's professional urgency.

She took the picture downstairs and measured it, knocked off early, and dropped by Lowy, the Upper East Side framer to the magnificent. She approached the woman at the desk: "Hello, I'm Lacey Yeager, I'm with Sotheby's. I'd like to talk about a frame for a Milton Avery."

Lacey's voice carried past the desk to the racks of luxurious samples, where velvet easels held pictures while corners of frames were laid over them. Customers stood back and imagined the other three-fourths of the frame. A man walked over to her. "Hello, I'm Larry Shar. How can I help you?"

"We have a Milton Avery that needs a frame. It's being auctioned in the next sale. Could something be done in that time?"

"Sure. Where's the picture?"

"Well, here's the situation. The couple who's selling it can't really afford a frame, so I was wondering if you could make a frame on spec. We could auction the picture stating that the frame is on loan from you. Whoever buys the picture would certainly want to purchase the frame. Your work is so good."

"We usually—"

"And if they don't buy the frame," Lacey added, "I will."

Larry said curiously, "What is your name?"

With that, Lacey knew he had consented.

7.

LACEY LIKED THE GAMBLE, and she flew home with other thoughts of how to ratchet up the picture's appeal. She had noticed after it had been pulled from the frame that the picture was brighter where it had been hidden under the liner. Maybe the owners were smokers or had hung the picture over a fireplace, where it had been layered with grime. Certainly the picture could be freshened. She had an idea that she could corner Tony, the conservator from downstairs, and persuade him to give it a light cleaning.

When she got home there was a message on her machine from Jonah Marsh: "Hey, want to do X tonight? I've got some."

Sure, Lacey thought, let's do X.

Jonah Marsh arrived at six p.m., minutes before dark. Lacey threw a maroon scarf over a lamp, reddening the room. Outside, the streets were wet from a sudden, cooling rain. Lights were coming on in windows across the street. Jonah produced the pills, displaying them in his hand like buttons. "Supposed to be excellent and very clean," he said.

Lacey poured two glasses of tap water and momentously swallowed a pill, then laid the other pill on Jonah's tongue, gave him the water, and kissed him as the pill was going down.

"You've done it before?" asked Jonah.

"Yes, once."

"What was it like?"

"I saw my goddess."

Huh? thought Jonah.

Minutes passed. He lay on her bed, and Lacey lay down next to him, not with romantic proximity, but at the polite distance of two travelers sharing a bed. The sex that Jonah had anticipated now seemed very distant to him. Lacey breathed deeply, and an eerie wave shimmied up her body. She gripped the bedspread beneath her and hung on until the unpleasantness passed. She comforted herself and had closed her eyes again, when, unexpectedly, a stronger, final flood of chemistry saturated her body from head to toe, placing her in its ecstatic grip. In this dream state, she saw her mother extending her hand toward her. Her mother led her through her childhood home, swung her on the backyard swing, held her close. She led her to the Maxfield Parrish, where she saw the silken girl that was her grandmother, whose luminosity Lacey had inherited, who was now in Atlanta, lying so ill in her bed. Lacey wondered whether her grandmother was looking backward over her life, finding her face reflected in one of Parrish's pools, or if she was in the present, staring into the face of death.

One hour had gone by. Jonah and Lacey were now suspended in an artificial nirvana. They loved their friends and understood their enemies. They loved their mothers and fathers, they loved the bed they were in and the street noise outside, they loved the person next to them. Jonah, in a low mutter addressed to himself, whispered, "Wow, wow," as though a revelation had just transformed him, a thought that he brought to himself in cupped hands after holding them under a fountain.

Nighttime had fully arrived, and Jonah slid the covers lower, to Lacey's waist, and looked at her without the cloud of sexual desire. She was a ceramic, her skin reflecting light, the ribs highlighted, the slope of her stomach shading into desert tan. His palm glided over her upper body, hovering like a hydroplane, a few fingers occasionally touching down. Lacey then sat up like a yogi, and Jonah did the same. Lacey pulled the curtains shut.

The drug made Jonah a perfect lover. Time was slower, making his normal masculine drive turn feminine, while Lacey's normal masculine overdrive downshifted into the pace of a luxurious Sunday outing.

"I love you," said Lacey. "I love you so much."

In the morning they stirred, relapsed into sleep, and were at last out of bed at eleven a.m. They moved like slugs around the apartment until Jonah pulled on his socks, his pants, and the fancy shirt that he'd thought he was going to need last night. He looked out the window and said, "Thank God it's gray. No sunglasses."

He told Lacey, "Last night, I saw a painting. Now I'm going to go home and paint it." It was a momentous night for each of them. The only problem was that when Lacey told Jonah she loved him, he believed her.

8.

I MET LACEY at the Cranberry Café near 10th Street on an unexpectedly blessed spring day, which appeared after a string of cold weekdays that blossomed into sudden glory on Saturday. Her conversation was full of spit and vinegar, and her complaints about one person would effortlessly weave themselves into praise for another person, so it wasn't as though she hated everybody. She gave me every detail of the Ecstasy trip, recounted all the complexities of her work life at Sotheby's, and even managed to inquire how I was doing. Having my torpid accounting of my last few months spill out in such proximity to Lacey's salacious and determined adventures made me feel all the more dull. I had just had a two-year relationship end because of boredom on both sides. Even the breakup was boring.

Lacey was anticipating the sale of the Milton Avery in a few weeks. She had focused on pumping it up to the exclusion of all other interests, including returning Jonah Marsh's forlorn phone calls. Lacey, I believe, liked to know that he was hanging on, that he was hers when she wanted him. She would occasionally leave him an affectionate message—crafted to be both enticing and distancing—when she guessed he wasn't home, just to keep the pot stirred.

Then Lacey leaned in, as though she were going to tell me a secret.

"I was in Atlanta last Sunday. It was so vivid when I saw my grandmother dying, I went."

"Is she lucid?" I asked.

"More than you, not as much as me," she said. "The Parrish print I told you about? It was across from her, and its presence was almost cruel. She's so withered, but the print is bright. I took it closer to Gram; she wanted to look at it. I looked at it, too." Then Lacey started to talk more excitedly. "Daniel, I've known that print all my life, but I..."

She paused, strangely, as though she were distracted by the implications of the next sentence. I could almost see her head bobbing along to the words like a bouncing-ball sing-along.

"But what?" I said.

She was silent. It was as though she were trying to retract what she had told me. Her mind was turning something over, then she looked up at me and stammered through the rest of the meal, as though she had an idea she needed to hang on to.

Outside, as we rambled around the East Village, Lacey would throw exaggerated looks to me as we passed the overweight, the underclothed, and a wandering family of tourists who looked as if they were at least forty blocks away from where they wanted to be. I laughed shamefully every time as Lacey parodied each sorrowful personality with a quick, exact facial expression.

Then I found myself participating in an unpleasant coincidence. We rounded a corner and Jonah Marsh was walking toward us. Spotting him, Lacey did an awful thing: she took my arm. Guessing that Jonah was probably dumped by Lacey, I instantly tried to look as nonthreatening, as nonromantic, as I could. But Lacey's bearing didn't change; she clung to my arm as though we had just gotten engaged.

Then, "Oh, Jonah! I've missed you!" she cried, and hugged him like a returning army husband. "How was your birthday? I'm sorry I couldn't come... This is my friend Daniel. Daniel is a great art writer. He should see your pictures."

"Hi," I said.

Jonah tried to let nothing show, though he may have lightened in color. He knew that Lacey was up for anything and that my hip-nerd look was something that she might go for.

"Jonah, are you doing anything now?" she asked.

I guessed that whatever Jonah might have been doing would be thrown aside if Lacey was implying anything from a tryst to a walk around the block.

"Not right now," he said.

Then Lacey turned to me. "Were you headed midtown?"

"Yes," I said.

"I think I'll stick around here, okay?"

"Sure," I said, and after one of those intense, show-off hugs from Lacey, I headed for the subway. I don't know what happened after that.

9.

BY MAY 1995, Lacey had become conversant with American painting up to 1945 (because that was where the auction catalogs stopped) and it was becoming her default specialty. Default because although she had a collegiate overview of art history, her heavy lifting had taken place in the Sotheby's sales department. She had learned to differentiate good pictures from bad ones, but because prices usually followed quality she was now learning the difference between good pictures and desirable pictures. What lifted a picture into the desirable category was a murky but parsable combination of factors. Paintings were collected not because they were pretty, but because of a winding path that leads a collector to his prey. Provenance, subject matter, rarity, and perfection made a painting not just a painting, but a prize. Lacey had seen the looks on the collectors' faces as they pondered various pictures. These objects, with cooperating input from the collector's mind, were transformed into things that healed. Collectors thought *this one artwork* would make everything right, would complete the jigsaw of their lives, would satisfy eternally. She understood that while a collector's courtship of a picture was ostensibly romantic, at its root was raw lust.

From her experience with men, she knew that lust made them controllable, and she wondered if this principle could be applied to the art business.

Unfortunately, the Avery was not a picture that would arouse lust.

It was a respectable girlfriend you would take home to Mom, without stopping first to have sex in the car. After Lacey had tweaked the picture in every way it could be tweaked, it hung in the galleries during the Sotheby's previews, wearing its new frame like a bridal gown. Lacey explained this change to Cherry Finch by simply saying, "I reframed it," as though this were the most natural thing in the world. Because this strategy had been used at Sotheby's before, Cherry assumed Lacey was implementing a standard practice, not, as Lacey believed, creating one. Lacey had connived to have the picture hung in the main gallery, near the star lot, a nearly perfect Homer watercolor of a trout squirming on a fishing line. She would pass by the picture during viewing hours to see who paused, who commented, who nodded. A particular couple, the Nathansons, had swung by the picture a few times and, quickly sizing her up as an employee, turned to Lacey, who had been eavesdropping.

"Do you know the condition of this picture?" they asked.

She was not supposed to answer floor questions, but she couldn't resist. "It's perfect," she said. "We gave it a light cleaning, that was all."

"Could we see it under a black light?"

"Certainly," dared Lacey. "Just a moment."

She dashed to the in-house phone and explained the situation to Cherry, overstating the haphazardness with which she happened to be gliding by. Because time spent with a painting created an interested buyer, Cherry was eager to have pictures flipped over, hefted, and examined. She told Lacey to bring the Avery to room 272, where a black light would be produced and Cherry, too, if she could make it.

Saul Nathanson—his suit was dapper, but his tie wasn't—leaned back and looked at the picture as it hung on a universal nail in the cramped viewing room. His wife, Estelle, her hair a bit too orange but otherwise just as turned out as Saul, stood by, commenting.

"We knew Milton," she said.

"Lovely guy," said Saul. "Do you mind?" he said, indicating he would like to take the picture off the wall. He held up the picture and looked closely at it.

"He likes to hold pictures. I say why do you have to hold them?"

"She's right," Saul said amiably, "I don't know what it means, but I do it."

"You do it a lot," said Estelle.

Saul grinned at Lacey. "See what I go through?" Then he turned his attention back to the painting. "Avery knew Rothko and Gottlieb. He may have influenced Rothko with his flat planes of color."

Cherry Finch, slightly harried, opened the door. Cherry knew the Nathansons, so Lacey figured they must be regular customers. Everyone milled around the picture, and Cherry explained that it had never been on the market, which made Saul nod, pleased.

"When's the sale?" asked Saul.

"Next Tuesday," Cherry said as they began to exit the room.

Lacey, reminding them of her presence, said, "It's a very beautiful picture, and a great year, 1946." Cherry glanced at Lacey.

After the Nathansons left, Cherry turned to Lacey. "Lacey, some advice: You don't have to sell paintings. All you have to do is put a good picture in front of a knowledgeable collector and stand back."

10.

AS THE WEEK WENT ON, the public viewing of the American pictures drew only light crowds. Tanya Ross was officially on the floor, but Lacey made detours across the gallery, whenever possible, to promote the Avery when Tanya might lapse. Tanya—her back turned—was on the far side of the floor when Lacey came upon an unlikely customer, a young man, Jamaican, perhaps, his head circled in a scarf with sun-bleached dreadlocks piled on top, looking like a plate of soft-shell crabs. He was paused in front of the Avery.

"If you have any questions…," Lacey began.

The young man turned. "Who's this?"

Sensing this was not a knowledgeable collector, Lacey went through her pitch: "American Modernist…America's Matisse," she spouted, and then threw in her latest slogan: "Deeply influenced Rothko." Through Lacey's compromised history, Avery now "had deeply" influenced Rothko rather than "may have." The man didn't have the savvy of the Nathansons, but there was still an aura of money about him.

"Do you have a card?" he asked.

Lacey said she was out but told him: "You can reach me here, I'm Lacey Yeager."

The man wandered away, looking puzzled as he surveyed other pictures in the gallery. It was then that Lacey realized he was not a customer, and she had a dim visual recall: he had followed her in from the subway and had just wangled her name and phone number.

When she arrived at the office floor, there was a phone call already waiting for her, but she backed away from the friendly secretary and waved it off, miming, "Take the number."

Over the next few days, several people inquired about the Avery, but Lacey didn't know who they were, and Tanya wouldn't tell her.

Lacey took one extra gamble. She manipulated Tanya into predicting the outcome of the Avery in front of Cherry Finch. Assuming an air of indifference, Lacey said in her most casual voice, "What dya think that Avery's going to bring?"

"High estimate at most," said Tanya.

"So seventy-five?" Lacey said, making sure the number registered in everyone's brain.

American sales started at ten a.m. Unlike the flashier Impressionist and contemporary sales that began at a glamorous seven p.m., where people dressed in their showcase clothes, the day sales attracted attendees who wore brown pants with blue blazers and shirt collars that lay crushed under their lapels. Lacey had improved her single invitation from Heath Acosta to attend one sale into a standing invitation to attend any sale, and nobody seemed to notice.

The auction started off with a few alarming bumps. An uncharacteristic John Singer Sargent oil, decent enough, died a lonely death without a single bid. The failure was made even more visible because the auctioneer quickly escalated false bids against the reserve to give the illusion of furious bidding, only to promptly sputter out upon reaching the reserve, where he was forced to dwell in a few lingering seconds of ringing silence. It felt as though a shroud of death had fallen over the room. This was especially alarming as last year a Sargent had stunned the crowd, topping out at seven million dollars. Sargent was desirable, more desirable than Milton Avery, and Lacey felt a nervous chill as she acknowledged to herself that the sale could have a disappointing outcome. One would think that the seven-million-dollar figure would motivate at least one buyer to pop for a hundred grand, even for a not-so-great Sargent, if only for the signature, but the auctioneer had to muffle his obligatory announcement, "Passed," by saying the word exactly as his gavel struck the lectern.

The Avery now seemed like an outside shot to reach even the reserve. There was a sign of life as a Whistler watercolor, expected to bring between sixty and eighty thousand, sparkled enough to double the estimate, and Lacey's emotions began flip-flopping like one of Winslow Homer's just-landed trout.

The carousel turned and the Avery swung into view. Now she worried about the frame. Sotheby's tarted-up lighting reflected harshly off its expensive silver leaf. Thankfully, an art handler, who rode in with each picture, tilted it forward to diminish the glare, and the picture looked better than ever.

"Let's start with thirty thousand..." Then the auctioneer quickly manufactured a frenzy with an ersatz bidding war: "Thirty-five, forty, forty-five thousand, fifty thousand..." One would have thought there were a hundred bidders in pursuit of this bashful Avery, but really there were none. Then there was that ugly pause. The next bid, fifty-five thousand, would mean that the picture had sold to an actual, existing buyer. A savvy collector might read this pause, if no bids followed, as an opportunity to buy the picture after the sale at a discount and would sit on his hands instead of bidding against the reserve. Lacey looked around to the few recruits, including Tanya Ross, who were manning the phones, hoping for movement. Tanya stood poised, listening, when her heel slipped off the dais, and she clumsily fumbled the phone, dropping it over her counter, where it swung by its cord. Tanya held up her hand to the auctioneer, as if asking for a time-out. This produced the kind of laugh one hears in a restaurant when a waiter drops a stack of plates. She pulled up the phone and stuck it to her ear. Then, raising her finger as if to make a point, Tanya said meekly, "Fifty-five."

A paddle was raised in the center of the room: "Sixty." Then, the pall broken, there were raises and reraises, taking the picture to eighty-five thousand, after which there was again, in the room, stillness. But this time the auctioneer didn't show a detectable squirm. Rather, he turned his body fully toward the phone and waited patiently. "Ninety," relayed Tanya. Then, turning his body back to the floor as if he were on a spindle, he stared into the face of the floor bidder, whom Lacey could not see. "Will you make it ninety-five?" The ninety-five came and went, the picture crossing a hundred, edging further from Tanya's prediction and more toward Lacey's. The auctioneer brought the price up and up and finally, when he felt there was no more, said, "Last chance... selling, then, at one hundred fifty thousand dollars." Smash. He looked over at the phone. "Paddle number?"

And Tanya replied, "Five oh one."

Lacey was elated and disappointed. She had won her self-imposed contest, one in which she had enrolled, without her knowledge, only one other contestant, but she had hoped the picture would land on her magic number, one hundred seventy thousand, making her victory more memorable.

After the sale, she blitzed back to the office, trying to make her absence less conspicuous, and she was already in place when Cherry came out of the elevator. Cherry saw Lacey, an armload of superfluous papers held against her stomach, and said, "Good one, Lacey, you hit it." Lacey was thrilled that her guess had even been remembered, that her plan for professional notice had succeeded, and especially pleased that Tanya Ross had to witness her win.

"I was a bit over, but I thought it was a good picture," said Lacey, feigning modesty.

"What do you mean?" said Cherry. "You hit it within a few thousand."

"How?" said Lacey.

"The buyer's premium, twelve percent added on," said Cherry.

The addition of the buyer's premium streaked in like a come-from-behind win at a horse race. Lacey felt like a prom queen, even if no one else in the office felt it was that much of a triumph, as numbers routinely bounced around the staff for weeks prior to an auction. But Lacey knew that she was firmly impressed on Cherry's cortex and that above the name "Lacey," whenever it slipped across her consciousness, was a shining gold star.

11.

LACEY'S BANK ACCOUNT—A parental send-off for her life in New York—had halved in the two years she had worked at Sotheby's. New York was cruel to cash reserves, and her Sotheby's check, even with the routine raises, failed to replenish the pot at the same rate of depletion. Lacey always had magic happen to her at moments of financial crisis, but New York now seemed to vex her. She didn't believe in guardian angels, except for the guardian angel of her own self, and usually she laid the groundwork for financial salvation way in advance, and often in such unconscious ways that she didn't even know she was doing it. Her independence kept her from friends offering money, but her cleverness kept it sputtering in. But the past few years were unusually fallow.

My own life was on a gentle gradient moving quietly upward. My contributions to art magazines—I wrote the capsule reviews, usually unsigned—gave me a life and got me out of my apartment, and I found myself with continuing work. There were also relationships, almost romantic, that seemed to lack ignition. My style is courtly, which fails to excite those who anticipate drama. I had to introduce myself to gallery owners a half dozen times before my face started to become familiar.

12.

LACEY HAD, in the course of her work, come to know the Upper East Side. After lunch at 3 Guys, a coffee shop gone crazy with a menu as expansive as a Nebraska plain, she made routine stops at various nineteenth-century galleries along Madison Avenue. Hirschl & Adler, an elegantly staid establishment on 70th Street, held sway in the world of American paintings; they had a knack for polishing and framing a picture so it glowed, and they knew the location of just about every American picture of quality. Next, on 57th Street, was Kennedy Galleries, which had hoarded enough masterpieces to keep it active in the American market but was being sapped of its pictures through the attrition of time. All great pictures flow toward museums. They are plucked off the market by hungry institutions snaring them one by one as the decades march forward. (There are dozens of masterpieces in high apartments along Fifth Avenue, in sight of the Met, longing to make the leap into its comforting arms.)

Lacey had made herself known to the dealers, inquiring about prices and even occasionally helping them out by researching a provenance question about a picture that had passed through Sotheby's, and her name started to come up irregularly when I traveled above 57th Street.

On one of these afternoons, as summer approached and also the end of the art season—leaving the galleries' air-conditioning blazing and floors unpopulated—she wandered into the Kenneth Lux Gallery, which

41

Mug, Pipe and Book, John Frederick Peto, circa 1880
Size unknown.

specialized in more moderately priced American paintings. On the wall was a small picture by John Peto. Peto was a nineteenth-century still life painter who presented books, pipes, and mugs arrayed on a tabletop. The still lifes were rendered in dark greens and browns, the books ragged at the edges, close-ups of a tenement dweller's humble routine. Peto was forgotten until the early 1950s, when a scholar, Alfred Frankenstein, noticed that the most popular of the nineteenth-century still life painters, W. M. Harnett, whose pictures were quite valuable, appeared to have two distinct styles. One was photographic; every object in those pictures was vivid and defined. The other was looser; the edges of the books and tabletop objects seemed to evaporate and blend softly into the surrounding air. Frankenstein discovered that the second version of Harnett's work was

Herald, William Michael Harnett, circa 1878
Size unknown.

actually by Peto. Fakers, wanting to cash in on the more valuable Harnett, erased poor Peto's signature on any of his pictures they could find and added crude monograms of Harnett. When the decades-old fraud was revealed, Peto's prices shot up, nearly matching Harnett's.

Lacey, trying to determine a price for a Peto that was coming up at Sotheby's, asked Ken Lux what the cost of the small picture was. "Thirty-five thousand dollars," he said. Lacey thought the picture was fine and asked for a photo for comparison to Sotheby's picture. "Sure," he said, and gave her a small transparency. Then, continuing her walk, Lacey went around the corner to Hirschl & Adler, where, coincidentally, another small, comparable Peto was hanging. She inquired about the price. "Sixty-five thousand," was the reply. Lacey, stuffed from a deli sandwich she had devoured at 3 Guys, hiccuped. The two pictures were so close in subject matter, they could be a pair.

"Oh," she said, and she walked outside and scraped Ken Lux's label from the transparency. Lacey had heard that art dealers don't communicate with one another, trying to keep their offerings private so rival dealers can't bad-mouth them. This would be a test.

She walked back into H & A, transparency in hand. "Is there someone I could talk to about a Peto I have for sale?"

"Certainly." The secretary asked her name, then buzzed upstairs. "You can go on up to the third floor." And she pointed to an elevator just big enough for two.

She was greeted by Stuart Feld, the powerhouse American dealer with a critical eye for pictures that could make a boastful collector wither. Feld not only sold nineteenth-century pictures, he *felt* nineteenth century. He looked perfectly suited—his suit was perfect—for sitting in his favored neoclassical American furniture. She pulled the photo from her purse. Feld held it up to a light box.

"How big is it?" he asked.

"Eight by twelve inches," she said.

Silence was his response until, "Where is it?" he asked.

Lacey's first real dealing in the art world incorporated tiny lies into its construct. "It's at another dealer's, but he's deliberating. The owner is looking for the money now." It was the perfect response. There was enough truth in the statement for it to be convincing, and it inadvertently sparked Feld's competitive spirit.

"We don't make offers," said Feld. "Tell us what you want."

Lacey calculated the asking price on Feld's Peto, discounting it appropriately.

"Forty thousand," she said.

"That's a bit rich, but perhaps, providing it's in good shape," he said.

Lacey went around the corner to Ken Lux but could only get him

AN OBJECT OF BEAUTY

down to thirty-three thousand. Still, seven thousand dollars was not bad for a walk around the corner. Ken was a dealer who began in the 1960s, when pictures were hard to sell and were easily let out of the gallery to hang in a collector's house for a few days' trial or even shipped out of state with only a promise by phone to secure the painting. The deals were conducted on handshakes alone and often without even that. It wasn't until the prices started jumping in the mid-1980s—and a few dealers went to jail for selling the same picture twice—that paperwork became necessary. Ken knew Lacey well enough from the floor at Sotheby's, and relying on old-fashioned instinct, he let the picture out of the gallery with just a one-page contract and a promise to pay in two weeks. (Once he had put a painting out for approval to a motorcycle gang, who for some reason wanted a picture of bears frolicking in human clothes. He got paid the next day, in cash pulled in wads from the gang's pockets.)

With the picture under her arm, she rounded the corner once again to H & A, got a check, and pocketed seven grand. Lacey hadn't really lied, she had only been crafty, but she had tasted honey in the art market, and she momentarily felt smarter than Stuart Feld, Ken Lux, and the rest of the dealers who were burrowed in the brownstones stippling Madison Avenue.

13.

THE NATHANSONS had called Sotheby's—yes, they had bought the Avery. Could it be delivered to D.C. today? It would be an object of conversation at their dressy dinner party tonight. Was there a walker who could escort the picture and deliver it? It's only a four-hour train ride. Sometimes the lowliest employees get the best jobs, and Lacey was on a train by ten a.m., with the Avery wrapped in cardboard, bound with a splintery sisal string affixed to a wooden handle, and fully insured. This seemed like a snow day to Lacey, although there was no snow in sight for six months.

The wide train windows looked onto verdant pastures, soot-smudged buildings, and shuttered storefronts like a rapidly unscrolling panorama as the train whizzed past them. Her wrinkle-proof dress clung statically to her legs, and each move of her arm pulled it this way or that above a knee, which was noted by a slouching youth facing backward and adjacent to her.

Lacey had picked D.C. highlights from her mental guidebook of sights to see. The National Gallery and the Hirshhorn Museum had moved up the wish list every time they were cited in illustrations as being the home of her favorite paintings. All she had to do was crib some time from the Nathansons to devote to holiday sightseeing in D.C.

The Avery, stowed overhead in the steel-pipe luggage rack, was projecting out just enough to thwack a man on the forehead. Lacey's rifle response, said before she even turned her head—"You can sue me, but I've got nothing"—charmed the man enough that he said, "Is this seat taken?"

"Sit down, father figure."

He was older, professorial. Wearing a suit and tie and crowned with a muss of gray hair. He muttered his name, but Lacey didn't catch it.

"Who's the artist who clobbered me?"

"Milton Avery," she said.

"Milton Avery? That's a big name for such a slow train. Shouldn't he be on the express?"

"I would have preferred it. I don't think the painting cares," Lacey said.

I should tell you now about Lacey and strangers. She loved codgers and coots, truck drivers and working folk, any sort of type that she wasn't familiar with. She would engage them in bars and parks, focusing on their accents and slang, probing them for stories, and the slightest accomplishments, including whittling, elevated them to heroes. The man next to her didn't qualify as a folk hero, he was too well dressed for that, but Lacey liked the opportunity for repartee and felt she could keep pace with anybody.

"How do you know about Milton Avery?"

"I try to be a gentleman of taste, even when it comes to getting clocked in the head." He glanced up and down, taking her in. "What do you do?" he said.

"What do *you* do?" she said.

"What do *you* do?" he said.

"Okay. You outmaneuvered me. I work at Sotheby's and I'm delivering a painting to Washington."

"Oh, Sotheby's. Then perhaps you can answer a question I've been mulling over. Or maybe you're too young."

"Just give me the question."

"How is it that rich people know about good paintings?" he said.

Lacey said nothing but implied that he should continue.

"Well, think about it. How do they have the eye for it? Why is a five-million-dollar picture always a Velásquez or some other fancy name, and not a Bernard Buffet?"

"Maybe you just explained it to yourself," said Lacey.

"How?"

"You said 'fancy name.' Maybe they're just buying fancy names."

"But then a lousy Velásquez would bring as much as a good one. They actually seem to know which one is better. How does a steel magnate or a car dealer or oil baron learn what scholars take years to learn?"

"I'm going to need some train wine," she said.

"I'll get it," he volunteered, loosening his tie. Minutes later, he reappeared holding two plastic cups that didn't bother to imitate wineglasses. Lacey took a sip, "Acheson, Topeka, 1994."

After he had settled in, now using his briefcase as a table, he relaxed deep into his seat's leatherette cushion.

"I see it this way. Paintings," he said, "are Darwinian. They drift toward money for the same reason that toads drifted toward stereoscopic vision. Survival. If the masterpieces weren't coveted, they would rot in basements and garbage heaps. So they make themselves necessary."

She laughed and stared at him with a pixie face. "I must be drunk, because I think I understood you," she said, and cranked her body sideways to better see his pleased response.

The noontime wine wore off just as the train pulled into the station. The gentleman stood, saying, "Lacey, have a great day. You shortened the trip for me."

Lacey, responding with warmth, said, "You too; you have a great trip, too."

Lacey never knew the man's name until a month later when she saw his photo on the inside of the book's dust jacket. It was John Updike.

14.

LACEY ANGLED THE PICTURE into the backseat of a taxi, its corner sticking into her knees because of the drivetrain hump on the floor. She braced it with her palm for self-protection as well as for its own good as the taxi bounced and rattled from one stoplight to the next. The taxi pulled up to a Georgian brownstone with gardens neat and trimmed and a crisp white door with a brass knocker. On the street were laborers unloading party chairs and caravanning them into a side door. She got out of the taxi, and the driver, a vociferous cabbie with a resonant voice who had entertained her by singing the songs of John Lee Hooker, pulled the picture from the backseat. The white door of the brownstone swung open with a faint jingle-bell tinkle, and Saul Nathanson waved with full panic, shouting, "Don't come up the steps!"

So many interpretations. Was he shouting at Lacey, the painting, or the taxi driver? "Don't step on the walkway!" Was the concrete wet? But Saul ran toward them more sheepish than commanding, and they all stayed put.

"I thought by having you bring the picture," Saul said, panting, "that we were taking delivery of the picture in Washington. But it seems to be disputable that this might constitute taking delivery in New York."

Lacey looked at Saul, then at the taxi driver. He pulled his cap back and scratched his head. "Oh yeah, sales tax," he said.

"What?" said Lacey.

"My wife sells jewelry. There's always a sales tax issue."

Saul pointed at the driver with a silent "bingo." "We've got to have it shipped to us from New York by a reputable carrier."

Lacey muttered, "I'm reputable."

"But unlicensed. We've got a questionable situation here. You've got to take it back. It's a difference of almost ten thousand dollars," said Saul.

The statement hung in the air, until the taxi driver said, "You mean that box is worth a hundred and fifty thousand dollars?"

Lacey turned to him. "Who are you, Rain Man?"

Saul was balanced on his toes. "I'm so sorry, Lacey, we tried to turn you around, but we just learned it an hour ago. Here's something for you"—he handed her a folded hundred-dollar bill—"and don't let the painting touch the walkway."

"I'll be a witness," said the grinning taxi driver, implying there could be another tip due.

"I can't even invite you in," said Saul. Then he turned to the half-opened door. "Estelle! Wave hello to Lacey!"

Estelle poked her head out of an upstairs window. "Hello, Lacey. Saul's insane!"

Saul, standing away from them as though the state boundary line ran right down the middle of his sidewalk, pressed the driver. "Could you put it back in the taxi, please?"

"I'm not touching it," said the driver. "It could be an insurance nightmare."

"Well, I can't touch it," said Saul.

"I got it in once; I can get it in again," said Lacey, hefting it toward the still open cab door, as Saul stuck to his side of the imaginary line that separated him from a ten-thousand-dollar tax bill.

The driver was now gliding the taxi around potholes and speed bumps and slowing the car with the gentle braking that he reserved for fares involving infants and the elderly. "Rats," said Lacey. "I wanted to go to the museums, but now I'm stuck with Pricey."

"You can go," the driver said.

"What do I do with Pricey?"

"Check it at the museum, in the cloakroom. There's nothing but guards around there. Safe as a bank."

"Hell, I had it on a train. You're the one who spooked me about how much it's worth. Okay. Let's go to the National Gallery."

The taxi arrived, and Lacey pulled her burden from the cab. She gave the driver a healthy tip, all to go on Sotheby's expense tab. "Thank you so much, O kindly taxi driver."

"Adios, amigo. By the way, my name's Truman," he said. "What time you coming out?"

"An hour?" she answered.

Lacey went to the cloakroom, deposited the Avery, then passed through a security check so lax that she instinctively swung her head back to the cloakroom to see if the Avery was still there.

She wound down the vast interior stairs of the National Gallery. The cavernous entrance had little art to be seen. Only a gigantic, though airy, Calder mobile, swaying from above, indicated that this was an art museum and not an intergalactic headquarters.

With little interest in contemporary art, she headed underground to the west wing, where she speed-walked past neglected masterpieces in the near empty galleries of American art. There was a surprise around every corner: she had only seen John Singleton Copley's 1778 painting *Watson and the Shark* in two-by-three-inch reproductions in books, and the picture, a dramatic tableau of a rowboat staffed with sailors, in waters turned hellish by a circling shark that has just bitten off the leg of a thirteen-year-old boy, stunned her with its monumental size and perverse beauty. *Jaws,* the beginning, she thought.

Lacey later told me that while she was steaming past the pictures,

Watson and the Shark, John Singleton Copley, 1778
71.75 × 90.5 in.

she had a sudden, comic overview of herself in motion. She saw her head leaning forward as she entered a picture's sight lines, her feet trailing. Then her head would slow down while her feet caught up and advanced, so her eyeballs could spend as much time with a picture as possible without retarding her forward motion. Her upper body remained slow and steady, with her feet a futurist blur below.

After twenty minutes in the downstairs picture gallery, Lacey found that her time at Sotheby's had instilled in her a new way to experience a museum. In addition to her normal inquisitiveness about a work, who painted it and when, and a collegiate hangover necessitating a formulaic, internal monologue about what the painting meant—which always left her mind crackling with static—she now found she had added another task: she tried to estimate a painting's worth. Lacey's internal wiring had been altered by her work in Manhattan.

Her acceleration in the west wing meant that she had time to do the same sprint in the east wing. Here, the giant modern pictures loomed over her. Even the Copley was small compared with the antic Jackson Pollock. At first, she didn't catch the phallic silhouettes of Robert Motherwell's *Elegy*, but on instinct her head turned back, confirming, "Oh yeah, a dick and balls." A Rothko offered just two colors, more or less, but it made Lacey downshift a gear to take it in, and an Andy Warhol silk screen of a newspaper headline, which seemed so haphazard after the persnickety detail of the nineteenth-century flower pictures and desktop still lifes she had just seen, left her suspicious and not impressed.

There was a special exhibition of works by Willem de Kooning, and she stopped in front of one showing a female figure as grotesque totem. In the 1950s, de Kooning had aggressively painted women, and in the 1970s, these pictures endured the wrath of feminism. They were regarded as angry, misogynistic depictions of the female as beast: once again, it was claimed, a male artist was on the attack, reducing women to animals.

But Lacey, staring at de Kooning, taking in the roiling flesh and teeth, recognized herself. This painting was not an attack; this was an acknowledgment of her strength. de Kooning painted women not as horrific monster but as powerful goddess. Lacey felt this way about herself every day. Yes, she had a ghoul's teeth; yes, she had seductive breasts, long, pink legs, and a ferocious sway. She knew she had sexual resources that remained sheathed. But one day, when she used them, she knew her true face would resemble de Kooning's painted woman.

She went down the stairs of the National Gallery, heading toward the coat check. There was no line, but there were three security guards

Woman I, Willem de Kooning, 1950–1952
6 ft. 3.875 × 58 in.

talking into shoulder mikes and a smartly dressed woman in glasses, standing next to Lacey's cardboard box, which had been leaned against the marble wall of the foyer. Lacey instantly read the situation. Her first thought was, Oh shit, and her second was, What fun. She then put on her toughest face, graveled her voice, and said, "I think I'm the one you're lookin' for." She turned backward and put her wrists in handcuff position. So far, no one had changed expression, which meant that her comedy routine had bombed.

"Oh, I'm sorry," she said, turning back, "I'm with Sotheby's and I'm delivering that picture. It's a Milton Avery. Here's my card."

The smartly dressed woman spoke: "Do you mind if we open it?"

"Not at all."

Lacey felt a shiver at her fleeting thought that the Avery had been mysteriously replaced with the National Gallery's Watteau and that she would be sent up the river, unable to explain it even to herself. But the guard sliced open the tape, revealing the still pristine picture, while the woman radioed to someone, giving them the date and title and size of the painting. After a moment, the woman said, "Not one of ours. I'm so sorry, Miss... Yeager. I'm sure you understand."

As a guard with paper tape sealed the cardboard back up, he turned to Lacey and said, "Nice Avery."

Lacey stepped into the street, and before she could raise her hand, Truman's taxi sped into view. The window rolled down. "I waited for you... slow day."

"Okay, let's go, Truman. My last tip includes this. The Hirshhorn, please."

Lacey did the same routine at the Hirshhorn. She almost left the Avery in the taxi because she now trusted that Truman was a good fellow and a working-class hero. But a preview unspooled in her head of how she would feel if she came out and there was no taxi and no Truman; so she hauled the picture inside and got an institutionally authorized claim check.

In the Hirshhorn, she sped along with the same gallop as at the National Gallery, racing by masterpieces with her head swiveling. One picture, however, stuck her feet in cement. Painted in 1967, Ed Ruscha's large canvas depicted the Los Angeles County Museum on fire. Devoid of people on the grounds, the museum was shown in cool tones and sharp outline, while flames blew out from behind the building. The picture was so unlike the slash-and-burn canvases of the abstract pictures she had just seen. Those pictures asked for an emotional response. This one asked for an intellectual response. Was this a tragic image or a surreal one? The horror going on inside was unrevealed and only imagined. And where were the people? Then, as she waited in front of the picture for a thought to congeal, Lacey's mental gears cranked down,

Los Angeles County Museum on Fire, Ed Ruscha, 1968
53.5 × 133.5 in.

the questions stopped, and for a moment, her brain stopped churning and she just stared at it.

Lacey glanced at her watch as she headed toward the Hirshhorn's coat check, worried that a kerfuffle over the Avery would slow down her schedule, which now demanded precision. But nothing happened, the picture was retrieved and Truman sped her to the depot for the long ride home.

Lacey crawled into her apartment at ten p.m., still lugging the picture. Her tired body longed for a Scotch, which she poured over ice. She lay back on her bed. Light from the street lamps, diffused by summer leaves, gave her room movement. The idea of the Scotch hit her even before the alcohol did, so she was relaxed at just the taste. Her window was cracked open enough to let in the light summer breeze, and her eyes meandered around the dim room, moving slowly, high and low, from a vase of flowers, across her half kitchen, to a photograph, to a lamp. Her eyes drifted toward a closet door and the Avery that leaned against it. It's here, she thought. Why not hang it?

She unwrapped the Avery with care, more care, she felt, than was given it at the National Gallery, and hung it on the wall. She took a lamp off her chest of drawers and put it on a low stool in front of the

Avery, so that light was thrown upward on the picture from below. Then she lay back again. Without looking, she reached out and her hand landed perfectly on the glass of Scotch.

Would Leonardo's *Annunciation* be as beautiful hanging crooked in a messy college dorm at a party school in Florida? No, not as beautiful as it is in the Uffizi, framed, lit, and protected as the prize it is, while two thousand years of history flow by in the Arno outside. Context matters, but in Lacey's apartment, where nothing exquisite had ever been, where just the two of them looked back at each other, the Avery was the most beautiful thing she had ever seen. This moment was a secret among the Avery, the Scotch, and Lacey, and she saw clearly something that had eluded her in her two years in the art business. In a few minutes of unexpected communion, she understood why people wanted to own these things.

She rescanned the room. Where before she saw a photograph, a kitchen, a vase, she now added an adjective: she saw a *student's* photograph, a *student's* kitchen, a *student's* vase. The painting was an adult object, by and for people with grown-up eyes. This apartment, these things, were instantly in Lacey's past. They were on the way out, ready to be sold or boxed. The Avery had dipped her in an elixir. She wanted fine things, beautiful things, like the Avery. She wanted to grow up, no longer to live like a student. Lacey knew that what she needed was an amount of money that could support her rapidly evolving taste. This need repainted moral issues that were formerly black-and-white into a vague gray, and a dark idea that she had formed in her head as hypothesis now had to become actual.

Lacey called me late that evening. "Oh Daniel. I need you to do me a favor," she said. I agreed because her incomplete explanation made it seem like an adventuresome art world lark. I did not know that, if its nature were ever revealed, this favor would jeopardize my budding career as an art writer.

PART

II

15.

BY 1997, the art market, becalmed over the previous seven years, was beginning to catch wind. A day spent trekking from Sotheby's to Christie's with a lunch stop at Sant Ambroeus on Madison Avenue was a collector's version of the Grand Tour. Increased foot traffic at galleries and auction houses indicated a widening public interest. Prices were now reported in *The New York Times*, and even though I was somewhat acclimated to the art world while writing my fledgling reviews for *ARTnews* or *Artforum*, I was still surprised that no belligerent letters appeared in the paper condemning huge sums spent on art that could be better spent on children's hospitals. The public seemed to accept these sudden escalations with either resignation or glee, I couldn't tell which. I can't imagine that art prices reported around the water cooler were ever responded to with a "That's fantastic"—except the water cooler at the auction houses—and more than likely they were met with a dismissive sniff or complaint.

In the spring of 1997, Lacey sat at her desk, which had not, as yet, a cubicle around it, and saw, through an open doorway to the executive office, a picture leaning on an upholstered easel. It was covered with dark green velour, weighted at the bottom by a brass rod. A hand lifted the velour to reveal a Van Gogh drawing so fine that the only improvement it could make would be to turn itself into a painting. It showed Van Gogh's finest landscape subject, wheat fields being harvested by workers loading wheat into a hay wain. The velour, in place to keep sunlight off the drawing, was lifted only on occasions of aesthetic contemplation or for reasons of commerce. The person doing the lifting was Tanya Ross, and the person doing the viewing, Lacey later learned, was Barton Talley, whose cup was full with equal amounts of notoriety and respect.

Barton Talley's history was part glorious résumé and part rap sheet. He wore pale blue suits and expensive shoes, which were a sartorial trademark. He had a PhD in art history from Yale and had vaulted into fame and position with essays, art scholarship, and charm. After a decade in a curatorial position at the Boston Museum of Fine Arts, he had been let go for using his known and respected expertise to advise collectors on purchases and then receiving gifts of appreciation with dollar signs in front of them. Among the legacy trustees, he was still thought of as sullied.

He then formed a gallery in New York City, Talley, with funding that seemed bottomless, and he specialized in Very Expensive Paintings. He was a rare entity in the art world: a dealer with the credentials of a scholar. Most dealers knew only their own area, and it seemed that dealers in contemporary art knew nothing that happened before 1965. But Talley knew it all, except for the very latest. His familiarity with the ways of the rich, learned during his malfeasant tenure at the Boston Museum, as well as his own financial ease, gave him the clout of equality with international collectors. He never pushed to close a sale, making him the chased rather than the chaser.

Talley didn't like the artificial light in the small display room, so he brought the Van Gogh out to the offices, where ambient sunlight would make any flaws in the drawing more visible. He hovered around Lacey's desk, tilting it this way and that, looking for fading, looking for foxing. Lacey presumed he didn't notice her, but when he said, "A beautiful thing…a beautiful thing," Lacey, at her desk, said, "I do my best."

Talley looked at her, gave her an approving smile for her chutzpah—though neither of them could claim ethnic rights to the word—and then angled the drawing so he could see it under the raking light. Without moving his eyes from the drawing, he said, "Is there a lot of interest in it?"

Looking down at her desk, Lacey said, "There have been three or four people in to look at it, but let's keep that between us friends." Tanya Ross peered across the room at them from behind her doorway but sensed nothing unusual. They were like two spies looking at a sunset while they exchanged top-level information.

That spring, in London, the drawing achieved an exhilarating fourteen million dollars, and the auction room froze for a few seconds of unusual silence after such a spectacular price, before ripping into applause reserved for Derby winners and sports matches. Reports of cheering in the auction room when a painting soared past its reasonable limit and into the unreasonable stratosphere sound like a crass symptom of our age, but auction applause dates back centuries. Auctions were, and still are, spectator sports, where the contestants are money. In the nineteenth century, pictures were wheeled out to hoots and clapping, like boxers entering the ring, and the spectators responded to escalating bids as if they were hard lefts and roundhouse rights.

The Van Gogh represented one of a few stunning prices that had perked up the market in the last few years. Gossip and awe reverberated around Manhattan when rumors of fifty-million-dollar private sales began to circulate. Those overachieving paintings had great names attached to them: Picasso, Renoir, Degas. Prices were beginning to recall the glory days of the previous decade, and Lacey found herself rubbing elbows not only with these mighty names from the past, but with the well-funded dealers and collectors of the present. Sotheby's Impressionist and Modern Art divisions, however, were fully staffed and immutable. No one in this upturning market was going anywhere, and there was no nook that Lacey could be wedged into without popping someone else out from the other side.

Cherry Finch liked Lacey, which also inhibited her transfer from American to Modern Art. Tanya Ross, Lacey's slight superior, did not like her. She perceived that Lacey's genie bottle of charm was uncorked when the Sotheby's elite were on parade and recorked after they passed by. Although she saw this habit as good business sense rather than manipulative evil, Tanya correctly understood that she was the next person up the ladder whom Lacey could displace. So Tanya was attentive when Lacey was called into Cherry's office, and she watched Lacey cross the room, the door closing behind her.

"Do you know who Rockwell Kent is?" asked Cherry.

"Somewhat," said Lacey. "Illustrated *Moby-Dick*, right? Painter too."

"Painter, mainly," replied Cherry. "Not one of the top Americans, but rare. Plus, he had ties to Robert Henri, and the Canadians, Lawren Harris, Group of Seven. Landscape painter, mostly. Greenland was his big subject. Icy fjords with Eskimo dogs in tiny perspective standing by their masters. During his lifetime everyone admired them but nobody bought them. Communist sympathizer, 'man for the people' type. He ended up owning most of his own major works. Then in the fifties, at the worst time for a citizen to be sympathetic to Russia, he snubbed America and donated most of his work to 'the Russian people.' What already looked bad became actually bad.

"Now forty years have gone by and nobody remembers his Communist bent, and people who want a Rockwell Kent *of size* can't get one, and there are about eighty large paintings sitting in Russia, and Russia couldn't care less."

Cherry shuffled some papers, as though she were waiting for Lacey to figure it all out. Finally, Lacey said the only thing she could think of:

"What are they worth?"

November in Greenland, Rockwell Kent, 1932
34.25 × 44.5 in.

"A top, top Kent would bring about four hundred to six hundred thousand dollars."

"Times eighty," said Lacey.

"Not really," said Cherry, "because you couldn't put them on the market all at once, and some are better than others. But placing a few pictures in conspicuous museums, and releasing one or two a year onto the market could be a nice annuity for someone."

Lacey wondered for whom. "But you can't get them out of Russia?"

"That's what we're going to try and find out. Could you meet Barton Talley at his gallery on Monday, around eleven a.m.?"

The weekend was a long one for Lacey. She wondered what possible involvement she would have in the Rockwell Kent endeavor, and she was excited because the request indicated career movement—and not just stolid up-the-ladder movement, either, but a skip-step that put her near the center of the action. At parties, Lacey's fearlessness always guided her to the top person in the room, and her cleverness made the top person in the room believe that he had guided himself to her. But the Sotheby's feeler seemed to come from nowhere, maybe even merit. She figured out that Talley had called Cherry, and Cherry had recommended her for something. What, she did not know.

16.

LACEY NOTED THAT days moved faster when nightlife was involved, so she planned to meet up with Angela and Sharon in Chelsea for drinks. Art galleries populated the area, but Lacey didn't normally frequent them. She was East Side, and the art she represented was understood; Chelsea was West Side, and the art it represented was misunderstood. She had been meaning to go but never did, as her travel in Manhattan was vertical, not horizontal.

Lacey's new dress was, as she described it to me, "schoolgirl with possibilities." She knew that the conservative quality of the outfit set her apart from the other females who stuffed themselves into jeans and four-inch heels on Saturday night and then, after two too many drinks, bellowed in the bar with resonant horse laughs. Her rule for weekend dressing was excess during the day and sophistication at night. After pulling tight her wide patent-leather belt and leaning over and shaking her hair into a perfect mess, after hurriedly sticking blue Post-it notes on furniture in her apartment that she meant to get rid of, she taxied sideways across town to catch a few galleries on their last gala Saturday before the onset of summer.

The confidence that she wore so comfortably on her home turf was less present on the new shores of West 25th Street. She had touched down like an immigrant and hadn't even planned a route. For a moment, in the midst of an active street crowd that didn't need her, she experienced a rare feeling: invisibility. She passed active galleries with wide windows and unmarked entrances, with modest signage announcing artists she had never heard of. She stood on the street and looked down at dozens of galleries from which new art was mined and then trucked into Manhattan residences.

By the time she got to the end of the street, after quick ins and outs, shouldering through crowds for partial glimpses of this and that, she had a movie montage in her head of artworks spinning in an aesthetic vertigo. These objects were not old paintings bound in gold frames like their uptown counterparts; these were free-growing sprigs of wild grass, curving around corners and hanging from ceilings. They were lying on floors, making noise, glittering with mirrors and alien parts, stuck in the walls like spears, and looking at you with human eyes. There were good old college tries mixed in with older artists on the edge. There were blatant messages hanging opposite indecipherable jabberwocky. There was kid's stuff, crass stuff, smart stuff, and porn stuff. There were labor-intensive works that sold for two thousand dollars and flimsy slap-ups that cost thirty thousand. And taking it all in were the muscled, the pretty, the pretty strange, and the thoughtful. Lacey felt like a Martian lander, scooping up dirt samples and having no luck analyzing it. As exciting as the carnival was, the art she saw left her unmoved. It was not comparable to the Picassos and others she navigated around every day, but her addiction to energy kept her pushing on, snaking between Tenth and Eleventh Avenues, down to 20th Street and beyond, until the mood gave way to mundane galleries presenting new art made in the old way.

Lacey met Angela and Sharon at Cointreau, where they sat at the hundred-decibel bar for thirty minutes, until they were shown to a table. Of the three of them, Lacey was the easiest to pick up, Sharon was unlikely, and Angela was impossible. This rule also coincided with their physical appeal, with Lacey at the top, though it was Sharon who was often pointing Lacey toward mischief, like a dare, because she knew Lacey was often up to it. Angela saw intrusions suspiciously and couldn't open up to lengthy chats with strangers at the table. But Lacey was also loyal to girls' night out and never flew away before the evening was officially over. If Lacey met a man she enjoyed, it was she who was the sole determiner of the sexual possibilities, and if emotions were invested, they were his and not hers.

The three of them, well dressed but a mismatched trio of varying styles, made outsiders wonder at the nature of their dinner. Three women who couldn't get dates? Impossible. Each was appealing in her own way. Lesbians? Too easy a guess, the fantasy of frat boys, who were not to be found in the pricey restaurant. The way they talked in animation, leaning forward with palms on the table, stifling giggles that led to champagne hiccups, said clearly that they were having a good time, hadn't seen one another in a while, and were quite sufficient on their own.

In the room was a noted television actor, Stirling Quince, who was forming a collection and hosting fund-raisers. He was in rare company: Larry Gagosian, the powerful art dealer with growing influence reaching to Europe and Los Angeles, whose eye for pictures made him competitive with museums of the world; Roy Lichtenstein, the most congenial of the new old masters, anointed at a time when consensus took twenty years rather than months to point its finger at genius; his wife, Dorothy, the most likable of all the artists' spouses. At the actor's side was Blanca, a Czech model whose body seemed to be assembled from schoolboys' dream bits.

Neither Angela, Sharon, nor Lacey knew who anyone was by sight, except the actor. Yes, he was handsome. Yes, he was smart. Such a man, Angela and Sharon agreed, but Lacey balked.

"A man? He wakes up every morning and goes into makeup."

Angela caught the conversational trend: "And holds a pretend gun."

"And shows his bare ass on TV," Sharon added as she slapped the table a bit too hard.

"His girlfriend is supposed to be smart," said Angela.

"Smart?" said Lacey. "She's supposed to be smart? She *poses*."

When the check came, Lacey reached for it. "No!" said Angela.

"I've got it," said Lacey.

This was not a cheap bill. The routine was that it would be split, as none of them could easily afford to treat except at the cheapest of restaurants. The ease and snap with which she picked up the check had a second-nature quality that said Lacey was not extending herself uncomfortably. Both Angela and Sharon thought this was odd.

On the street, Lacey hailed a cab, and they all bowed low as they filed in. "Driver," said Lacey, "follow that street," and her finger pointed uptown.

"Where're we going?" they chirped.

"I'll show you," said Lacey.

The cab wheeled up to 83rd Street and Broadway and, according to Lacey's exact command, hung a left, meandered over a few streets, and stopped at a corner. Lacey rolled down the window and leaned out, and so did the other two as best they could.

"Look up," Lacey told them.

"What are we looking at?" asked Sharon.

"Count three floors up and look at the apartment on the corner, then count five windows in."

They did and saw a nicely framed window in an old building. From what they could see of the apartment, it was empty, freshly painted white inside, and illuminated by a contractor's light standing in the center of the room.

"It's my new apartment," said Lacey. "I move in tomorrow."

"You bought it?" said Angela.

"Yes."

The girls were stunned. As recently as several months ago, they had shared financial recaps, and both Angela and Sharon knew this apartment was out of Lacey's reach.

"Lacey," said Sharon, "how'd you pay for it?"

"Think of it as magic," she said.

Lacey had come into money not by magic, but by prestidigitation. No one had seen her sleights except her and me, and I was bound to silence by complicity. I was guilty, too, but I did not know exactly of what. Lacey and I had collaborated on a feint—I delivered on the requested favor—for which I went mostly unrewarded, but Lacey had seen hundreds of thousands of dollars come her way. It was her will that brought money to her, and it was my lack of will that kept it from me, so I considered her deserving of this newfound rootless cash. But sometimes money falls like light snow on open palms, and sometimes it falls stinging and hard from ominous clouds.

17.

MONDAY MORNING, Lacey climbed the steps of Barton Talley's gallery on East 78th. She rang a buzzer, looked into a videocam, then pushed on the door when she heard a solid click. She entered what was once the foyer of a grand residence, now painted white and accommodating half a dozen paintings of varying size and period and one freestanding Miró sculpture, illuminated only by reflected sunlight as the gallery lights were off.

There was no assistant on duty, and she faced a carpeted staircase, at the top of which sunlight spilled around a curve of banister. Voices, too, tumbled around from somewhere up above. She stood, not knowing what to do. Then two men in narrow suits and cropped hair appeared at the top of the stairs, talking low to each other as they descended the steps. One of them said to Lacey, "He said to come upstairs and walk back to his office." The two men left, and Lacey thought how in the art world even well-dressed, intelligent-looking men could look like misfits.

At the top of the stairs she entered a hall, unsure which way to go. She looked left, toward the street, to a sunny, blindingly white front room, then right, to a hall that extended back to another half-open door, which she guessed was her destination. She walked down the hall, passing a few offices housing an art library, open books on desks, transparencies leaning on light boxes. She got close enough to the end of the hall to see, through a door cracked open not more than a few inches, a sliver of a painting on an easel, an old master type, of a woman singing in a parlor.

"Not there, behind you," Talley said. She turned and saw Talley silhouetted against the window, waving his arm for her to come the other way. "That way, evil and darkness; this way, goodness and light," said Talley, then added, "We're all in here."

"Thank you, Mr. Talley. I'm Lacey Yeager, just in case—"

"Oh, I know," he said. "Thank you for coming. This is Patrice Claire..." Lacey saw the open-collared European whom she had met briefly at Sotheby's a little over three years ago.

"We've met," she said, recalling a memory that had set firm in her by a feeling of premonition.

"Ah, you remembered," said Claire.

"Ah, *you* remembered," said Lacey.

Lacey sat; they all sat. "Have you ever been to Russia?" Talley asked her.

"It's on my to-do list," she said.

"Well, move it up a few notches. Did Cherry explain about the Rockwell Kent situation?"

"Yes, she—"

"So the Russians have these pictures that they really don't care about, but America does care about. Mr. Claire has some pictures that the Russians really do care about, and we don't care about at all."

Patrice Claire picked up the story. "I collected about twenty nineteenth-century Russian landscape painters through the years. All these Russian pictures are painted tight, very photographic, very realistic, the respected standard for the period. Russian artists never got into Impressionism until it was practically over—"

"Neither did the Americans," Talley interjected.

"Yes, neither did the Americans. A hundred years later they turn out

73

to be unimportant, pretty pictures, but they are still amazing. Amazing light, amazing detail."

"Patrice contacted me with the thought of an exchange, a sort of prisoner exchange," Talley explained, "and I contacted Sotheby's for added clout. The art world wants an opening in Russia, and this could be a civil way to begin. We need an assistant for the trip, someone with an American look and nature, preferably from Sotheby's, and Cherry recommended you. Do you think you might have an interest?"

Not wondering, or caring, whether she was picked as a sexual possibility on a lengthy trip for gentlemen, Lacey said yes.

"We would leave in a week for a three-day trip to St. Petersburg. Many of the pictures are at the Hermitage, stowed away. My Russian pictures are being sent there now. Russia's a bit chaotic these days, so it might be easier to make a deal now than in five years."

The conversation loosened; anecdotes were told about travel, foreign ways, differences between Europeans and Americans, and everyone relaxed. Barton Talley fussed with a letter opener, finally laying it precisely square on his desk, leaned back in his chair, and said, "One night in Paris, I was faced with the choice of flying to the South of France to meet Picasso, or staying in Paris and fucking Hedy Lamarr. I chose to fuck Hedy Lamarr.

"That I would call a mistake."

"I'll try not to make the same one," said Lacey.

18.

WITH LACEY ACTING as passport holder and ticket captain, the three of them landed at the St. Petersburg airport, which had a lonely, neglected quality. Weeds grew in the centers of the runways. Broken-down Aeroflot jets seemed to be parked randomly, but upon closer look, Lacey realized they were not broken down at all and there were rattled passengers disembarking from them.

After a sour-faced customs agent rubber-stamped their papers, they checked into the Grand Hotel in St. Petersburg on a rare hot day of the Russian summer. The hotel was built around an indoor courtyard that was now a mecca for the traveling businessman. In 1997, Russia was "between regimes," and a Wild West lawlessness gripped the major cities. Danger marked the streets, and Lacey had been warned that evenings out could be trouble, and that the food in restaurants could not be trusted. It was wisest to eat only at the hotel and walk no farther than around the block. This made her job as tour guide and car arranger easier. Everything was done through the hotel desk.

Before sundown, Lacey took a jet-lagged stroll in the permitted area. Magnificence surrounded her, but the city was tattered at the edges and had a run-down feeling that affected all the stately buildings, except for the busy churches. The government buildings were shabby and tired; she could imagine the hunched shoulders of weary Kafkaesque protagonists trudging up their unending staircases. Street vendors sold assembly-line paintings only a few blocks away from the Hermitage, which made the junky pictures seem better by its beatific proximity.

Cavernous government offices had been converted to gigantic marts with stalls that offered household cleanser next to plastic baby Jesuses, and the variety of products from stall to stall was so extreme as to be illogical. The streets were alive, though; the warm day brought every-one out as if to stockpile sunlight and warmth for the battering winter. The people seemed to be of two types only, sculpted beauties or squat beer kegs. Lacey's flirtatious imagination made fantasy contact with a few of these Adonises, but she knew that if she was to sleep with anyone on this short trip, it might as well be one of her employers.

The food plan for the day would be the same for every day: breakfast in, lunch in, cocktails in, dinner in. Tomorrow morning they would be given a private tour of the Hermitage, tomorrow afternoon they would meet with the director, and the next day they would fly home. So they would be three musketeers for the next few days, all for one and one for all, relying on, or perhaps stuck with, one another for camaraderie. When Lacey returned to the hotel, she saw Patrice Claire already in the bar, talking to a man in black. He saw her and signaled her over just as the man was leaving.

"Are you passing secrets?" said Lacey.

"Oh no, just making use of my time here for commerce. How about a drink?"

"I'll have a black Russian...oh, wait, you said drink. Scotch." The joke didn't make it through the language barrier, and Patrice ordered the Scotch.

She slid onto a stool. "So, Patrice, what's with the hair?"

He looked at her, puzzled.

She continued, "You know, what's with the oily look?"

"I am European. It's what we do."

76

"Maybe forty years ago . . . but come on."

"Anything else you find objectionable?"

"Just the gold chain. And the open shirt. Chest hair doesn't have the same effect on American girls. Oh, and I'll pay for your drink. It's the least I could do."

"I should pay. I'm so grateful for the personal instruction."

"Just thoughts."

"If I don't grease my hair, it's like an Afro."

"No way. Euros don't have Afros. Something matte would do it. Same effect, no shine."

"Now should I criticize your hair?"

"You can't. Unfortunately for you, I have perfect hair. I have hair that women sit in beauty parlors for hours to try and achieve. Natural streaks, natural highlights. I think my breasts are slightly low, so I'm vulnerable if you want to get even."

"Do you get a lot of complaints?"

"No," said Lacey, then flatly: "Oh, my God, it was a trick question."

"Tell you what," said Patrice. "After dinner, come to my room. I'll show you something."

Lacey went to change for dinner. Her "luxury" room, one third the size of a room at a Holiday Inn, had electronics from the 1940s and buttons for valet, maid, and room service, all out of commission. A fat hunk of telephone sat by the bedside. Out her window, she could see the Russian Museum, which she found uninviting. Its repeating vertical windows reminded her of a pair of wide, frilly underpants.

She lay down on the bed for just a minute, and the overwhelming weight of jet lag settled on her. Lying there, unable to lift even an arm, she went into a trance of sleep, waking only a few minutes before the eight-thirty dinnertime. She forced her body to sit up, her head still hanging heavy with double gravity. She sleepwalked to the bathroom and dipped her face in cold water. She looked at herself. Passable, she thought. She bent over to let the blood run to her head, rose slowly, and got dressed.

At dinner, Lacey didn't uncap her wit; she thought it would be inappropriate. She was there to listen. She quietly smiled at Patrice, whose hair was now minus the sheen of whatever it was he had been greasing it with. She understood this dinner could be an opportunity to learn something, and her serious question—do museums often swap works of art—was answered quickly by Barton.

"Oh yes," he said. "How do you think the National Gallery got its Raphael? Andrew Mellon swept in and bought a ton of pictures after the revolution because the Reds thought paintings were bourgeois."

Diners in Russia smoked feverishly at the table, and when Barton pulled one out, Lacey inhaled the secondhand smoke and eventually, wanting the nicotine boost, asked for one herself.

After dinner, Lacey, wrongly assuming her rendezvous with Patrice was a secret, excused herself, said good night, and left. At eleven p.m., only a few minutes after dessert and coffee, she rapped on his door, heard shuffles and voices, and the door was opened.

Patrice invited her in—his room was a suite—and she saw the man in black who earlier had spoken with him at the bar. Patrice introduced him, Ivan something. He spoke French with Patrice, English with her, and Russian whenever he felt like it.

"I wanted you to see this," Patrice said, and gestured to the man, who laid an ostrich briefcase on a table. The man turned the case toward them and opened it presentationally. In the case, against black velvet, was amber. Amber rings, amber necklaces, amber jewelry.

The salesman stood with firm confidence, as if he were getting out of the way of a knowledgeable collector and a premier object.

Lacey sat at the table. "May I?" she said.

"Certainly."

She picked up several pieces, rotating them in the light, seeing fissures in the honey-colored transparent stone that pierced the gem like frozen lightning bolts. Occasionally there was an insect trapped in the petrified resin, which brought a vivid picture of the amber's formation, the slow ooze of ninety-million-year-old tree sap flowing over a prehistoric bug.

"Pick something," said Patrice.

Lacey chose a small pendant, with the amber hanging from a filigreed silver claw, laid it across her neck, and smiled. "It's so lovely."

Patrice pointed to two other pieces—Lacey figured they were for other girlfriends—and the man in black scooped them up with, "Excellent choice. Beautiful, so clear."

Lacey held her pendant, warming the amber to her touch as the two men finished their business. She sensed that the amber jewelry was not that expensive, but connoisseurship mattered from piece to piece.

The man in black left, leaving Lacey to wonder what was next.

"Vodka?" said Patrice.

Ah. Vodka was next.

"Sure." Sounds of pouring as Lacey pinched the amber between her fingers and held it to the lamplight.

"Come look out the window."

She went to the window, which was in the bedroom, where the lights were off. Moonlight and city lights gave the room a blue hue, and the fanciful, spiraling towers of cathedrals could be seen poking up over the top of the city's otherwise rigid architecture. Patrice pointed with his finger, circling his arm around her, resting it on her shoulder. He turned half toward her. Sensing permission, he slid his other hand to her breast and caressed it, to the accompanying crinkle of the starch in her blouse.

"I haven't been felt up since high school."

He said nothing but continued his exploration. There was a moment of unbuttoning, and his hand edged toward her skin, which was becoming dewy from internal heat. He stood there like a boy, holding, cupping, grazing her skin with his fingertips. His lips brushed her neck and shoulder, and Lacey's arm dropped. The back of her hand moved toward his pant leg, where she felt what she expected. Minutes passed without advancement, just a steady state of touch.

They stood at the window, in the darkened room, in the same posture, without an instinct to relocate, her hand exploring him, unzipping, reaching in, to which he responded by lifting her skirt and pressing the back of his hand against her. Their heads were both bowed now, their foreheads resting against each other, breathing in what the other breathed out. Lacey lifted her leg against the sill, widening his access to her. He moved her underwear to one side and his fingers slipped in effortlessly, as though they were being drawn up by osmosis. Lacey reached between her legs, lubricating her hand and moving it over to him. They now understood that they were not moving from the window, that this stance was to be the extent of their dalliance. Their breathing intensified; there were adjustments of their bodies, rings clunking on metal, and shoes hitting walls. Lacey's back rested on the windowsill, and one arm stiffened against the opposite side to hold her firm against his hand while her other hand pulled and pushed on him until the end came for both of them.

Lacey got a towel from the bathroom for the gentle mop-up, and then, their legs shaky from their unbalanced stances, they laid themselves on the bed.

"Whoosh," said Lacey.

"You are a very beautiful creature."

"Well, I'm definitely a creature."

There was an unawkward silence.

"Tomorrow," said Lacey.

"Yes, tomorrow. Tomorrow the Hermitage."

"Are you a dealer?"

"No, definitely not. I must move pictures around only to acquire more."

"You have the collector's disease."

"Not a disease. A disease makes you feel bad. I have a mania, an acquisitive gene. Pictures come through me like a moving train through a station. I only need to own them once."

"Like you owned me tonight."

"I don't think of it that way. You, pictures, two different things."

"Momentary objects of desire." Lacey was cornering him, in a friendly way, and she could tell he was rethinking.

"It's true," he continued, "that both you and paintings are layered. You, in the complex onion-peel way, dark secrets and all that. Paintings operate in the same way." He didn't say anything more.

"Uh. Hello? Go on," said Lacey.

"Well, first, ephemera and notations on the back of the canvas. Labels indicate gallery shows, museum shows, footprints in the snow, so to speak. Then pencil scribbles on the stretcher, usually by the artist, usually a title or date. Next the stretcher itself. Pine or something. Wooden triangles in the corners so the picture can be tapped tighter when the canvas becomes loose. Nails in the wood securing the picture to the stretcher. Next, a canvas: linen, muslin, sometimes a panel; then the gesso—a primary coat, always white. A layer of underpaint, usually a pastel color, then, the miracle, where the secrets are: the paint itself, swished around, roughly, gently, layer on layer, thick or thin, not more than a quarter of an inch ever—God can happen in that quarter of an inch—the occasional brush hair left embedded, colors mixed over each other, tones showing through, sometimes the weave of the linen revealing itself. The signature on top of the entire goulash. Then varnish is swabbed over the whole. Finally, the frame, translucent gilt or carved wood. The whole thing is done."

Lacey grasped his forearm and squeezed it, as if to signal that the extremes he went to were all right with her. They lay there for a while, sounds of traffic in a light rain coming from outside.

Lacey got up. "That was a nice shortcut. I don't have to get dressed." She made a move to the door. "Does this mean I have to sleep with Talley, too?"

"They say he's got a girlfriend somewhere. No one knows who."

"Maybe it's a boyfriend."

"You make me laugh, Lacey."

"We'll see," she said.

19.

THE NEXT MORNING, Lacey sat in the courtyard with her breakfast, and when she saw Patrice turning onto the landing from the stair-
well, she opened her legs and lifted her skirt slightly, showing him a
flash of polka-dot underwear.

At ten a.m., they got in a limo to take them three blocks to the Hermitage. They stopped on a wide street along the Neva where the side
entrance was. The museum was closed today, and they were provided
a special tour. Tall wooden doors swung open into a small anteroom,
where they were given a brief security check, and a guide appeared—a
woman with short dark hair and wearing a worn, ill-fitting uniform—to
escort them around. Even though the corridor had layers of green paint
that reminded Lacey of her high school cafeteria, the oak wainscoting
and interior doors had a mellow patina that spoke of history. They were
led up a small staircase that opened onto a stairway of renown: wide,
hushed, and grand. Then they stepped into the first room of paintings.

The gallery was paneled and dark—translucent shades over the tall
windows were raised only a few feet, pinching off the light. The ceilings
soared up twenty feet, Lacey estimated, and on the walls were a few
Rembrandts, Ruysdaels, and unidentified, musty masters. All the pictures were dingy and brooding, with ornate carved frames that seemed
to foam around them.

"This is the beginning of our seventeenth-century collection," said the guide phonetically.

They stood in the center of the room and circled their wagons, each with a back to the other. Lacey wondered why these paintings, made in a century lit only by candlelight and fireplaces, were so dark. How could anyone have seen them? It seemed that Impressionism should have been invented immediately, not only for visibility, but for cheer.

The guard waited patiently, staring toward the daylight with an expression of having been caught in a stagnant pool of unending time. Talley, looking at a nighttime seascape, whispered to Lacey—because whispering was the voice that the hallowed gallery inspired—"You know what I like?" He pointed toward the seascape. "I like it when the moonlight is reflected on the water." He said this as though he didn't want anyone to hear a thought so mundane, as though it were a confession for his priest, who would no doubt impose penance of the harshest kind. Lacey wondered how this connoisseur, this scholar, a man who dealt in Picassos, Braques, and Kandinskys, could care about moonlight on water, a simple effect used by both masters and Sunday painters.

As they moved on through the Hermitage, the ceiling height seemed to grow with every room. Past Jan Steens and even more Rembrandts and through hallways whose second floors, lined with oak paneling holding entrenched libraries, looked down onto galleries below. The tour was punctuated by the appearances of babushkas, stubby little women who served as museum guards and whose word was law. They stood like garden gnomes, wearing head scarves and peasant dresses, and they lurked in the corner of your eye, giving the feeling that if you looked at them, they would vanish into a hidden passage, moving as if on clockwork rollers.

They came into a large hall, tall, wide, and supremely ornate, with glass vitrines extending the length of the room, containing a vast collection of bejeweled clocks and golden boxes, the result of intense craftsmanship applied to useless loot. The quantity of stuff made the most exquisite reliquary seem inadequate when compared with the even more refined one sitting next to it, and after a half hour spent in the room, their response to this treasury had dulled.

They were then led upstairs, to the highest floors, where the oak paneling was replaced by industrial paint and track lighting. However, there was compensation for this depressing change in ambience. The transition from the lower floors was like being taken from the river Styx up to an ascendant sunrise in paradise. Here hung the Matisses and Picassos from the first decade of the twentieth century, paintings so startling, then and now, that they provided a fulcrum on which twentieth-century art was hoisted. To Barton Talley, being in the presence of these pictures—Matisse's colossal painting of elongated figures the color of red clay, dancing against a turquoise blue sky, and Picasso's Cubist women, painted in dark greens and grays—was like being in the presence of the singular gravity around which the modern art world revolves.

Lacey knew she was seeing something she could not quite comprehend. She didn't feel equipped to appreciate these paintings, but she suspected it was a moment that would acquire meaning as her life went on.

She leaned in to Patrice. "How did they get to Russia?"

Talley, looking over to be sure they were the proper distance from the guide, intervened.

"It seems the revolution developed an eye for pictures. Two great rivals, Morozov and Shchukin, were the only two Russians who saw Matisse and Picasso as collectible. They were fantastic competitors, and each made sojourns to Paris to gobble up as much as he could. They double-hung them in grand apartments, until, of course, the Marxists stole—uh, *nationalized* that which the State would never in a million years have collected." Talley looked around warily, as though he might be shackled at any moment.

They toured the rest of the galleries, the endless Kandinskys and Braques, and every picture was enhanced by Talley's sometimes enigmatic expertise ("Poor old Chagall," he said, not adding anything), until they were exhausted by art and longing for food. They went back to the real world, the busy courtyard of the Grand Hotel, where they ordered American sandwiches and rested up for their afternoon meeting.

At three p.m., they met in the lobby and were taken to the director's office in the Hermitage. The director spoke English and welcomed them cordially. "Did you see our few pictures?" he joked. "Come..."

He opened a side door onto a large library. In the room, resting on the waist-high shelf that ran around the bookcases, were eight large Rockwell Kents, the Greenland pictures, inhabited by sled dogs and

The Bay of Naples by Moonlight, Ivan Aivazovsky, circa 1850
47.6 × 75.2 in.

Greenlanders, ice floes and midnight sun. On the opposite railing were a dozen paintings by the Russians Aivazovsky and Makovsky, landscapes, mist-scapes, and village-scapes, some of size, some small and resting on the floor. Not as magnificent, Lacey thought.

"Russia is getting interested in its own," said the director, and with that ensued a negotiation as tough as a missile crisis under Khrushchev. Lacey sat, pretending to make notes in order to justify her presence. Forty-five minutes later all sides were exhausted, and the result was the same as if one of them had said in the first five minutes, "How about twelve Russian pictures for eight Kents?"

They were offered vodka, and they sat around the center table, eventually laughing and toasting. The director looked up at the Kents. "I'm going to miss these pictures."

"Ah, you spent time with them?" said Talley.

"No, this is the first time I've seen them. I didn't know we had them, but they are quite beautiful. Couldn't be hung here, of course. Next to the Rembrandts and Matisses, they would look like...what is the word? Slang for shit."

"Uh...," stammered Talley, "turds?"

"Ah, turds. That's the word I'm looking for. Yes, they would look like turds. What about Kent? Wasn't he a...what did you call us? Commies? Wasn't he a Commie?"

"Never quite," said Talley. "It's mostly forgotten now. He's too rare to collect; that's been a problem."

"You want to see something? You want to see something wonderful?"

"We would like to see something wonderful," said Patrice.

The director rose, went to his office, and called out, "Sylvie, bring in the gouache we were looking at."

A minute later, a striking brunette entered the room, so beautiful that Lacey's normal confidence was dimmed. She observed the men's response to this sylph, noticing that Patrice was doing the gentlemanly thing and faking oblivion, while Talley stared at her between neck and knees. She brought in a Van Gogh watercolor and set it on the railing.

"Please, take down the Aivazovskys," said the director. "It's for their own good."

The brunette leaned the two paintings on either side of the Van Gogh on the floor, giving the gouache breathing room. The director turned to Talley. "Do you know this picture?"

The subject was a green boat on yellow sand next to a blue sea, eighteen by twenty-four inches, under glass. "Of course I know the painting, but I didn't know there was a gouache. It's wonderfully fresh," said Talley, standing and examining it. Lacey came close. The signature, "Vincent," made her feel the artist was nearby, that his brush had just lifted off the paper.

There was among them—five of them now—a sudden, communal silence. They stood motionless for several seconds, as though the desire to remain still had coincidentally struck each of them at exactly the same time. These were thoughtless seconds. The object was not for sale, not for trade; it had already ascended. It was for them only, to be seen by them only, as though the artist himself had placed it before them, a holy thing. The object seemed, in this brief encounter, sentient. It sat quietly, and everyone was quiet. It spoke in silence, because that was the language of the moment.

"Well," said the director, "thank you, Sylvie." Sylvie picked up the picture and started in motion, a double whammy of beauty. "It's leaving, sadly," said the director. "We've owned it since the war. We got it from the Germans, as spoils, after they looted us and we looted them back, and we kept it all these years. Now we make nice. Give back."

The director poured another round of vodka as Patrice moved the

Aivazovskys off the floor and back to their makeshift easel. Several Russian pictures had been excluded from the trade, the too small and the too inconsequential. Lacey looked, through affected eyes, at one minor Aivazovsky, lit by reddening sunlight, of moonlight on the water. The Aivazovskys were looking more beautiful to her now.

20.

LACEY UNDERSTOOD the ways of men, but she did not know how clever they could be. That night at the hotel, she walked into the bar and saw Talley and Claire sitting at a table with Sylvie. She could not remember any contact or any efforts made in that direction. It all must have taken place after they left the museum, by phone, which was impossible to use, or by messenger, which was even more impossible to imagine, since she was the travel coordinator and had never run across anyone like a messenger. Lacey, in rare confusion, didn't know whether to join the table, but everyone's eyes met at the same time and there was no other alternative for anyone.

"You met earlier at the Hermitage. Sylvie is one of the curators of drawings," Talley said.

Curator of drawings? Lacey thought. Jesus Christ, she can't be thirty.

Sylvie was a five-language European with a soft voice that was raised only to laugh at stories about rich-world: so-and-so's yacht or a Greek's rowdy behavior at a restaurant that ended in broken plates. All this seemed very cosmopolitan to Lacey. She did, however, remain composed. Lacey wondered if Sylvie had been so beautiful from birth that she didn't know her power was unearned. Like the cooing attention lavished on a three-legged dog.

Talley spoke: "Too bad you have to give back the Van Gogh."

"He's not giving it back. He just likes to say he is."

"He can do that?" said Claire.

"In the new Russia, lies and truth are indistinguishable. He may give it back, but it will take years. We gain years of diplomacy with only announcements."

"Will our deal stick?" said Claire.

"Stick?"

"Will our deal *hold*?"

"Oh yes, it's too insignificant. These deals go on all the time. There's no supervision."

Lacey pried into the conversation. "That little Aivazovsky, how much?"

"What do you mean?" said Claire.

"How much is it?"

"It's worth around fifteen thousand."

"I didn't ask how much it's worth. How much is it to buy?"

"You want to buy it?"

"I might."

"It's twelve thousand."

"That's what it's worth," said Lacey.

"I said it's worth fifteen."

"Same difference. Fifteen, twelve. The same."

"I'll sell it for eleven."

"You have nothing in it. You made enough today that your cost is covered. I'll pay you what you have in it. Nothing."

"Maybe you should pay her to take it," Talley added.

"I'll pay six thousand."

Lacey was doing two things at once. She was letting the table know she was funded and letting Patrice know that he owed her. She persisted: "You don't want to take it back. I can put it in my suitcase."

"I would be doing you a favor at ten thousand."

"You would be doing me a favor at six thousand."

"She's eating you alive," said Sylvie, displaying rapport with Lacey and facility with English.

"I've got ten thousand in it."

"You've got nothing in it. It's all profit to you. I'll give you eight thousand."

Talley, amused, spoke: "You are whimpering and wounded, Patrice."

"All right. Eight thousand. But only if I buy the drinks."

Sylvie laughed, Talley laughed, Patrice laughed, Lacey laughed.

Later, in her room, the phone rang. She knew who it was. She did not answer.

21.

SHE HAD WRAPPED the Aivazovsky in a bathroom towel, wedged it safely in her suitcase, and transported the émigré back to the Upper West Side of New York, where she realized, after sending Patrice Claire a check for eight thousand dollars in Paris, that she hated it. It was half as good as an American picture of the same period, and it did not accomplish in her uptown apartment what the Avery had accomplished in her downtown apartment. This was an eight-thousand-dollar souvenir, the price tag on an exotic and egotistical moment far away. However, it was the most expensive thing she owned, so she hung it in a place of honor in her new flat, where absolutely no visitor, art-wise or not, ever noticed or commented on it.

22.

LACEY'S NEW DIGS brought small quakes to her accustomed way of life. Old friends were now subway rides away instead of around the corner, local restaurants had to be scouted, and her route to work was now on a crosstown bus, which meant that on rainy days she had to dodge slush much more frequently than when she was downtown. However, movie theaters abounded, and bars were classier and friendlier to her new, upscale life. On weekends and holidays, she bicycled down the West Side bike path toward Chelsea, sometimes meeting the girls for lunch, dropping into galleries on Saturdays before work, and on Sundays she circled the entire city of Manhattan if the day was lazy enough and warm enough. Nearby, Central Park grew into an oasis of biking, jogging, strolling, street music, tanning, fashion, summer theater, and solitude. For nightlife, though, she eschewed the Upper West Side and would head below 14th Street on weekends for a taste of rambunctiousness.

Barton Talley had given her high marks, and Lacey was more entrenched than ever at Sotheby's, but the summer was under way. The art world was moribund. Promotions and pay increases were unlikely when there was no money coming in. August made Manhattan bake and stink, and her trek to Atlanta for, she assumed, a last look at her grandmother did not relieve the oppression, as Atlanta was under a tidal wave of humidity. There were solemn moments in Granny's bedroom, but in the living room, there were small, quiet talks of inheritance, and Lacey could gather that with priorities going to her mother and aunts, little would come her way. She was thankful for her own sudden wealth.

Labor Day weekend stretched long and slow, and I met her for lunch at Isabella's on Columbus—at an off time, thank God—when we could sit outside and idle away several hours without guilt of table hogging. Lacey's art knowledge had trebled, and she related the entire Russia trip. My face stayed in a frozen grin while she told me of her liaison with Patrice Claire, hiding my real feeling of envy for the lucky Patrice.

"You know what I think now?" said Lacey. "He didn't fuck that Sylvie person. But, oh well, I wasn't up to a second night of high jinks anyway. Plus, I never have sex on the second date."

"Only the first," I said.

"Zackly," said Lacey. "So, Thursday," she continued, then stared at me.

"Thursday. What's Thursday?"

"It's the beginning of the high holy days."

"What are you talking about?" I said.

"The art season! The art season opens Thursday. Why do you think Barneys stays open on Labor Day? To sell clothes for Thursday!"

I laughed. I was removed from the money side of the art world, but I liked that so much excitement was stirring around a subject I had decided to devote my life to.

"There's a show opening at Talley, Giorgio Morandi. Let's go," she said.

"Jeez, Lacey, and then we hop over to Hirschl and Adler for some real kicks? Let's go to Chelsea. There're about a dozen openings that night."

"We'll get Angela and Sharon to come, too."

I said yes, and then I said, "So . . . how is . . . you know, the thing?"

"We are fine," she said. "You and I are fine."

23.

I MET LACEY at her apartment. Wet, robed, mouth full of toothpaste, she pointed me the few steps toward the living room and then flitted into the bathroom. I looked around. I had never been in a young woman's quarters that bore the appearance of success; the ones I'd seen looked assembled from hand-me-downs and junk stores. Bedrooms, if I ever made it that far, usually held a lonely futon. Lacey was no longer dragging furniture from her past life into her new one. Her apartment, now furnished in Craftsman style, with mica lamps and hooked rugs, contradicted its inhabitant, this girl who was barely tame, whose businesslike demeanor was a curtain she closed and opened.

When Lacey reappeared, I changed my opinion. Wearing a dress that uptown looked smart and downtown looked vintage, I realized she was of two worlds, able to exist in either of them without denying her own personality. She had always had flair, even when she had been struggling. She was the type that would be photographed on the street wearing mud boots by *The New York Times* with the implication that, yes, here was commanding style. Yet this was the first time I saw her that she looked like a woman and not a girl.

Lacey had made mint juleps from a *Times* recipe, and we sat by her window at a small round table, sipping them like two grannies. Her window faced south, which meant that the impending sunset ricocheted down the street, turning windows gold and opaque. Lacey always managed to find her light, though I don't think it was conscious: she looked as beautiful as I'd ever seen her. Then we hailed a taxi to the Upper East Side.

People in coats and ties were milling around the Talley gallery, and on the wall were the minimally rendered still lifes by Giorgio Morandi, most of them no bigger than a tea tray. Their thin browns, ashy grays, and muted blues made people speak softly to one another, as if a shouted word might curdle one of the paintings and ruin it. Bottles, carafes, and ceramic whatnots sat in his paintings like small animals huddling for warmth, and yet these shy pictures could easily hang next to a Picasso or Matisse without feeling inferior.

Lacey scanned the party and instantly gave me a look that said, "What are we doing here?" The attendees were on the other side of sixty, and Lacey, observing the clothing of the men, with their gold-button

Still Life with Wine Bottles, Giorgio Morandi, 1957
12 × 16 in.

blazers, plaid pants, and striped shirts topped with starched white collars, said to me, "Are they all admirals?"

Talley came over to us and gave Lacey an extraordinarily warm greeting, hugging her like an old friend. I suppose the adventure they had shared made them comrades. "Isn't Morandi marvelous!" he said. "Every one is the same and every one is different. I opened the season with him because he is uncriticizable! I'd like to hang him in a room with Edward Hopper and see who could outsilence the other. Lacey," he continued, "if you ever get bored at Sotheby's, call me. I could use you in all kinds of ways." Lacey knew there was no double entendre in Barton's invitation, and she felt flattered.

Angela and Sharon rolled in, looking like dressed-up secretaries, which they were, and I could read on their faces the desire to back out the door, hoping no one would notice. But we corralled them, did an obligatory walk around the gallery, and then were standing on the street in perfect September weather, now officially on the town. I realized we were really on the prowl not for art, but for a party. We took a taxi for luxury and charged into the steaming heart of Chelsea, energized and wearing our best outfits. People spilled out into the streets, and the gallery fluorescents did, too, lighting up the sequins on dresses and other glitterati. The plastic wineglasses were appropriate here, where at Talley's they seemed like a lapse in critical thinking.

The gallery names downtown stood out from the stolid uptown houses: Exit Art, 303, Atelier 14, Deitch Projects, Feature, Generous Miracles, Metro Pictures. Some of the names sounded more like bars than galleries, and there was a parallel. Here, the attractive waitresses were the attractive gallery girls, the macho bartenders had become the less-than-macho gallery guys, and the customers' eyes were ever darting around the room, searching for eye contact. The spaces had the buzz of a noisy restaurant, and there were lots of handshakes and kisses for people who only ran into each other at these events. The art on the walls—or on the floor—was duly noted, but if a cynic wanted to make the case that the art was there as an excuse to socialize, he could.

Our group hit about five galleries, in and out, in and out. There were paintings that were intentionally bad, which was an easier goal to reach than those trying to be intentionally good. One gallery had an artificial flower sprouting out of the ceiling; another gallery's interior was coated with dense wax the color of rosé wine, in which the artist had scratched the names of all his rivals; and another gallery had a robotic machine that either saved or destroyed snapshots according to the whim of the viewer. Some of the art made Lacey laugh, some she admired, some made her turn to me and make a vomit sign with finger in mouth.

One artist with the pseudonym (it was natural to assume) of Pilot Mouse had taken over a gallery and installed...another gallery. We viewers went in one at a time, and inside was a simulation of an uptown gallery, complete with gallerygoers—really guerrilla actors—who walked around and looked at the antique store paintings on the wall. It was, I supposed, a comment on gallery going, though I don't know what the comment was. The actors uttered phrases like "The artist is commenting on the calculation inherent in our society" or "The artist is playing with the idea of dichotomies." These phrases were the smarty-pants version of a car dealer's "This little baby only has eight thousand miles on it and gets fifteen miles a gallon." But Pilot Mouse had created something intriguing: I felt a mental disorientation knowing that everything in the room was fake, including the people, especially having just come from a similar real situation uptown; and after I went back into the real world, the feeling lingered uncomfortably. Lacey reported that she had engaged one of the actors in a conversation about a picture, during which neither of them broke character, meaning that she too had become a fake gallerygoer. Afterward, as we walked down the street, Lacey turned to me and said, "How the hell do they sell that?"

The Robert Miller Gallery had one foot in uptown and one foot in downtown, and his image was that of a reputable dealer who had a good eye and knew the market. We wandered in, ambling through a show of Alice Neel paintings, which to me could qualify as either fine art or a student's MFA thesis show. Lacey separated from us and found herself looking through a sandwich of glass that divided the offices from the gallery. She had noticed a small fourteen-inch-square silk screen of flowers.

"Is that...?" she said to one of the employees as he walked into the office, balancing three plastic cups of wine.

"Andy," he said, letting the implied "Warhol" appear in Lacey's head.

She looked at it again, thinking of the few Morandi still lifes she had just seen, thinking it was Morandi deprived of all its energy, squeezed of its juice, that it was as dead as a thing can be, thinking that it was a joyless illustration of one of earth's wondrous things, that it could hang in a dentist's office. After her years of looking at pictures that were working so hard, here was something that exerted no effort at all. And yet, hanging there on the wall, lit, it looked strangely like art.

We finally left Chelsea, our night of art-looking over, but Lacey was about to confront the problem of Andy Warhol.

Andy Warhol died in 1987 and, surprising many historians and connoisseurs, nestled into art history like a burrowing mole. He inched up in stature, casting a shadow over the more accomplished draftsman and less controversial figure Roy Lichtenstein, and could be referred to by

Flowers, Andy Warhol, circa 1965
48 × 48 in.

his first name only, like Jesus or Madonna. As with them, the reference could be either sacred or profane. As Warhol's prices escalated—some said by canny market manipulation from a handful of speculators—there was a strange inversion of typical market reaction. Formerly, when a masterpiece sold for an unimaginable price, as Picasso's *Yo, Picasso* did in 1989 for nearly forty-eight million dollars, it pulled up the prices of equivalent pieces by the same artist. Then, when Van Gogh's *Irises* sold for an equally unimaginable price in the same year, it pulled up the prices of *all* masterpieces. But when Warhol started to achieve newsworthy prices, the value of contemporary art, including art that was yet to be created, was pushed up from behind. Warhol's presence was so vivid, so recent, that he was identified not with the dead, but as the first nugget of gold from Sutter's Mill. The rush was on.

If Andy Warhol had lived to see his conquest of the art world, his response would have probably been a halfhearted "Oh wow." His artistic legacy is rich, but his legacy as a news item is equally rich. He mastered the laconic interview, never seeming to care how he came off and never caring whether he answered the question. He possessed an indifference that said he was not trying to be popular, which had the converse result of making him popular. When asked once what he would do if he was given a million dollars to make a movie, Warhol replied, "Spend fifteen thousand on the movie and keep the rest." This makes sense, when you remember that one of his early films was a seventy-minute continuous shot of his friend Taylor Mead's ass.

If Warhol had stepped into the Cedar Tavern bar, where all the tough-guy Abstract Expressionists hung out, he would have certainly been beaten up for ordering a milk. The shift from muscled, dynamic strokes of an angry brush, intended to reflect inner turmoil, to slack-armed pulls of silk-screened burlap, intended to pose as wallpaper, meant that the slow evolution of art had been upended. Art was no longer tough-guy stuff.

It was easy to give Pop critical status—there were lots of sophisticated things to say about it—but it was tougher to justify the idea that repetitive silk screens were rivals of great masters. If Cubism was speaking from the intellect, and Abstract Expressionism was speaking from the psyche, then Pop was speaking from the unbrain, and just to drive home the point, its leader Warhol closely resembled a zombie.

If you were older and believed in the philosophy of art as rapture, and didn't expect the next great development in art to be a retreat from beauty and an exploitation of ordinariness, then you couldn't endorse Warhol as the next great master. But if you were young, with essentially no stake in art's past, not caring about the difficulty of paint versus the ease of silk screen, you saw the images unencumbered, as bright and funny, but most of all ironic. This new art started with the implied tag "This is ironic, so I'm just kidding," but shortly the tag changed to "This is ironic, and I'm not kidding."

Lacey had been primed in the old art world, so the leap she was about to make took effort, but her heart was leading her head. The flower picture had piqued her interest, and the next day she slipped out of her office, five minutes at a time, to thumb through the library, turning page after page of Warhols, until her desire for the picture had risen to overflowing. She also checked auction prices on Andy Warhol flower paintings. Made in 1964, they were the least expensive of his significant pictures, rounding out at about fifteen thousand dollars for one of the small ones. She came to the conclusion that if Warhol was about deadness, the flower pictures were the deadest of them all. This was, as far as Lacey could remember, the first time she was affected not only by the object itself, but by its theory.

The next Saturday, Lacey went to the Robert Miller Gallery to check in on the picture. It was no longer on the wall, but she didn't let that bother her; pictures were often moved around at galleries. She inquired about it and was taken into an office where the picture had been rehung. A rep came in, a Ms. Adams, who startled Lacey with her youth, and gave her a pitch on the painting. "Comes from a collector who knew Warhol...in excellent condition...signed by Warhol on the back, which is rare...is approved by the Warhol estate." Lacey was instantly relieved that a problem was solved that she didn't know existed. After some haggling, she bought the picture for sixteen thousand dollars.

Robert Miller came in to congratulate her and meet this unknown new collector. "It's a lovely piece," he said.

"Yes," said Lacey, "it reached out and snagged me."

"I like these rich blacks, and how defined the stems are in the background. It's a wonderful example," said Miller, "and it's got great wall power."

"It stopped me from thirty feet away."

"Don't you love the relationship of the colors?" he said.

"Well, yes, but..." She hesitated. "I guess what I really love is..." Miller hung on his toes and looked at her through her long pause. "I love the way the moonlight is reflected on the water."

24.

IN A COUPLE OF MONTHS, Lacey had spent, quite unexpectedly, twenty-four thousand dollars on art. To feel comfortable spending that much in a short time, one must, I assume, have a multiple of that at least ten or twenty times. That is, unless you are far gone. I think Lacey was far gone for several months, perhaps deprived of oxygen from her long Russian flights. She also must have put forty thousand down on her apartment, and she had been generally liberal with cash at restaurants, and tips flowed like Bacchus's wine. No matter what amount she came into, I knew Lacey was not like a lottery winner who would wind up paranoid and broke, muttering, "It's all gone." She saw every action as bearing a response: every penny spent, somehow, would have a return, if not this year, then another; if not in kind, then in another form. But in spite of this practicality, she also—and this is what confuses me—could be rash. She was rash with people, with her body, her remarks. Lacey had an extraordinary sense of position: who was above her, who was below her. However, she considered no one her peer. She was equally reckless with all. So where was I in Lacey's world? I was, officially, a supporter of Lacey, like Angela and Sharon, told I was great, told I was loved. As she would say, "I need you guys so much."

25.

THE WARHOL QUICKLY displaced the Aivazovsky, which was moved to the bathroom. Having an eight-thousand-dollar picture in the bathroom amused her for about a week, then she thought of possible damage that could occur, including being lacquered with hairspray, bubbled by heat from a hair dryer, or sprayed with steam from the shower, and she moved it to the bedroom. For the next month or so, whenever she passed the Warhol, she felt her head crane toward it, as if it were a kid in a cradle that had to be checked in on, not only to see if it was all right, but for the sake of looking at something in which she had so much invested. She did not check in as one would on a stock, to see how the price was doing, but to see how her emotional investment was doing. When visitors came, if they didn't admire the picture—or worse, didn't notice it—she would think them stupid or confused, and they were moved to the bottom of her list of worthwhile people.

In the past few weeks, Lacey had unintentionally balanced her lopsided art world equation: She now knew what it was like to stand on the other side of a transaction. She had experienced the lunacy that can overtake the mind when standing before its inexplicable object of desire, in this case the Warhol, and she had felt the sudden, ego-driven impulses that spark the irrational purchase, in that case the Aivazovsky. She had, in just a few weeks, experienced buyer's remorse, buyer's rejoice, and the extremes of nervousness associated with first dates and executions. She was now able to put herself inside a collector's head, know that she was treating a blessed illness, and determine the appropriate bedside manner.

One night, she lay on her sofa peering over a book at the Warhol, and she retraced her route toward it, which led her to think about Ms. Adams at the Robert Miller Gallery. She liked that Ms. Adams was dealing with customers, unlike her backroom work at Sotheby's, and thought, I could be her.

26.

BECOMING MS. ADAMS began sooner than Lacey was expecting. The 1997 American paintings sales were listless, even though they were given a small boost with the sale of the remains of the property of Andrew Crispo, an ex-dealer whose precise eye for American art was complicated by his proximity to sordid sex scandals—one a brutal torture-murder—and jail time for tax evasion. In the 1980s, he had sold over ninety million dollars in American paintings to Baron Thyssen, and many of them now hang in Thyssen's museum near the Prado in Madrid. Acquitted of the especially seedy sex murder in 1985 that involved leather masks and mouth-balls, he was also a victim, if one could call him that, of tabloid excess when it was reported that sado-masochistic leather masks were found in his gallery, thus indicting him, at least in the newspapers. The press didn't realize that these masks were the work of artist Nancy Grossman—intellectually distant from those found in adult sado-shops—and unwearable. Crispo had vanished from the art world for years, three of which could be accounted for by time spent in the slammer; but this year he poked his head into a Christie's preview, and it was as though the other dealers in the room were pointing at him, shouting, "Unclean!"

But even as slow sales eroded the glamour of older American painting, there was an unexpected upswing in contemporary sales, and Lacey was still a valuable employee who was making connections with collectors and dealers. When Cherry Finch called her into her office in January 1998, Lacey was expecting good news. Tanya Ross watched her go in the office, watched the door being closed, watched and waited, knowing that if the rumor was true, Lacey would be coming out worse off than when she went in. A half hour later, Lacey had been fired, and she explained why to no one.

27.

IT WAS THE coldest day of February when Lacey flew to Atlanta for Kitty Owen's funeral. This conjunction of dire events was not Lacey's world crashing down around her: her grandmother, at ninety-six, was old enough that it felt as though her death had already happened even before it happened, and Lacey's release from Sotheby's was quiet enough and even accompanied by a vague but believable letter of recommendation from Cherry Finch. She told her family in Atlanta that she was moving to a gallery, which was true—that is, if events that have yet to happen but probably will can be counted as true.

Lacey's parents, Hart and Meg, were intelligent and cultured, two qualities that ride along effortlessly in households where the discussion of art is routine, though it's difficult to tell which is the chicken and which is the egg. The memorial was sensible, held in their living room in the early afternoon, with people speaking solemnly about the departed; a delightful letter was read aloud, written seventy-five years earlier from Maxfield Parrish to Kitty, and the Parrish print was featured over the fireplace. The early dark of the afternoon segued into cocktails after the children were trundled off. Hart and Meg had been the ones to attend to Kitty during her waning years, and the estate was passed down to Meg, though there was a will to be discussed, essentially a dispersal of gifts to friends and family.

As Lacey wandered around the house she grew up in, each bit of décor provoked in her waves of either affection or revulsion. The sixties modern stand-alone record player, bought as furniture and now used only for its radio, repulsed her. It had become an antique in her lifetime and had no mystique for her. But she felt an affection for the old records she discovered still stacked inside it, the ones she had played with microscopic precision, laying the needle in the groove like a skilled DJ. She held the jacket of the sound track to *Xanadu* next to her nose and inhaled it as though it were a madeleine, then removed the disk and saw written on the sleeve in her own hand, "Property of Lacey Yeager, age 10." There were antique dishes and silver plate place settings, there were framed paintings that Lacey now knew were worthy only of a junk shop, there were reproductions of famous paintings that showed her parents' good taste. Their furniture was in the style of Danish Modern: pieces that had never been near Denmark, and had been manufactured in the sixties, one decade too late to benefit from a growing craze for authentic fifties furnishings.

Lacey liked her parents, especially her father, but couldn't trace her character to either one of them. Her father's gentleness made her wonder where she got her mean streak. Her mother was practical, but hardly a prototype for her scalpel personality. Lacey was, however, bused as a child to a tough school. She'd often had to defend her modestly better financial status, exemplified by a pretty dress or lunch box depicting the latest TV fad. The usual options for coping were stoicism or aggression, but Lacey chose another: cunning. It had been cultivated from her childhood reading of age-inappropriate literature, encouraged by her mother and book-learned aunts. In children's literature, the clever foxes were often the bad guys, but Lacey never thought so.

Meg took Lacey into a side bedroom. "Lacey, Mom left a little will."

"I don't want anything," said Lacey. "You keep it."

"No, sweetie, it's not money. She wanted you to have the Parrish print. She said you're the one in the family who looks most like her and you should have it."

Lacey sat on a divan with a look of shock on her face, which changed into a suppressed laugh. "Oh, that is so sweet," she said. "I'll keep it forever; I want you to know that." No one at that time knew that her response, which sounded like gratitude, was infused with relief.

Lacey took the print back to her new apartment and shuffled a few things around on the walls until it finally found a home low on the wall, beside her bed. She poured herself a glass of wine, sat in her sole bedroom chair, and stared at the picture, thinking that she had experienced incredibly good luck.

28.

BY THE LATE 1990s, artists' output ranged from the gigantic to the minuscule, from the crafted to the careless, the thoughtful to the thoughtless. Richard Serra made art measured in tonnage, while Tom Friedman carved his self-portrait on an aspirin. Work ranged from macho to fey, regardless of the sexual preference of the artist.

Pilot Mouse edged into the art scene when he spray-painted black bats on walls and doorways around various neighborhoods. He parlayed these art attacks into money by following Jeff Koons's and Damien Hirst's template—and, incidentally, Rubens's and Rembrandt's: he maintained an art factory. The studio, a derelict warehouse teeming with volunteer assistants, produced paintings and sculpture, and in spite of excoriating critical response, the market responded with cash.

His breakthrough had come when collector Hinton Alberg, the American equivalent of the dynamic English collector Charles Saatchi, swept through a modest downtown show and bought every one of Mouse's paintings. The paintings, in retrospect, weren't that good, but when Hinton Alberg bought them out, they suddenly *became* good. The theory of relativity certainly applies to art: just as gravity distorts space, an important collector distorts aesthetics. The difference is that gravity distorts space eternally, and a collector distorts aesthetics for only a few years.

But this purchase was not what made Pilot Mouse a star. It was a

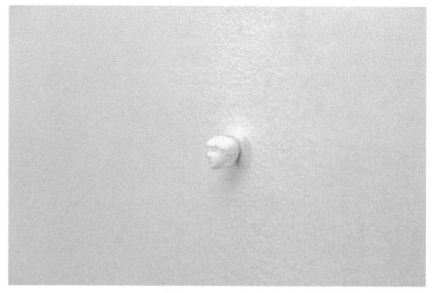

Untitled, Tom Friedman, 1994
.25 × .375 × .375 in.

revelation, made a few weeks later, that guaranteed he would have at least a decade of tenure as an art star. But to explain it, it is necessary to know a little bit about the eccentricities of Hinton Alberg.

Alberg was a collector with a quick purse, which delighted those on the receiving end of things. He donated to the most offbeat art functions, as well as to MoMA, Dia, and the Whitney, and therefore had made himself essential to the goings-on of New York art culture, both newfangled and old established. He had a body shaped like a bowling pin and would sometimes accidentally dress like one, too, wearing a white suit with a wide red belt. His wife, Cornelia, was thin where he was wide, and wide where he was thin, so when they stood side by side, they fit together like Texas and Louisiana. There was always a buzz when he entered a room, a buzz that could be described as negative.

There was a certain unfairness to the bad buzz because Hinton Alberg had at least a sense of humor where his collecting was concerned.

"I went to the Basel art fair last year. Before I left, Cornelia told me to try to slow down. " 'Don't buy everything, honey,' she told me. I told her, 'Darlin', don't you know I'm a *crazy man?* ' "

He described his overstuffed warehouse, where he stored his paintings, as either "a junkyard with gems or a gemyard with junk." But he was shy, too, so word of his humor did not leak into the main body of art society; and there was a disdain for his wealth, which was rumored to come from Cornelia's old Detroit money.

Hinton probably had many quirks, but one was highly visible to everyone in the room. He did not drink or abuse himself with anything except food, but he had cultivated or inherited an extraordinarily developed sense of smell, which meant that food was not only devoured but inhaled. Before each meal, he leaned into his plate, sometimes putting a napkin over his head to create an aromatic bell over the food, and took deep, elongated sniffs. From across the room, it looked as though Oliver Hardy had fainted into his food. This exercise was not limited to the entrée, but was employed at appetizer, dessert, and whatever else might appear. It was considered disgusting when a plate of hors d'oeuvres was passed around standees at a cocktail party and Alberg's nose was suspected of grazing the delectables. Once, it is said, he entered a town house off Madison and sniffed the underside of an antique Italian table.

After Alberg bought out the show, Pilot Mouse released the news that when he learned Alberg was coming to the gallery, he came in, took down every painting from the wall, turned them backward on the floor, and daubed the stretcher bars with light touches of truffle oil. He then rehung the pictures. When the story broke, Mouse spoke to *The New York Times* on the phone, saying that he was mocking collectors who bore the smell of money, by making paintings with an odor that was best discerned by a pig.

This comment made Pilot Mouse popular.

29.

BARTON TALLEY HIRED LACEY. She was now the first person a client might see after the receptionist. She was allowed to quote prices, but only after she had judged the client not worthy of Talley. This was a shortcut to success, because what she had learned at Sotheby's was that the Known don't always buy pictures; it was often the Unknown who converted from lookers into unexpected buyers. She had to bone up on a new set of artists, this time ones with famous names: Renoir, Modigliani, Balthus, Klee. The bins, unlike those at Sotheby's, were upstairs, at the end of a suite of offices, and sunlight dribbled in. She had space in one of the many alcoves, even had a private computer. Downstairs was a dimwit receptionist, Donna, who paged her for almost every question that needed answering.

There was less to do here than at Sotheby's. Three or four pictures a month came in or went out. There were shows built from inventory, like "Renoir and His Peers," which needed only one Renoir to ten works by anyone else who had been alive at the same time. "Works on Paper" meant anything that was on paper, regardless of theme or era. Talley also mounted the occasional miniblockbuster, all Giacometti, all de Kooning, some of the pieces borrowed from museums, some from collectors who swore their pieces weren't for sale but who would succumb to an extravagant offer that came after Talley suggested to a client that the owner was reluctant to sell. In fact, Talley did an extensive trade in pictures that weren't for sale, because he understood that anything was actually for sale at some price, and it could be harder to sell something that was for sale than it was to sell something that wasn't for sale. At least in the art business.

Lacey got used to being the front man—attending cocktail receptions, greeting clients—and found she had suitors. Too many repeat visits by a young man asking prices and wanting to be shown other pictures meant that Lacey was the draw, not the art. These were not downtown guys who wanted to fuck her and whom she wanted to fuck back. These were men with jobs who wanted to take her out to dinner and "see if it worked." They wanted to put their best foot forward, which often meant that she couldn't intuit who they would be when the courtesy stopped. The young men downtown were always clearly broke; the men uptown could pay for dinner on credit cards, but maybe they were broke, too.

The downtown men were tolerable because Lacey always viewed them as short term. The uptown men were intolerable because they were presenting themselves as long term. And there was always something fishy about them. She knew what a struggling artist was, she knew what a deejay was. But what was someone in finance? Her worst dates were those on which the other party tried to explain what he did, which was usually prefaced by "This is really boring, but..." and then the explanation would be reeled out in detail. Once, Lacey responded, "You lied when you said it was boring. You should have said it was beyond boring."

There was also a humor gap. Lacey's own wit seemed to blunt itself for lack of response. She thrived on feedback and interplay, but her lines and sparkle seemed to tumble off a cliff before arriving at their destination. The simple problem was that when she was "on," it was a one-man show, and when she was "off," she didn't like herself. But she also knew that her downtown boyfriends were like her downtown furniture: in need of upgrade. So she viewed time spent in the land of the normal as an investigation into the world of marriage-worthy men, even if she was unsure about her own interest in marriage. There must be one solid citizen who also had a spark of life, a sense of humor and adventure.

Lacey was becoming known as an up-and-comer, and her release from Sotheby's was perceived not as a firing, but as conventional art news: who was moving from what gallery to where. People did it all the time. In fact, her position at Talley was seen as a promotion of sorts, and stories about her, stories of audacity, were transmitted along the strands of spider silk that connected the art world.

30.

BARTON STOOD in the middle of his gallery while two art installers stared questioningly at him. He called to Donna, "Please ask Lacey to join me in the main gallery."

Lacey, as if from the ether, said, "I'm standing right behind you."

Barton turned. "Oh," he said. "What do you think? Hang it here?"

"Yes, but it needs to come up a foot."

"You think?"

"Too low," said Lacey.

"Up ten inches," Talley said to the installers. "And Lacey, I donated, unwillingly, to the new Institute of Contemporary Art in Boston. Sunday there's a benefactors' party, but it's, shall we say, 'open' to the Boston Museum board, an entity I'd like to avoid until its current members are dead and replaced with bright, shiny new ones. I think I should have someone there. Can you put in an appearance for me?"

When Talley was unavailable or too tired to show up at the latest cocktail party, he sent Lacey as a rep, because he believed a rep was essential, and a pretty rep had an effect beyond his own venerable powers.

31.

THE DELTA AIRLINES commuter plane to Boston was like having a private jet on call. It left every hour, no reservations necessary, and a ticket could be bought from a machine, so there was very little waiting in line. It returned every night up until eleven p.m., so Lacey could be home in bed by one a.m. She certainly would be given a little grace to arrive late to work the next day, but she preferred to show up on time because otherwise Donna would be in charge and might burn down the place.

She laid out three outfits for the trip: one for the plane ride, one for the evening cocktail party plus boring speech, and one for the next day's trip home. Lacey never chose comfortable clothes for travel, unless it was coincidental, as her instinct was to look at least cute at all times. Naked or well-dressed, was her dictum. And because she was feeling a strong rise in her libido and couldn't foresee a sexual circumstance in Boston that would be appropriate or wise, she reached in a bedroom drawer and selected a vibrator, in this case the one that looked least like a vibrator so she could pass through the X-ray without a glance or wink coming her way. She sometimes used one to promote sleep, although it usually woke her when it finally rolled off the bed and banged on her wooden floor.

Lacey's solo entrance into Boston was less important than Christ's entry into Jerusalem, but not to Lacey. She was a certified representative of a major gallery in Manhattan, and Boston was an outpost of Manhattan that needed to know about her. Lacey had misread Boston as simply a tourist town, but even a short walk from her hotel on this spring day gave her chills of patriotism. She passed the Old North Church and then found herself standing in front of Paul Revere's house. She could feel the immediacy of its revolutionary citizens and the clashes that stirred the community and evolved into legends. Lacey was, in a surprise to herself, moved.

She went back to her hotel for a nap and primp before the evening's cocktail party, but the nap was replaced by a session with a guidebook, in which she read the relevant entries about what she had just seen.

Lacey took a last look at herself: her hair, fuller and longer than usual and still variegated blond even though summer had long since been over; her skin, white against the blue wool of the business suit she had purchased and had fitted just for the trip; and a pair of absurdly high heels on which she was still learning to navigate. Her final swing toward the mirror was one of those moments in a woman's life where she thinks she looks more beautiful than she ever thought she could.

No rain or wind meant that Lacey could walk to the event in Boston's Back Bay without risking a disturbance to her appearance, and it took her only a few yards to find her balance atop her spikes. She stood outside the ICA, a foundation that, if tonight's fund-raiser helped, would be relocated to wider and whiter corridors on Northern Avenue. The current building was too dowdy and cramped to house the needs of contemporary art, which was becoming more hungry for space almost daily. Lacey planned an early arrival so she could familiarize herself not only with the surroundings, but with the guest list. There was a foyer with a table hosted by two young men guarding what Lacey guessed were gift bags to be distributed at evening's end. On each bag was an envelope with a name. There was also a pay phone in the foyer, and Lacey, in a fit of inspiration, went to it, entered in her credit card information, and called Barton Talley.

"It's me."

"Where are you?"

"I'm in the lobby of the ICA."

"Good..."

"And I can see the gift bags for every guest. With names."

"Read them off."

"Mr. and Mrs. Donald Batton."

"Ignore."

"Shelby...something...Fink?"

"Frink. Ignore."

"The Whitzles."

"Oh, my God, run for your life."

"Gates Lloyd."

"Huge collector. Don't ignore."

"Ms. Tricia Dowell."

"Don't mention my name."

"Hinton Alberg."

"Big collector, don't ignore."

The list went on, and Lacey did her best to remember the important ones. As the party expanded to the elite fifty, she introduced herself, was chatty with almost all, and ignored only the most dangerous. Even though she was by far the youngest person in the room, her prettiness was unthreatening because she used it so subtly. She latched on to one group, introducing herself enthusiastically with, "Boston is *beautiful*...I had no idea it was so art-friendly. Hello, I'm..." From this group, she would gather information about another group ("The Frinks are restoring a home on Beacon Hill..."), then walk over to the

Frinks and say brightly, "I heard you're restoring a home on Beacon Hill. That is so exciting!" The Frinks would bestow on her another tidbit, and thus she made it around the room like a square dancer, changing partners when a new bit of information was called out. When asked where Barton Talley was, after she explained her presence, she would say, "He's in Europe."

Droopy canapés were passed around by volunteers, stopping only when a man clinked a glass with a spoon to quiet the room. Everyone halted where they were, and Lacey found herself standing next to a rotund man in brown and his big-haired wife. The man who had clinked the glass spoke with the ease of a natural-born fund-raiser: "Because of you, the ICA is in position to go forward with our grand plans..."

Lacey stood listening, wondering if she was in the best group. She spotted a few married men looking over at her, then noticed the rotund man signaling for canapés. A young woman brought them over, balancing a tray on her open palm, offering a paper napkin with the other. The man bent over the tray, took a whiff in the shape of an S, and then selected one, then two, then three. The tray was offered to Lacey, and she leaned over, took a whiff of similar length, and selected only one. The man looked at her, wondering if he had found a compatriot or a satirist, and Lacey said, "I'm with you."

Cornelia Alberg leaned over to Lacey and said, "You have a friend for life."

After the speech, Hinton and Cornelia Alberg introduced themselves. Lacey was a perfect art crony for them. The Albergs collected contemporary and Lacey sold modern masters, two very different fields, so there was no feeling that Lacey might have ulterior motives; but here was a person, they thought, who should be converted to the new. Yes, they knew of Barton Talley, "marvelous eye, marvelous eye."

"But," said Lacey, "he deals in modern."

Alberg puffed up, and a big grin spread out across his big face. "But we love it all! Lacey Yeager, we love it all!"

Cornelia looked at Lacey and, erroneously, saw herself at a younger age. "We're having a private tour of the Isabella Stewart Gardner tomorrow, why don't you join us?" she said.

While Lacey was hearing Barton Talley's voice in her head saying, *Hinton Alberg, don't ignore,* her own voice was speaking: "I would be thrilled."

She walked out of the event, mingled with a few people who stood outside with drinks, and started her walk home. She was approached by two men—Lacey thought stealthily—who seemed to have been waiting for her. They were not more than thirty, wore suits and thin ties, and one said, "Excuse us, Miss Yeager?"

"Yes."

"You work with Mr. Talley?"

"Yes."

"Sorry to disturb you, but we were told you could deliver this to him."

He pushed a small manila envelope toward her. Lacey thought the men seemed oh-so-American, like handsome heroes in adventure movies.

"Yes, I could."

"It's important, and fragile, if you don't mind."

"I'll take care of it." And the two men left.

That night, after placing the envelope in the safest part of her bag, Lacey bent back her guidebook pages that referenced the Isabella Stewart Gardner Museum. Isabella Stewart Gardner was a grand dame *terrible* of late-nineteenth-century Boston who inherited an inexhaustible fortune and spent as much as she could on art. She built a Venetian fantasy palazzo in demure Boston and, to fill it, began an art sleuthing partnership with the scholar and quasi-dealer Bernard Berenson.

Berenson located and authenticated masterpieces for her that were then spirited out of Europe, sometimes disguised as worthless antique store paintings. This was at a time when "spiriting" was a polite word for "smuggling," but also at a time when nobody cared that much.

The house was three stories high and surrounded a courtyard filled with exotic plantings, Moorish tiles, and ivory carvings. Gardner dedicated it not only to the housing of art, but to concerts, salons, lectures, and company of the bohemian kind, creating a lively and, presumably, stimulating life for herself.

Lacey met the Albergs, now with their son Joshua along—perhaps this was the purpose of the invite?—at the front of the Gardner Museum at ten a.m. Joshua, who was a very young twenty-six, and Lacey, who was an old twenty-eight, recognized each other as compatriots. His parents, longing for a romantic match, failed to recognize their son's guessable homosexuality and Lacey's need for much more varied sexual intercourse before marriage. The parents' illusion of their compatibility was strengthened by the excited squeals of gossip between Lacey and Joshua, which passed for romantic spark.

They were greeted at the door and checked through a metal detector, which Lacey thought was extreme thoroughness given the status of the Albergs.

A guard led them into the dizzying grandeur of the house, which was dark even on sunny days. They were met by a docent who necessarily had to stay with them for the tour, and when the docent asked if there was anything they specifically wanted to see, Alberg replied, "Sargent."

"Sargent?" Lacey said to him. "How do you know about Sargent?"

"I know about Sargent because my father owned one."

"Still have it?" was Lacey's autoresponse.

"That's the dealer in you. Long gone, sorry to say."

At the end of the wide corridor, she saw a painting so familiar that it made her gasp.

125

"Look at this," said Alberg. "If my knees weren't bad, I would kneel."

In front of them was Sargent's *El Jaleo*. At almost twelve feet long, it had not been imagined by Lacey to be so monumental, and she felt now that as she approached it, the picture would engulf her. A Spanish dancer, her head thrown back, an arm reaching forward with a castanet, her other hand dramatically raising her white dress, steps hard on the floor. Behind, a bank of guitarists strum a flamenco rhythm that is impossible for us not to think we hear, and one hombre is caught in midclap, a clap we finish in our minds. Another is snoring. The scene is lit from below, as though by a fire, throwing up a wild plume of shadow behind the dancer. The frenzy and fever of the dance, the musicians, and the audience are palpable.

In Lacey, the picture aroused her deeper hunger for wild adventure

El Jaleo, John Singer Sargent, 1882
93.375 × 138.5 in.

that could not be fulfilled by a trip to Boston in modern times. She longed for wanton evenings spent in a different century, her own head tilted back, flashing a castanet and a slip of leg, and sex with young men no longer among the living. Just then, Joshua leaned in to her and whispered, "That dress is fantastic."

Hinton spoke: "The amazing thing is, Sargent painted this in his Paris studio *from memory.*"

"Mr. Alberg...," said Lacey.

"Mr. Alberg?" replied Mr. Alberg. "Who's that? I'm Hinton."

"How do you know all this?"

"Honey, I told ya, I love it all."

Cornelia jumped in. "He's had more collections than the IRS."

"So why do you buy contemporary?"

"This stuff," he said, waving around the room, "you can buy one, maybe two every other year. Too rare. Contemporary is cheap. I can buy all day. 'Collector' is too kind a word for me. I'm a shopper."

The group marched up the stairs, which were lined with tapestries, odd birdcages, and furniture that, though authentic and valuable, was also grim and sullen. Through the low-slung hallway, they came into a room with soaring ceilings, again lightless except for courtyard windows stingy with the amount of rays they were letting in. They saw Sargent's portrait of Mrs. Gardner, a picture that looked as though the artist wanted to do something wonderful for the enthusiastic patron but couldn't. It suggested there might have been a wee lack of sex appeal about Mrs. Gardner, because if it were there, Sargent could have painted it. Perhaps she commissioned the portrait, longing to look like Sargent's exotic Madame X, but it's clear that she lacked the X factor.

Lacey stepped back from the picture and looked to its left. "Did she collect frames?" she asked.

"No, no," said Alberg. "Sadly, that's where the Degas was. They kept the frame hanging empty as a kind of memorial."

"Stolen?"

"Don't you know about this?" He turned to the guard. "When were the pictures stolen?"

"In 1990, sir."

"How many?"

"Thirteen, sir."

"They never got them back?" said Lacey.

"Never found them," said Cornelia. "They tied up the guards at gunpoint. There're empty frames all around this place. Vermeer, Rembrandt. I always find it sad to come here."

On the way out, they gave Lacey a brochure of the collection, and she put it in her overnight bag, stowed in the coat check.

"Got time for lunch, Lacey?"

"I'm trying to catch the two o'clock."

"Good. The way Hinton eats, there's time," said Cornelia.

"I don't eat that fast," Hinton protested.

"Remember the bag of marshmallows? I turned my back and they were gone."

"That's unfair. I put four of them in my pocket for later."

They stopped in a Boston chain restaurant, high up the chain because it was pretty good. Hinton got the waiter on his toes with, "We gotta catch a plane," then he leaned back in his seat and looked at Lacey. "Tell me," he said, "do you know who Pilot Mouse is?"

"If I didn't, I couldn't be in the art business."

"I've got nine of them I want to sell. Talley could sell them. Do you think he'd be interested?"

"Well, that's not his area, but—"

"That's the point. I don't want them 'on the market.' Quietly, to clients who aren't downtown every day. I want them to go to Mexico, Europe. Those are Talley's clients. I don't want it known I'm selling them."

"I know that Mr. Talley..." said Lacey, making up facts she hoped were true, "...has many clients who buy both modern masters and contemporary. He's perfect for this."

"He can keep it secret?"

"Have you ever heard gossip of any major sales by Talley? They're always discreet. I work there and I don't know anything. I didn't know who you are."

Lacey boarded the plane feeling she had impressed two men. One was Hinton Alberg, who had plucked her like the one bright rose from a monochrome Boston garden; and the other was Barton Talley. Not only had she ignored those to be ignored and attended to those who needed attending, she was returning with a consignment from one of the most freely spending collectors on earth.

32.

LACEY CHECKED IN at the gallery late Monday, stopped by the front desk, and asked Donna if there were any messages.

"Yes, one from the Goodman Gallery and one from Patrice Claire."

"Were the messages for me or Mr. Talley?" she said, hiding her exasperation.

"I'm not sure."

"Did Mr. Claire ask for me?"

"Yes, he did."

"Did he leave a number?"

"He said he's at that hotel . . . down the street?"

"The Carlyle?"

"Yes."

Impeccable and expensive, the Carlyle Hotel was art central. Its tower stood over Madison Avenue like a beacon. Buyers and dealers came to the Carlyle from around the world, but they were social pikers next to the princes and princesses, presidents, prime ministers, and mysterious international travelers who amassed there, and who thought nothing of paying sixteen dollars for a glass of room service orange juice and who didn't blink when the occasional actor crossed the lobby wearing jeans and a headband. Ursus Books was on the second floor, dealing exclusively in art books and rare editions, and was the place to go to buy the thirty-three-volume *catalogue raisonné* of Pablo Picasso at somewhere around fifty thousand dollars, which all Modernist dealers had to have, whether or not they ever opened it again. Across the street was the Gagosian Gallery, about to expand vertically, horizontally, and internationally. Up Madison was Sant Ambroeus, the flawless Italian restaurant where dealers gathered at feeding time. When Larry Gagosian, the champion art world muscle-flexing aesthete, and Bill Acquavella, the connected and straight-shooting dealer in Impressionists and beyond, were at their separate tables, the place had a nuclear afterglow. The rivalry between the two was friendly, since officially they dealt in different corners of the market, though temperatures could rise to boiling when their merchandise overlapped. Picasso was implied to be Acquavella's, and Cy Twombly was implied to be Gagosian's, but what if some Saudi prince wanted to swap his Picasso for a Twombly? Star wars.

"Is Barton upstairs?" said Lacey to Donna, who sipped coffee with no steam coming from it.

"He left. But he said for you to call him."

Lacey turned toward the stairs. She remembered the first time she'd climbed them, before her Russia trip. Like an echo, one that reverberated with memory rather than sound, she recalled that the two men who handed her the envelope in Boston were the same two men she had passed one year ago when she came to the gallery for the first time. She paused, her eyes downward, letting the memory come back fully. Then she moved up the stairs and into her office.

Lacey called Barton at home, but there was no answer. She left a message, then called the Carlyle and asked for Patrice Claire.

"Oh, Lacey. I'm in town. Let's have a drink. Where are you?"

"Hi," said Lacey.

"Oh yes, hi. The Kents have done well. Let me buy you a drink."

"Not dinner?"

"I thought you hated me or something," he said.

"Hate can be so fleeting."

Patrice hesitated, trying to interpret her. "Well, good. Drinks and dinner. Where are you?"

"I'm at the gallery."

"I'll meet you there and we'll walk to Bemelmans and see where we end up. It's beautiful out."

Lacey consented and hung up the phone. She reached in her travel bag, took out the small envelope, and set it on her desk. She unpacked an outfit from her trip and stepped into it, changing her underwear and bra, too. This was a sudden fix-up that worked. Her hands went to the side of her head, and she raised and lifted her hair, fluffing it outward, making her look like what she was: reckless.

She walked the envelope down to Talley's office and set it on top of his desk. A Matisse hung on one wall, a Balthus drawing in colored pencil of a young girl hung on another. The Matisse was sublime. It was an unreal thing, a windowsill still life with the colors in the wrong places, where flowers were black, and trees were blue, with a pink sky above a floor that was plum purple; and it was, incidentally, a painting at the impossible end of Matisse prices. The picture was being encroached by a harsh streak of sunlight, so Lacey canted the blinds.

The Matisse seemed to respond to the decreasing light by increasing its own wattage. Every object in the room was drained of color, but the Matisse stood firm in the de-escalating illumination, its beauty turning functionality inside out, making itself a more practical and useful presence than anything else in sight.

Lacey retrieved the envelope from Talley's desk, because now she had plans for that desk, and walked back to her own office. She picked up the intercom, almost saying "Dopey," but she caught herself in time. "Donna, you can go home. There's nothing to do here now. I'll lock up."

"Should I set the alarm?"

"No," Lacey said, "I'm still inside. I'll take care of it." Lacey put the small envelope back in her purse.

She watched from the window until she saw Donna leave, then walked to a drawer in Barton's office and pulled it open until she could see bottle tops. She picked out a vodka and made herself a drink, meaning she poured an inch into a glass without a mixer or ice. Then she drank it down.

It was twenty minutes before she looked down and saw Patrice Claire's head at the gallery door. She buzzed him in and met him in the downstairs gallery. Patrice's hair was now straight, combed back over his head, his collar was buttoned higher than his chest hair, and he appeared to have undergone a stylistic transformation.

"Bonsoir, Lacey!"

"Bonsoir, whoever you are."

"You like my new image? I took a look around me and cleaned out the closets."

"How's it working?"

"Fewer European girls, more American girls."

"Good for you."

"I'm joking, Lacey. I've been all over. Europe, Brazil, Mexico. But I still remember Paris."

"It was Saint Petersburg."

"To me it was Paris."

"Patrice, you can also lose the winking."

Patrice peeled off to look at the walls. "Nice Gorky drawing. Hard to find. You still have your Aivazovsky?"

"Neatly in place."

"Barton here?"

"Nobody's here."

"Just the three of us?" asked Patrice.

"Three?"

"You, me, and crazy you," he said.

"You want to see something great?" said Lacey.

"Absolutely." He knew she meant a painting.

"You won't mention it to Barton?"

"I never mention the surreptitiously viewed thing."

She flicked off the downstairs lights, leaving on one ghost light in the back gallery.

Patrice kept his eyes on Lacey as she led him up the stairs. "We sold a Kent in Canada. Sold one in New York. One to a dealer here," he told her. "Our Russian trip was successful."

They turned into the upstairs hallway, toward the office. "You want something to drink?" she asked him as they entered. She set the rheostat to half, spotlighting the Matisse.

Patrice stopped at the doorway. "Oh, that's so nice," he said.

"Vodka? Is it calling you?"

"Yes. Vodka. Thanks."

Lacey poured, got ice from a small refrigerator, handed him his drink, and leaned back on a bookshelf while Patrice stepped around the room, looking at the picture, farther back, closer, farther back. "Nice condition."

It was dark outside now, and Lacey had decided she wanted to have sex under the Matisse or thereabouts. Things slowed a bit as they looked at the Balthus, a sexy image that became officially unsexy when the age of legal consent started to settle in America's mind. They had second drinks, and Lacey sat on the sofa opposite the picture.

"I don't know where to look," said Patrice, who was starting to get the idea. He moved toward her. "You're moving up in the world, Lacey."

Lacey shrugged it off as if it hadn't even been said. He started to speak again, but she put her finger to her lips. "Shh. Lights," she whispered.

"Lacey, let me take you to dinner first . . ."

She stared at him. He continued, "All right, I'll take you to dinner after."

He walked over and pulled her up from the sofa. His hands ruffled her clothes as he felt all around, finally raising her dress, his palm on the back of her leg. He moved her over to Talley's desk, then pulled down her underwear, and Lacey stepped out of it. He sat her on the desk and slid down the length of her body until he was on his knees, his head pressed against her skirt. Slowly he lifted the cotton fabric until his head was between her legs. With a deep breath, Lacey leaned back, and, stiff on her arms, spread her knees by inches. Patrice's hands were on her thighs, his head now covered by cloth. She raised her eyes and saw the Matisse. She pulled up one leg, hooking the heel of her shoe on the desk, and she stayed in that position until it was all over.

There was a lot of neatening done to Talley's office. Lacey tried to get herself back together, but it had been a long day for her.

"Patrice, let's go to dinner now. I flew in from Boston and I'm dead."

"We'll go to the Carlyle," said Patrice. "Nobody will be there this early."

"Will that make us nobodies?" said Lacey.

The maître d' at the Carlyle went over his reservation sheet for a solid minute before allowing these walk-ins to get a table. He seemed to be on their side, scanning the list as though it were a long equation in which he was trying to find a scientific loophole, even though the place was practically vacant. At last, yes, there was a table. He took them into the blissfully old-fashioned restaurant, with French wallpaper bearing rococo vignettes of women stepping up into carriages, a dining room lit by chandeliers and sconces, and a center flower display that had to cost as much as ten dinners. They were seated at a dream corner table, on a tufted banquette, catty-corner to each other, and the only other people in the restaurant were stragglers just paying their check for afternoon tea.

"Lacey, just so you know, I didn't call you up to have sex with you."

"And if you had?" said Lacey, implying that would not have been a problem.

Patrice angled himself toward her. "Lacey, do you realize you've never said one thing to me that is not banter?"

"I'm doubly shocked," said Lacey.

"Why?"

"Well, one, you're right, and two, that you know the word *banter.*"

They ordered food and drinks, and Lacey settled back comfortably.

"There's a Warhol *Marilyn* coming up for auction. They're estimating it at four million," said Patrice.

"Four million," said Lacey, thinking of her own small Warhol; if the *Marilyn* did bring that much, there was a good chance some financial goodwill would spill over onto her flower picture.

"Want to go look at it next week?"

"Where is it? Christie's or Sotheby's?"

"Sotheby's."

"Uhh…maybe. I was in Boston today, at the Isabella Stewart Gardner. Have you ever been?"

"Don't think so. A long time ago, maybe."

"Look at this," she said, reaching in her purse and pulling out the black-and-white brochure from the museum. She put it on the table and flattened it with her palms. "Look at these pictures." She stabbed her finger at each one. "Stolen. Stolen. Stolen…"

"Oh yes, I remember that. A tragedy."

"Rembrandt. Degas. Manet. Vermeer…" Lacey stopped her finger on the Vermeer, and her expression changed to quizzical.

"What?" said Patrice.

"I've seen this somewhere."

"It's a famous painting."

"No, I've seen this, recently, I think. Where did I see it?"

"There was a Vermeer show in New York at the Met. I can't remember when."

"I wasn't in New York before it was stolen."

The rest of the dinner, Lacey would periodically renew her question, as if she were trying to remember a movie title that escaped her, shouting, "Oh, oh!" and hitting her head with her fist. But still, she hadn't found the answer. Patrice observed her like a child interested in an automated toy; he kept wondering what it would do next.

The lights in the restaurant were turned low. A pianist could be heard from the bar playing "The Way You Look Tonight," which worked subconsciously on Patrice. Lacey, now lit by candlelight, her hair relaxed and heading toward unkempt, her concentration diverted, would include him by holding his wrist with one hand and pounding the table with the other when the answer she sought appeared near. In these few seconds, deep inside him, so deep as to be insensible, a passion of viral intensity was slowly infecting him. In spite of their odd beginning, he was deciding not only that Lacey Yeager would make his life wonderful, but that her absence would make it tragic.

Outside, Patrice was shocked to learn it was nine p.m. That meant he and Lacey had spent at least four hours tête-à-tête, talking, eating, flirting, wooing and cooing, and oh yeah, much earlier, fucking. Lacey was exhausted and said good night to him in front of the Carlyle, and a further discussion of another meeting was aborted by the arrival of a cab. Lacey threw her bag in the backseat and said, "Au revoir, baby."

Lacey crossed the park at 79th Street and rested her head against the door of the cab. Her mind relaxed, allowing a sunken memory to bob to the surface. She had seen the Vermeer, or at least a sliver of it, through a crack in the door on her first visit to Barton Talley's gallery, when she was there to be interviewed. She straightened up and the image came into focus, a young girl singing to a gentleman whose back was to the frame, all in Vermeer's unmistakable colors.

She hurried into her apartment, standing vacantly in the center of her living room, wondering what to do. She saw her message light blinking. There were three messages from Talley, saying, "Call me when you get in," "Call me when you get this," and "Where are you? Call me."

She picked up the phone and dialed.

"Oh, Lacey. Gee, darling, where were you? I left word everywhere. I'm getting you a cell phone. Did you get a package? Did someone give you a package?"

"An envelope."

"You got an envelope. Where is it?"

"I have it here."

"Is it thick? Thin?"

"Thin, they said it was fragile."

"Can you bring it over? Can I come get it?"

"You can come get it. I'm dead."

"I'll be there in a few minutes. Where are you again?"

Lacey hung up the phone and went to her purse. She took out the envelope and examined it. It was stiff in the center but otherwise flimsy. She filled her electric kettle with water and turned it on. She took out a white cloth napkin and laid it on the counter. She went and lay on her bed, closing her eyes, not to rest but to blot out the overhead light, her heart beginning to accelerate. The kettle started to spit.

She went to the kitchen, picked up the envelope, and began to steam it open. After a while, there was success, though she left a few faint tears in the flap. She opened the envelope and poured its contents onto the cloth napkin. She saw two pieces of shirt cardboard, cut to about the size of a playing card, taped together and bulging slightly at the center. She went to her bedroom and got a pair of scissors and a roll of tape. She cut one end of the tape and squeezed the cardboard like a change purse. A small, rectangular piece of canvas fell out, ragged at the edges as though snipped by shears, hard and stiff like plastic.

She turned it over and saw brown, old brown paint made rigid by layers of varnish, and she could see its amber tint affecting the color of what was underneath. She put it under the light. She could see words, and she read, written in script, "Rembrandt van Rijn."

Lacey took the piece and sealed it back inside the cardboard package. She went into the bathroom and turned on her hair dryer, aiming it at the flap while she stood and waited, waving the envelope through the blasting air.

Her doorbell rang. She checked the envelope, which looked good, and put it back in her purse. She buzzed in Barton Talley, and his first words were, "I'm glad I remembered where you live. Do you realize you gave me the wrong address? You inverted two digits."

Yes, Lacey thought, while saying, "Oh, sorry, I do that sometimes."

The teakettle gurgled. "You want some tea?" Lacey asked him.

"No thanks, too late for me. Did you have a good trip?"

"Fabulous. I got a consignment from Hinton Alberg."

"Really?"

"Nine Pilot Mouse paintings."

"Well, that will be interesting. Difficult and interesting. How are we supposed to sell those? Anyway, good job. Fill me in."

"Tomorrow, I'm so tired. Here's the envelope..." Lacey started to root around in her purse. "What's in it?" she said, handing it over.

"Come in an hour late tomorrow, Lacey. You've worked hard."

33.

THE NEXT DAY, Lacey banged around the office like a sit-com wife signaling anger. She shut doors with extra force, slammed phones down on their cradles, walked with harder steps on wooden floors. Talley's door was shut, and Lacey was stuck outside like a cat who wanted in. His phone line would be lit for a solid hour, then he would hang up for seconds, and it would light again for another forty minutes. His voice could be heard, but the closed door gave the effect of a voice in the next room of a cheap motel: you could hear someone was talking but couldn't understand one clear word. Once, he got angry and his volume rose.

She heard: "Well, they're idiots! They're not art people. These people are not art people."

Lacey continually checked his door and his phone extension light. Closed and on. She went down the hall to the bins, treading lightly even though the bins were a normal place for her to be. The paintings were arranged on shelves covered in carpet and separated by cardboard flats to keep frames from knocking into each other. Some of the pictures were sheathed in bubble wrap, some were in their own pasteboard containers, and some merely had gaffer's tape stuck on the sides of their frames with the name of the artist written in marking pen. She was familiar with most of the visible stock, but the bins lined both sides of the room and the dark areas toward the back wall remained unexplored.

She wandered down the aisle, her hands touching the frames, left and right, her head doing a tennis match scan of the shelves, pulling the unfamiliar ones out a few inches to check labels. Her head twisted around to the wall phone, and she saw that Talley's light was still burning. She got to the end of the storage and saw in the last, lower bin a picture wrapped in cardboard and sealed tight with wide, clear tape. Under the tape was written a number, 53876, which she committed to memory. She estimated its dimensions by spreading her hand and counting spans. She had long ago measured this distance for quick calculation of a painting's size.

She then went back into the hall, which was lined floor to ceiling with art reference books. A never-used section on museum collections had migrated to the bottom row—because nothing in them was ever for sale—and there she found a Gardner catalog published before the theft, in 1974. She didn't want to be caught holding the book in case Talley suddenly emerged, so she quickly turned back to her office, impressed at her own detective work as she edged out of sight. All this sneaking around was making her agitated, even though every one of her actions could be considered ordinary office maneuvering.

She opened the book and went to Vermeer. There it was, *The Concert*, one of the world's masterpieces reproduced in muddy, out-of-register ink. Its size was printed as "0.725 x 0.647." What the fuck does that mean? she thought. She figured it was metric, but there wasn't as yet an omnipresent Internet to confirm it. She called the Carlyle and asked for Patrice, but he wasn't in. Before she hung up, the hotel operator came back on the line and asked, "Would you like to leave a message?" The Carlyle was one of the few remaining hotels where unanswered room calls didn't default to voice mail.

"Yes," replied Lacey, "ask him how many centimeters are in an inch."

"Please hold," said the operator, whose accent placed her in the heart of Queens. Thirty seconds later, she came back on the line and said, "It's two point five."

Lacey computed that *The Concert* was twenty-eight inches by twenty-five inches, and she added three inches all around to allow for the frame and another inch for packaging. Yes, the package was the same size as the wrapped, stolen Vermeer. She was convinced that this was the missing painting.

A moment later, Lacey heard Talley's door open. She quickly put the book on the floor under her desk. "Lacey, are you here?" he called.

"Yes," she shouted. "Let's meet."

Talley was flush and distracted. "So what about Hinton Alberg?" he said.

"I called him this morning," Lacey told him. "He's sending us transparencies. Nine early paintings by Pilot Mouse."

"Early? The guy's thirty."

"Yes, but it seems that in the contemporary world, early can be four years ago."

"What's the deal?"

"He paid a hundred eighty thousand for them, and he wants to double it."

"Can we?"

"Well, if they were on the New York market, we could, but he doesn't want them on the New York market because he doesn't want it known he's selling."

"Well, we'll do our best."

"Who's your collector in Mexico? Flores? He bought a Hirst, didn't he? It was in the *Art Newspaper*," she said.

"Flores buys Légers and Braques."

"He also buys Hirst."

"Who's Hirst?"

"He's my dry cleaner."

"Are you joking?"

"Yes, Mr. Talley. You've got to get out more."

"I'll call him. Tell me about Pilot Mouse."

"I don't know much about him. He was with a small gallery, Alberg bought all the paintings, then Pilot Mouse jumped."

"Jumped?"

"Jumped to another gallery with a higher profile. Then he started doing conceptual pieces, and raids."

"What are raids?"

"Like happenings. He fills the gallery with nudes, nudes standing around, lots of things banging and sound effects, clatter. He calls them raids, as in raiding the conventional art establishment."

"Sounds unsalable."

"I agree. That's the part I don't get."

"What's he look like?"

"Never seen him."

"What do I tell Flores?"

"You just say Pilot Mouse and he's either heard of him or he hasn't, I guess."

Talley was not used to talking about living artists. "The deader the better," he would say. The antics of the long dead, like Duchamp sending a signed urinal to an art show or Salvador Dalí giving an interview with a lamb chop on his head, had transformed in time from pranks to lore, while the actions of Pilot Mouse just sounded juvenile or, at best, lacking in originality. But Talley was not stupid. He knew that "derivative" was an epithet used erratically and that generations of collectors grew up believing that the art of their time, however derivative, was wholly new. He understood that markets could be blinkered, with activity hotly occurring and nobody ever hearing about it. So while Pilot Mouse's status as an artist of importance was doubtful, his status as a name that could be sold, at least for a while, was probably assured.

I met Lacey for lunch, and she alternated between fretful and enthused. She described the trip to Boston and the consignment from Alberg. When she told me about the office tryst with Patrice Claire, again I felt an involuntary electrical jerk pulse through me, which I interpreted to mean not that I had a crush on Lacey, but that I wished she had commandeered me instead. When she elaborated on the intrigue, she never once asked me what she should do. I only listened. Once she said, "Am I in trouble?" but she answered her own question by placing herself at such a distance from the initial crime that she tried and exonerated herself in a matter of seconds. Whether Talley was complicit or innocent was open to her. He could be working to get the pictures back, but if the Vermeer was indeed in his gallery, didn't that make him a criminal? And if Talley went to jail, would that hurt her career or help it?

Finally, Lacey said to me, "How are you doing?"

"I'm still writing, got a piece in *ARTnews*, doing an essay for a photography catalog. I keep trying to start a novel."

"About?"

"About my growing up."

"Daniel, jeez, get a subject."

"Well, I'm rethinking."

"Girlfriends?"

"They come, they go. Nothing sticks."

"You know what you are, Daniel? You're too kind. Girls like trouble until they're thirty-five."

"I thought I was an intellectual nerd."

"Wow, if you were an intellectual nerd who made trouble, you would be *potent*."

Lacey paid the bill, and we walked out of 3 Guys onto Madison Avenue, and in the air were the first real hints of summer.

34.

"IT DOESN'T MAKE SENSE to me, Mr. Talley."

"What is that, Lacey?"

"Why you didn't go to Boston."

"I told you—"

"I know what you told me, that you didn't want to see people from the Boston Museum. But that's never stopped you. You're not shy. And the room was filled with collectors. That's like Ho-Ho's to a fat man."

"I'm breaking you in, Lacey."

"Baloney. Is it that you didn't want to carry back what was in that envelope?"

Talley looked up at her. "What was in the envelope?"

"I don't know."

"Lacey, you carried something back. I didn't even know what it was. You have to stay out of this."

"But I'm in it. Your fault."

"Aren't you afraid of being fired?"

"But you can't fire me now, can you? Can you put me loose on the streets?"

Not sure what she meant, Talley squinted fiercely and leaned back, and although he was taking himself farther away from her, his total area seemed to expand. "Oh, I could, Lacey. But truthfully, I wouldn't.

Go back to work. Zone out. Stare at the Matisse for a few minutes. Use it like Zen."

Lacey crossed her arms and looked up at the Matisse. "Wrong time of day," she said.

Busying himself at his desk, he said, "Well, take a last look because it's leaving. Sold it this morning."

"Oh, who bought it?" said Lacey.

"A European," said Talley.

"That's specific," said Lacey.

"A Western European," said Talley.

35.

LACEY WAS SURE she was going to open the wrapped picture, but she would let several weeks elapse without drama to make Talley believe that the matter was a blip, now forgotten. Auction season was settling upon Manhattan, so there was much to be distracted by. Patrice Claire invited her to the previews, and Lacey decided she couldn't avoid Sotheby's forever, so she made the trip on her lunch break, understanding that it would be Sotheby's lunch break, too, and perhaps she would not run into those she would rather avoid. As she stepped out onto the tenth floor, she saw a newly promoted Tanya Ross leading clients around the room. Lacey was not and never had been unnerved by her—she only resented her for being competent, nice, pretty, and prim. When Patrice, reacting to her "Ugh," asked her why she didn't like Tanya, Lacey said, "Because I'm a petty person."

They turned the corner into the main gallery and saw, in the premier spot where a 1909 Picasso had hung last week before selling for eleven million dollars, the Warhol *Orange Marilyn*, a silk screen done in 1964. While the Cubist Picasso had gravitas, the *Orange Marilyn* had exuberance: it was as though a fruit-hatted Carmen Miranda had just shown up at a funeral.

However opposite these pictures were, they both worked as historical objects, and they worked as objects of beauty. While the Picasso was deep and serious, the Warhol was radiant and buoyant. The Picasso

Woman with Pears, Pablo Picasso, 1909
36.25 × 28.875 in.

added up to the sum of its parts: artistic genius combined with powerful thought combined with prodigious skill combined with the guided
hand equals masterpiece. The Warhol was more than the sum of its
parts: silk screen, photo image of popular actress, repetitive imagery,
the unguided hand, equals... masterpiece.

"How," said Lacey, "can an artist have no effect on you for years and
then one day it has an effect on you?"

"What are you talking about?"

"Warhol. I'm a proud owner, you know. A small flower picture, but
still..."

"Darling, I call that the perverse effect. Those things that you hate
for so long are insidiously working on you, until one day you can't resist

Marilyn, Andy Warhol, circa 1964
40 × 40 in.

them anymore. They turn into favorites. It just takes a while to sort out the complications in them. Those artworks that come all ready to love empty out pretty quickly. It's why outsiders hate the art we love; they haven't spent time with it. You and I see things again and again whether we want to or not. We see them in galleries, we see them in homes, we see them in the art magazines, they come up at auction. Outsiders see it once, or hear about it after it's been reduced to an insult: 'It's a bunch of squiggles that my kid could do.' I would like to see a kid who could paint a Jackson Pollock. In a half second, any pro could tell the difference. People want to think Pollock's not struggling, that he's kidding. He's not kidding. You want to know how I think art should be taught to children? Take them to a museum and say, 'This is art, and you can't do it.'"

"And I thought you were just in the service industry."

"That's my night job," said Patrice.

They stopped at Sant Ambroeus for a panini at the bar. Patrice set up a dinner with her the next night at the Carlyle. "I'm leaving in four days, Lacey."

"Oh," she said with an edge of disappointment. "When are you back?"

"It depends on how the auction tomorrow night goes."

They ate their sandwiches, and Lacey left for the gallery. Patrice stayed seated and watched Lacey through the glass window as she spoke with a young man on the street whom she seemed to know. Lacey was so vital with him, so animated, that Patrice wondered if she was as vital and animated with him. This moment, innocuous as it was, functioned as an ax blow to a tree: it didn't knock him over, but it left him less steady. Then he was invited to join a Minnesota collector and Larry Gagosian at their table, where they would engage in a conversation about art so lustful that an eavesdropper would assume they were three randy guys discussing babes.

At the gallery, Lacey stopped by the front desk for messages. Donna, who had unveiled a new, unbecoming hairdo, handed her a few, and Lacey read them as she climbed the stairs. One was from Hinton Alberg, inviting her to join them for cocktails after the auction on Thursday. And one was from her old boyfriend Jonah Marsh, asking her to call back. Lacey hadn't thought of Jonah Marsh for three years, and she guessed he had heard she was with Talley now, and would he look at my paintings? Lacey threw the message in her lowest drawer.

Talley summoned her into his office. "Eduardo Flores is going to be in Los Angeles next weekend, so I'm flying out with a shitload of transparencies," he told her. "You'll have to hold down the fort. The town will empty out after the auctions, so I think you'll be fine. Just remember, 'First, do no harm.'"

"And if I sell anything, do I get a commission?"

"You won't sell anything."

"I'll settle for five thousand on every million dollars I sell."

"Oh hell, all right."

36.

LACEY ARRIVED AT the Carlyle for her dinner with Patrice. Her salary at Talley's had given her not only a living wage, but enough spare money, if there is such a thing, to keep her well clothed without having to dip into her reserves. She looked elegant enough that she could move across the lobby without a disapproving head turn, and in fact she got a few approving, inviting, head turns. Elegance in the Carlyle lobby was common, but *youthful* elegance was not.

She went to the desk and asked for Patrice Claire. The clerk rang the room—after getting her full name—then pointed to the elevator. The operator pulled aside a brass folding gate and cranked an iron lever around to 21. His head tilted back and he looked just above her eye line during the ascent. The elevator landed, and the operator did a precision adjustment to ensure there was no fault line between the cage and the hallway floor. "To the right," he said.

Patrice opened the door, and over his shoulder, the first object Lacey saw was a small Picasso drawing: a nude reclining against nothing, all line and space, set in a dusky gold frame. He gave her a European kiss on each cheek and brought her into the small corner apartment; a hotel room that he owned. A large window looked over the rooftops to Central Park as the lights of the city beyond it were starting to twinkle on.

Lacey looked out over the city, south to the Plaza Hotel and north to Harlem, and said, "This will be a nice place to watch the apocalypse."

She turned and looked at him up and down as he waited for her full attention. Patrice did look attractive. He had completed his transformation from the oily Euro she had met at Sotheby's almost four years ago into an Armani guy with regular hair that no longer made her queasy to touch.

"I thought we'd eat in the room. The food is from the restaurant, and with the view—"

"Let's go get a drink in the bar first," Lacey said.

"But we can have one here."

"Yes, but then no one will see how great we look."

They walked around the block first, each proud to be on the other's arm. The sun was just dropping, and the bedecked, bejeweled mannequins in the store windows were like saluting soldiers as they strolled in their enchanted state of opulent seduction. They walked a few blocks and asked for an outside table at La Goulue. They explained they were just going to have drinks, and even though prime dinner hour was approaching when the outdoor tables were prized, the restaurant could hardly refuse such a civility.

Like their drinks, their date was perfectly blended. Patrice, desirous of Lacey, was the subtle engine driving them back to the Carlyle, and Lacey's nonchalant "let's wait and see" demeanor kept the ending unknown to both of them. This was Patrice's chance to legitimize their previous dalliances with a full courtship press.

Now, feeling the kind of euphoria that can overtake you at this time of day, at this temperature, at this level of breeze, after one drink, when the person beside you is making you alert and keen and the idea of being with anyone else is not imaginable, Lacey and Patrice went back to the Carlyle. Patrice knew that tonight would be their first opportunity, if her signals were interpreted correctly, for real sex, real lying-down sex, not standing-up sex or sitting-on-a-desk sex.

They ordered room service, sat at their own corner table with views across and up Manhattan, and sipped a bottle of wine until there was nothing left to do but kiss, and kiss again, for anyone with a pair of binoculars to see. Lacey led him into the bedroom, where the hotel sheets were fresh and rich, where the lighting had been preset, and where, placed opposite the bed, illuminated by two candles that threw their light upward, was the Matisse that had overseen their last coupling in Talley's office. Patrice had bought the moment, and it had cost him six million dollars.

"So it was you," Lacey whispered.

"With what it had seen, I couldn't let it get away." Then they made love.

Afterward, Lacey put on a robe that swathed her like meringue, and Patrice ordered dessert, which was wheeled into the living room while Lacey waited hidden in the bedroom. When the door shut, Lacey emerged and they sat again by the window.

"And now...," said Patrice as he picked up the phone. "Auction results."

"Oh, yay," said Lacey.

Patrice dialed someone. "How'd the auction do?...You're kidding... Oh, really?" He covered the phone and mouthed to Lacey, "The Warhol *Marilyn* brought seventeen million dollars."

Patrice continued on, asking other prices, but Lacey was stunned. She knew not only that the price was phenomenal, news-making, but that there would be a sympathetic rise in all of Warhol's works and that her small flower painting had at least doubled in value while she had been in the bedroom with Patrice.

Patrice hung up the phone. "So," he said, "there's been a revolution."

Lacey looked at him.

"Warhol has brought more money than an equal Picasso. The baby boomers are starting to buy their own." What Patrice was saying was true. The vague rumors of strength in the contemporary market had

154

been made manifest, and contemporary art, over the next ten years, was about to inflate like the *Hindenburg*.

Lacey spent the night and left early to change clothes at her apartment. She said good-bye to Patrice with a kiss. He was flying out before lunch for Paris and had already made arrangements for flowers to be delivered to her at Talley's, with a note that read, "I am missing you right now." When Lacey got to her apartment, she paused in front of the Warhol. The feeling that swept over her was a bit like that of a gambler who gets lucky the first time out and leaves the table thinking, This is easy.

At work, Lacey bounced up the stairs and stiff-armed one hand on Talley's doorway. His eyes rose, and as she fluffed her hair with the other she said to him, "You owe me a commission on the Matisse." Then she turned and strolled down the hall, dragging her jacket by one finger before letting it fall to the floor as she turned the corner into her office.

37.

TALLEY PACKED A BAG and flew to Los Angeles, and Lacey went to the shipping room to get an X-Acto knife. She was going to perform surgery on the unknown carton in the bins, just as she had done on the envelope from Boston. The cardboard of the box had already been reused several times, so it wasn't likely that her tinkering would show. Donna never left her post downstairs, and Lacey was her overlord anyway, so she proceeded fearlessly, if secretly.

She turned the box upside down and sliced through the tape, then opened a flap that she bent back, revealing the framed painting inside. She pulled it a few inches from its sleeve, and even though it was now upside down, she could make out the distinct shapes of the now very familiar picture. She pulled it halfway out and bent her body sideways to make the view as upright as possible, and yes, there it was, *The Concert* by Johannes Vermeer. She slid the picture back in its case, retaped the bottom, turned the whole thing right side up, and seated it exactly where it had been. The whole enterprise had taken only a minute.

She walked back to her office and sat at her desk. She did not believe that Barton Talley had stolen a dozen pictures and tied up four night guards at gunpoint. She did believe, however, that Talley was involved in negotiations to get the pictures returned, but whether he was Jesse James or Marshal Dillon she did not know. What she did know was that she did not want to be a detective anymore. Her pulse was not handling it well, and she now, whatever the caper was, had her fingerprints all over it, literally.

Lacey went to the restaurant Sofia and sat upstairs, where she was nominally outdoors, and ordered a truffle-oil pizza. She never looked up while her mind rotated the facts, trying to see them from all sides, trying to piece them together into theory. All she could think was that she was flunking an IQ test.

38.

THE NEXT DAY was Sunday, and Lacey half-walked and half-rode her new bicycle over to the West Side bike path. The path, which ran from the George Washington Bridge all the way to Battery Park, was the great hope for bikers who were tired of dodging car doors that opened incautiously into the street. Even so, she noticed the occasional memorial to riders who were killed in action, a bicycle frame that had been painted ghostly white, including the tires, and bearing flowers that were usually desiccated and drooping. She also noticed that if she didn't wear a helmet and let her hair fly, male riders would tag along-side her for a hundred yards, as though it were all coincidence, hoping for an exchange of glances that Lacey never offered.

The bike path was her sacred time of contemplation, today espe-cially, as she tried to sort out whether she would go to jail for a hundred years or be a heroine who selflessly and cleverly returned a Vermeer to the nation. If she returned a Vermeer to the United States of America, it would be very good for her career. If she was implicated in grand theft, even though she would undoubtedly be cleared, it might be bad for her career. But while Lacey biked farther along, she began to imagine what she would wear on the witness stand, her handkerchief in hand to catch a sudden flood of tears, and the dinner parties she would be invited to. She pictured all the ears listening attentively as she told her story, and decided that either outcome would be okay.

She pulled off the route at 22nd Street, locked her bike to a tree, and strolled through gallery-rich Chelsea, looking in windows, seeing names that instilled in her a spore of initiative: Andrea Rosen, Mary Boone, Angela Westwater, all women who had opened their own galleries and succeeded. She then went to the Empire Diner—the busy café that served irresistible grits at any time of day and had a dozen unattainable tables on the sidewalk—sat at a back table, and ordered lunch. She took out a piece of stationery and carefully penned this letter:

To Whom It May Concern:
On May 10, 1998, I was sent to Boston by Barton Talley to attend a party celebrating funds raised by the ICA. On the way out, I was approached by two men who asked my name and confirmed that I worked for Mr. Talley...

Lacey went on to describe the entire misadventure, including her steaming open of the envelope, the discovery of the Vermeer, and her intent to confront Barton Talley. She expressed concern that if she exposed the presence of the picture without consulting him, she might ruin some plans to get the other pictures back, and that this letter was a dated testimony to her righteous intent in case there were developments before she could ascertain what to do by interrogating Talley. She then sealed the letter in an envelope and addressed it to herself. The idea was that if there was ever a trial, she would produce the unopened letter, with the postmark verifying when it was sent, to be opened in front of a judge, who would immediately send her home. She finished her meal, went outside, and dropped it in a mailbox. When she heard the letter hit the bottom, she realized its futility. Any crook could write himself a letter of righteous intent after a crime, but it wouldn't make him innocent.

39.

BARTON TALLEY'S SHOES were impeccable. He traveled with them in a separate suitcase, each shoe in its own velour slipcover and polished to a hard enamel shine. The Beverly Hills Hotel had expertise in the old world craft of shoe pampering, but Talley's care and maintenance was so self-contained and ritualized that he rarely used their service. Also, the hotel had recently changed hands and it was unknown if the degree of seemingly telepathic attention would remain constant, slide, or rise.

If cities could be given an EKG, New York's readout would be Andean and Los Angeles's would be a sandy beach. Talley already felt himself rocking to the slower rhythm. He dined Saturday night at the Ivy, a restaurant that years ago had ushered in the era of Cajun spices and had been in business so long that it had seen its initial clientele of young celebrities grow old, die, and be replaced by new ones. He ate with Stephen Bravo, a dealer with galleries on both coasts who had clout almost as thundering as Gagosian's. Talley showed him the Pilot Mouse transparencies, and Bravo bought four paintings essentially sight unseen. He wondered how Bravo could even see them as he held the five-by-six-inch transparencies up to the dim lamplight of the Ivy. But Talley understood. Contemporary paintings usually posed no condition problems or questions of authorship, they were valuable only by fiat, and there was rarely anything to research. Back at the hotel, he woke Lacey with a phone call to let her know of the sale and, unprompted, gave her her first small taste of profit participation.

His lunch the next day was taken alone at the Polo Lounge, the tourist-destination restaurant at the hotel. Agents and movie stars still patronized the place because its tables recalled Hollywood's most glamorous era. Out-of-towners who dared approach a celebrity table were nearly tackled by waiters or intercepted with a harsh arm signal of "foul" by the attentive maître d'. Talley ate a deceptive salad that had enough goodies in it to raise the calorie count to over a thousand and waved good-bye across the room to Bravo, who was off to catch a plane to somewhere kept secret from other art dealers.

There is art in Los Angeles that rivals New York's, but to see all of it you would need General Eisenhower to plan the attack. The Los Angeles County Museum of Art is miles from the Getty, which is miles from the Hammer, which is miles from the Norton Simon, which is miles from the Museum of Contemporary Art, and if the dots were connected on a map, you would see a giant circle running around the periphery of Los Angeles with no convenient route connecting them. The viewer of this map would realize that the best way of commuting among these five significant art museums would be by Swiss gondola or light aircraft.

But Talley was not there for the art museums. His main concern was dinner that night with Eduardo Flores. Flores was capable of expenditures the size of movie budgets, and to prove it he had just finished remodeling a house in Los Angeles that was the architectural perfection of 1961, before anyone thought of 1961 as a year of exceptional style. This was sixties modern, distinct from the kitsch California architecture of the same period marked by electrons swishing around nuclei on top of bowling alleys. But there was a high style floating around then, though no one knew it yet. It was the furniture of Knoll, Nakashima,

161

and the Eameses. Flores's house had been redone to satiny perfection, and the effect was spectacular. When you entered the house for the first time, it felt as though you had just stepped into the pages of a *Life* magazine layout of the modern home.

The house was walking distance from the Beverly Hills Hotel, but Talley wasn't about to risk it. Even a taxi or limo drive threatened to burr his shoeshine, and a walk would have to be done so carefully that he might look silly. So when he ran into Gayle Smiley, who was the highest-ranking representative of the Stephen Bravo gallery and who was also attending the dinner, he angled for a ride, as a front seat was safer for shoes than the backseat. But Stephen Bravo was Eduardo's number one dealer, and Gayle protected the franchise like a mother bear would a cub, claws and all. She did not want to arrive with Talley next to her, especially since she was morbidly unhappy that he had been invited in the first place. Gayle mumbled, stumbled, took a phone call, and withdrew.

In the end, Talley settled for a taxi. Though he was expecting to be berated by the driver for such a short hop, the turban-wearing cabbie said a cheerful good night and gave him his card in case he needed a ride back.

The houses in Beverly Hills were either low-slung or high-slung, and Flores's was as low as a sixties modern would allow. Yet the house had a view not only of its own sculpture garden, but of the city of Los Angeles. This mysterious effect belonged to many houses in Beverly Hills that appeared to be in the flatlands but were actually on an imperceptible uphill slope that positioned the house for a view to the sea. These views that skimmed just over the top of the city gave sunsets an extra redness and positively affirmed that Los Angeles could be beautiful.

Talley stood in the entry of the house, which he had been in before, and realized something was up. The art on the walls—formerly the modern masters that Talley sold—was now shifting toward contemporary, and because of it the house had been infused with energy. A

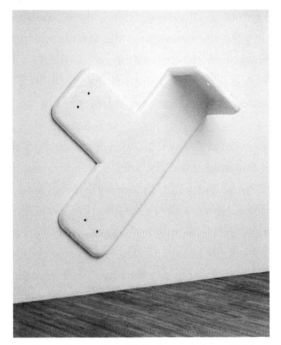

Three Parts of an X, Robert Gober, 1985
81 × 81.5 × 25 in.

Robert Gober sculpture, an interpretation of a porcelain sink that had been unfolded like a Chinese take-out box, hung on the wall in the dining room, and a Damien Hirst mirrored pharmaceutical shelf the size of a plate-glass window hung over the fireplace. The livelier environment felt good even to Talley. He was grateful to Lacey for delivering unto him some contemporary art that made him feel much more up-to-date. His normal world of modern masters made him feel snug and comfortable, but these new objects, hanging with such bewildering cheer, made him feel as if he'd already had one drink. One drink was not enough for any of this group, though, and they gathered in the living room, where the hard stuff was being served.

The host had not made his entrance yet, but Gayle Smiley had, and she made it clear that it was she who had sold most of these contemporary works to Eduardo. "Isn't the Gober fabulous?" She was already pumping the bellows for the art she was promoting. The party was livening with the arrivals of actor Stirling Quince and his enduring girlfriend, Blanca. Stirling had been a solid TV star for five years, and despite escalating annual salary bumps, he was still only *wealthy.*

Talley looked over at Gayle's purse, which she had put on a small divan. Sticking out from it was the very envelope containing the transparencies of the four Pilot Mouse paintings he had sold Bravo the day before. It was apparent to Talley that she was going to offer them to Flores. This made Talley slightly sick, as he knew he had the remaining transparencies at his hotel and hadn't brought them because, one, it was tacky, and two, he didn't know Flores had shifted gears. He also knew he had an advantage because he could beat Bravo's price, since he knew what he had paid for them. It wasn't that Talley wanted to make fifty thousand dollars; he simply wanted to sell Flores a contemporary painting right under Smiley's nose.

"Oh my," said Talley. "I left my inhaler back at the hotel."

Talley didn't really know much about inhalers, but he knew it sounded much better than saying "transparencies." He walked out the door, and because the hotel was downhill from the house, he made it in less than five minutes. This run was done with a strangely high-stepping gait, as each shoe had to come down squarely on its sole. At the hotel, he put the transparencies in his coat pocket and gave Lacey a quick call, waking her up for the second time in two days. "Give me the run-down on Robert Gober," he said to her.

"Sculptor, expensive, conceptual, very respected," she said. "Mention sinks, drains, and 'the playpen.'"

"Thanks, Lacey," he said.

When he walked back in, the party had grown to a total of ten, minus the host, who still had not appeared. One of the new additions was a stray young man whose name sounded like Fortunato, but Talley couldn't be certain and he was afraid to call him by name until it was verified. What worse blunder was there than calling someone Fortunato if that was not his name? The young man wore tight leather pants and a tight black T-shirt and would occasionally sally down the hallway, indicating he was a houseguest or perhaps more.

After one of these hallway dashes, Fortunato—yes, the name had been confirmed—appeared with Eduardo Flores on one arm. It was hard to tell whether he was escorting him in affectionately or propping him up, as Eduardo looked glassy-eyed.

Gayle, with rabbit quickness, bounded across the room to greet him. "Eduardo! The new Warhol looks incredible there. You were right!"

Eduardo said little as he was taken around the room and introduced to guests. Possibly he was uncomfortable with English, possibly he was just uncomfortable. But his discomfort was certainly social and not pharmaceutical, as he had the happy grin of a patient on morphine.

Talley looked into Eduardo's face and knew that neither he nor Gayle was likely to get his attention to look at transparencies. He would call Eduardo's curator tomorrow and make the pitch. The curator in Eduardo's case was a smart coordinator only, as Eduardo made all the final decisions with an uncharacteristically sober acuity. The group was then led around for a tour of the house, which was a showcase and had been meticulously detailed. Even the light switches were period and flawlessly installed; it was as though a heavenly contractor had floated in, waved a wand, and perfected every corner. In the bedroom, a surprising and satisfying art reference library was arranged alphabetically in a splendid Nakashima bookcase. Nakashima, who elevated the craft of driftwood furniture from beachside tourist shops to high art, was now being rediscovered after a lengthy fallow period, with Flores leading the way. Over the bed hung a Wilfredo Lam, the Cuban painter who was a Picasso acolyte but distinguished himself with a unique, surrealistic diversion from Cubism.

"Cubanism," joked Flores, indicating he was not as potted as he looked.

"Where the hell do you find one of those?" said Stirling, asking the question aloud that was on Talley's mind.

"Where'd we get that?" said Eduardo, looking around.

The other question that was on Talley's mind was one that only Stirling could answer: "What can it be like to sleep with Blanca?" Talley stood behind her and stared at her bare neck when he was supposed to be looking at the Lam.

The narrow hallway forced them to line up, Gayle shoulder to shoulder with Eduardo, squeezing Talley to the rear, making him leave the

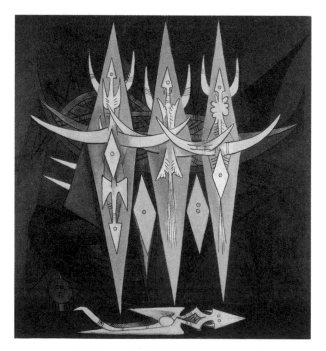

Initiation, Wilfredo Lam, 1950
72.8 × 66.9 in.

room last. But he could still hear her remark to Eduardo: "You know what would look good in the guest bedroom? Pilot Mouse! I have some transparencies I was going to show to Dean Valentine, but I'll show them to you first." This remark was intended to get Flores's blood flowing, as Dean Valentine made every other contemporary collector a pretender. Hinton Alberg's collection of seven hundred paintings seemed paltry compared with Valentine's twelve hundred. His sweet-science combination of a keen eye for new work and a vacuum cleaner mentality meant he got everywhere first. He once sneaked into a Manhattan art fair a day before it opened by disguising himself as a janitor in order to get first crack at the best in the show. But Talley thought Gayle had misjudged her man. Flores never thought of himself as a competitor; he just liked art.

Dinner was called. The service was stealthy and invisible; new plates were slipped in like playing cards. The conversation was exclusively about art, not so much art as spiritual metaphor, but art as advanced thing, with beauty being an asset like the sleek lines of a Buick: a really nice thing to have, but it still had to get you there. Gayle Smiley perked up at every mention of artists she represented and fell into irritated silence when any other artist was mentioned, including Goya. Talley scored points by mentioning Gober's playpen, but he still didn't understand what it was.

Gayle was more like a great basketball player than an art dealer: she unfailingly covered her man, making it impossible for Talley to throw him a pass. However, Talley knew that there would be a moment after dinner when Gayle would have to go vomit, leaving her man wide open. When she left, precisely after dessert, Talley took Flores aside and said, "I like the new direction. I left a transparency of a Pilot Mouse picture next to your bed. There could be some fakes out there, so be careful. This one is genuine. I'm assuming the Lam's not for sale, but if it ever is…"

Dinner wrapped up with everyone in a stupor, and Talley made his way to the hotel on foot, whistling drunkenly in the balmy night, one hand in his pocket, the other dangling his coat over his back with one finger like Sinatra. Back in his room, the phone rang.

"Hey, you in?"

"Yes, darlin', come on up."

A few moments later, Cherry Finch was at his door, and soon they were tugging at each other's clothes. These rendezvous remained undisclosed even to their closest friends, and their total discretion meant that they could go on forever.

40.

PATRICE CLAIRE was in Paris alone, and he didn't know why. Every bistro lunch, every café dinner, every evening engagement, would have been better with Lacey present. He wanted his social group to meet her, to like her, to see her as he did, as an extra measure of sunlight in the room. He knew she would stand up to his friends' rigid appraisals, because Lacey never tried to impress with manners; she impressed with wit and daring. He could imagine his stuffiest Parisian cohort tilting back on his heels, trying to get a wider look at her. Patrice wanted Lacey's take on everything in his world: what was the best food, which were his best clothes, what was his best quality.

It was eight a.m. in Los Angeles, eleven a.m. in New York, and five p.m. in Paris. Barton Talley was boarding a plane at LAX, and Patrice was calling Lacey at the gallery, his first communication with her since the rapturous Carlyle night. Donna put him through upstairs, announcing who it was. Lacey bowed her finger on the extension button.

"What are you doing?" he asked.

"Thinking about your dick," she said. Somehow, this was a more welcome response than if she had said, "How do I love thee? Let me count the ways." They talked for one hour, ending with phone sex that was as frustrating as it was fulfilling. Lacey's palm gripped the front of her chair as she rubbed against her wrist, her other elbow on the desk with the phone held under her hair. Afterward, she walked down the gallery stairs with a just-fucked look so evident that it made Donna wonder if a deliveryman had slipped by her.

Patrice had promised to be back in New York in two weeks, but Lacey knew he would be there by Thursday, so she kept her evenings open.

Talley stopped by the gallery after his plane landed. He looked exhausted, so she postponed until tomorrow the grilling she was about to give him. If he was going to be dragged off to jail, she thought he should be freshly shaven.

41.

I SHOWED UP at Lacey's that night at eight p.m. She was making pasta for Angela, Sharon, and me, the recipe for which she had gleaned from *The New York Times Magazine*, and tossing together a clarifying drink called an Aviation, which has to be made in a batch because after the first one you're too drunk to make any more.

When the drinks had taken effect, I was treated like the gay friend, privy to all gossip, allowed to hear the girls' most detailed sexual experiences. I even found myself retorting with catty comments that I imagined a stereotypical gay invitee might interject amid the squeals and coughing fits generated by spit takes. Lacey detailed the earlier phone encounter with Patrice and then would repeat it this way: she would say, "It was an ordinary, boring day, except for the..." then she would mouth the words *phone sex*. "Yes," she would go on, "except for the [mouthed] *phone sex*, it was a very ordinary day." Once, the phone rang during dinner. Lacey looked over at us and said, "That must be my *phone sex*." This sent us into fits whenever we could work "phone sex" into the conversation, and things got sillier and sillier as all of us contributed, intoning the unimportant words at full volume and finishing the sentence by mouthing the last two words only: "Now where did I put that *phone sex*?" We were aching so much that we imposed a moratorium on saying "phone sex," which, like an Arab/Israeli cease-fire, took longer to take effect than it should have.

During an interlude of sobriety, figurative only, we each filled in the others on our lives. Angela, the most practical of us, was likely to be married within the year and living in Seattle. Sharon had fallen in love with a downtown theater actor and was focusing on theater fund-raising so her boyfriend would have a place to act. And I had broken through at *ARTnews* magazine with an article on Jeff Koons's relation to Pop Art, where I made the case that Pop had become a genre unto itself, like landscape and still life, and was therefore no longer ironic by definition. I didn't get to explain the premise of my piece to the women, because my floor time had been cut short by a contest to see who could say the word *dirigible* without laughing.

Angela and Sharon shuffled out when the evening had deflated like a whoopee cushion after the joke's over, and I lingered because Lacey indicated for me to linger. She wanted to get my take on the Vermeer situation, and I sat rapt as she unfolded the story. She really didn't need me to hear it, because she never asked me what to do, and I had no clue what to tell her. I did think that it was symptomatic that her life fell naturally into states of intrigue, while I was always moving in a world where nothing changed.

Lacey finally arrived at the conclusion that the only questionable evidence was the Vermeer in the bins and that everything else could be explained as being on the right side of the law. This frustrated her. She wanted to go into work tomorrow steaming, but she couldn't quite. She finally found an angle that could work her up into a frenzy.

Tuesday morning she left a note on Barton Talley's desk: "I need to talk to you." Each word was underlined for emphasis. An hour later, Barton appeared at her office door with nonchalance, not picking up on the underlining.

Lacey looked up. "Oh," she said, "I need to see you."

"That's what the note said," Talley responded.

"In your office," she commanded.

Lacey was trying to funnel her energy into one pure welder's arc of white heat that would sear Talley's forehead, but she kept feeling herself slipping back into unwelcome calm.

"Sit down," Talley invited her.

Lacey, thinking she was being stern, said, "I'd rather stand," then she sat down.

"Look," she said, "why didn't you go to Boston?"

"When?"

"When you sent me."

"Lacey, do you realize you work for me, not the other way around?"

"You used me."

"You work for me. I'm supposed to use you."

"You used me in an off-contract way."

"We don't have a contract." Talley's responses were all said with a half-smile that indicated to Lacey he considered this repartee and not grounds for dismissal. So she went on.

"Why didn't you go to Boston?"

"I told you, I was trying to avoid a certain group of trustees."

"Okay, so that's bullshit. Next."

"Uh, you go next."

"As long as I've known you, you have never been shy, perturbed, or cowed. An art dealer doesn't live on tact. You sent me because of the two men. You wanted me to carry something back that you didn't want to be caught carrying back."

Talley got up, walked to the office door. "I didn't know what it would be," he said, and then he closed the door. "Do you know what it was, Lacey?"

"They showed it to me before they sealed it," she said.

Talley paused and thought over this statement, assigning numeric value to its possible truth. The number came up low.

"No, they didn't," he said.

"I steamed it open," said Lacey.

"Do you know what it is?"

"I think I do."

"It was like sending back a finger of a kidnap victim. Grotesque. I didn't expect it."

"And the two men?"

"FBI."

"Oh, good."

"Why 'Oh, good'?"

"Because if they were the crooks, you'd probably ask me to sleep with one of them. Wouldn't you."

There was a second of silence, then they both broke into laughter.

"Wouldn't you, you fucker!" said Lacey, simultaneously screaming and muffling her own voice.

"Only off-contract," Talley said.

Then Lacey got serious. "Don't mistake this smile for 'problem solved.' I don't want to be the dupe who gets ten to twenty."

"We wanted evidence that they had the pictures. The FBI guys acted as go-betweens to the thieves. I was expecting a photograph of the painting next to today's paper, something like that. But these jerks are not us. They don't handle with care. I didn't know they were going to deliver that night. I got a call and told them to give it to you. I didn't realize you were Nancy Drew."

"And why you?"

"It started years ago when I was in Boston. I was the expert; I had written essays on the Vermeer. The FBI came to me to authenticate if the situation ever came up in New York. The thieves tried contacting the FBI years ago, but the agent couldn't confirm that the picture they let him glimpse was the real thing, and the deal fizzled."

"So none of the pictures have been returned," Lacey said, which was her own test of authenticity.

"No. These pictures probably won't be returned until the next generation. Deathbed confession sort of thing."

Lacey had heard nothing but plausibility, yet everything Talley was saying was rendered implausible by the corpus delicti in the bins, and she didn't know how to handle it. But directness had worked so far, so she decided to produce the body. She stood up.

"Sit, just sit," she said to Talley, and she left the office. She went back to the bins, looked at the slot where the Vermeer still dumbly sat. She pulled it out and grabbed a box cutter on the way back to the office.

When she walked into the office with the package, Talley said, "Oh."

She carefully sliced open the tape and took out the painting while he sat. She rested it on Talley's office easel and stood back, crossing her arms.

"And?" said Talley.

"And you're under arrest if you don't explain."

"You're one to be talking about arrest, Lacey."

"What do you mean?"

"I've had a few conversations with Cherry Finch."

Lacey stopped still. She turned her attention back to the Vermeer. "What about this?"

Talley put the intercom on speaker and rang Donna. He indicated to Lacey to show him the edge of the cardboard box. "Donna, what's inventory item 53876?"

"Oh...okay...," said Donna, rattling around on a keyboard. "That's the...let's see...that's the Johannes Vermeer," she said, pronouncing the J in Johannes.

"Okay, thank you," said Talley. "Now, Lacey Drew, if Donna, who is my Connecticut client's quidnunc daughter—"

"What?" said Donna, who was still on the phone.

"Oh, sorry, Donna. I meant to hang up." Talley pressed the intercom button. "If Donna knows we've got a Vermeer in here, do you think we have a serious problem?"

Lacey put her index finger to her chin and shifted her hips, posing herself like a Kewpie doll.

"Turn the Vermeer around," said Talley.

Lacey did, resting it backward on the easel. "Read the label."

"Johannes Vermeer, blah blah, Metropolitan Museum of Art."

"What does that tell you?" said Talley.

"What's it supposed to tell me? It sounds like it's getting worse for you."

"Wrong museum," said Talley. "The stolen Vermeer's from the Gardner. The label says the Met. This is a nineteenth-century copy. Vermeer didn't bring much money until then; that's when the fakers got busy. Very precise, meant to fool. The size is correct to the centimeter. Bernard Berenson vetoed this one and found the real one for Mrs. Gardner. He was a dog, but he had a good eye. In the twenties this picture got donated as a study picture to the Met. There was a moment where we thought the bad guys were going to produce the real one as evidence, keeping the rest hostage while we examined it. We intended to swap the real picture out of its frame and stick in this pretender. The Met agreed that this was a lamb that could be sacrificed."

Lacey was deflated. "Rats. I wanted there to be a crime," she said. "It would have been so much more fun."

42.

PATRICE CLAIRE sat at his favorite restaurant in Paris, Le Petit Zinc, surrounded by cheerful friends who were toasting his fortieth birthday on a beautiful and still summer night when the sun wouldn't set until ten p.m., and all he could think was, What am I doing here? He had made several trips to New York during the summer to see Lacey, and each seemed to enforce his suspicion that she was in love with him. While his friends laughed and chatted, he left a phone message for Lacey: "Lacey, dinner Thursday?" He would fly to New York for no reason at all except to see her, unable to wait the two weeks to return to Manhattan that was his usual cycle. He had noted that phone sex with Lacey was better than real sex with his standby Parisian girlfriend, who once had intrigued him—but now looking at her was like looking at cardboard. Later that evening, when he told his standby that he was breaking it off, she responded with a "puh" so indifferent that he thought she had misheard him.

Patrice left Lacey a message with Donna, and wondered whether to go ahead and book the flight and just chance it. When he finally got a message back ("Come on over, sailor boy, I'll let you swab my decks"), he booked a Thursday Concorde, not because he didn't want to risk being late for dinner, but because he was so eager to get there that he wanted to arrive before he took off, which only the Concorde could accomplish.

As Patrice waited in the Concorde lounge, he noticed a change in the usual demographics. The Americans, English, and French were being displaced by Russians, Asians, and Arabs, who not only could afford to bring their entire families on the plane even though there was no discounted child's fare, but would also buy blocks of seats so no one could sit next to them.

A new level of wealth was emerging from the former Communists and the capitalist Chinese. Businesses lacking glamour, like mining and pipelines, bestowed riches on Russian entrepreneurs who had stunningly outmaneuvered organized crime and political kingpins. What one thousand dollars was to a millionaire, a million dollars was to the new billionaires. And what they spent on art was irrelevant to them and their lifestyles. Art was about to acquire the aura of an internationally recognizable asset, a unique and emotional emblem of the good life. While Patrice Claire was only a normal millionaire, incapable of the extended reach of the new global money, he had the advantage of expertise and intuition in a delicate business.

Even though the Concorde was sleek and magnificent, looking like a perfect robot bird, it was still a crate. It rattled like a jalopy as it hypersped down the runway, it jerked and clanked as it climbed, and it gave the illusion of stalling as engines were suddenly cut back because of noise regulations. And once aloft, it sailed dully like any other aircraft. The seats were cramped, and if someone took the seat beside you, it was easy to feel that your costly flight had been downgraded to a Bombay train.

When Patrice landed at JFK, he felt as though he had been inside a dart that was launched into the Paris sky and stuck into a passenger gate in New York. He called Lacey from the taxi, but six p.m. was a bad time to reach anyone, and he got message machines all around. He made reservations at Le Bernardin, which was intended to send a message to Lacey, and to himself, that this was a special night and she was worth every extravagance. It was seven p.m. by the time he arrived at the Carlyle, having already left another message for Lacey at her apartment. In case they don't connect, he said, meet him at nine p.m. at the restaurant. His actions, his mood, his methodology, indicated the presence of an unrealized kernel of hope in his soul: this night they would walk into the restaurant as two people on a deliciously serious date and emerge as two people in love.

The Carlyle was still old-fashioned, and phone messages were delivered on handwritten notes that were slid under the doorway by an unseen hand. After his shower, and after dressing in a looser-cut suit than his pre-Lacey, tight-waisted Parisian standby, Patrice noticed a small, folded message poking an edge out from under the doorsill. He opened it and read, "So sorry, something came up and I couldn't reach you. I'll call you later. Old friend in town and can't change." Patrice cursed the shower and sat on the bed, the message dangling from his fingers like a notification of death, and he wondered what had just happened.

What had just happened was this: Earlier, I had called Lacey at work and said, "There's an opening tonight at a small gallery in Chelsea. A not very interesting young artist, but Pilot Mouse is supposed to be there. They're friends or something. Want to go?"

"What time?" she said. "I've got a dinner tonight."

"The opening's six to eight. Party afterwards," I said.

"Where do I meet you?" she said.

"The bar at Bottino."

Lacey had picked up Patrice's message but hadn't responded, assuming she would meet him at Le Bernardin. But now there was a stronger pull elsewhere. She left a message for Patrice, not ringing his room, as she dashed out the door.

Lacey came into the bar wearing her usual too-small sweater and a cloche straw hat with a summer umbrella hung over her arm. When she came into the room, there was an adjustment in the hierarchy of women. The most beautiful remained undisturbed in their fixed positions, but Lacey shot to the top of every other list: cutest, sexiest, most fun. We had a drink, and a few other people joined in. Everyone was talking about Pilot Mouse and was he really going to be there. Yes, for sure, they said. He's supporting his friend's show. You know he's not reclusive, he's just wanted everywhere, so when he doesn't show up he's missed and mythologized. He's handsome, oh yes, he's handsome and mysterious. Doesn't speak much. Very serious. Gay? Maybe, someone said. I heard not, said another knowingly.

We all marched around the corner and entered an industrial building with a clanking elevator operated by a guy playing a radio. A dozen people crowded into the cab as it jolted and lurched to the seventh floor. The gab was already under way when the door screeched open and we spilled out into the hallway. We filled it like gas expanding and trooped our way around several bends, following hand-drawn signs bearing colored arrows. Finally, the gallery was in sight, indentified by a clutch of young people standing in the hall with plastic conical cups of white wine, a few of them smoking.

We entered the gallery, an unexpectedly large space for such a small door, where perhaps a hundred invitees, friends of invitees, and miscellaneous interlopers gradually raised the volume to crushing intensity. Lacey and I pulled away from our default group, heading toward the table of wine, which was pour-your-own. The art on the walls was the kind that resists normal interpretation: paper, sometimes cardboard, thumbtacked to the wall with collaged images taped or glued to its surface, and nearby, a plinth displaying a spool of thread, or a safety pin, or something else ordinary under a Plexi box. Lacey and I looked at one of these mysteries and then looked at each other, but I couldn't knock it because who knows? A lot of strange art had achieved classic status over the last twenty years, making criticism of the next new thing dangerous. Lacey, however, shrugged, leaned in to my ear, and whispered, "Spare me."

Even though there was no music, the gallery pulsed to a beat. Thursday is the standard night for openings in Chelsea, and when galleries' biorhythms aligned so that a dozen or more openings fell on the same night, there was blastoff. This was prom night for the smart set, a night to be smug, cool, to dress up or dress down, and to bring into focus everything one loves about oneself and make it tangible. It was possible for young men to set their sights on a particular woman and "coincidentally" run into her at three different galleries until there was enough in common to start a conversation, or rue for days one's failure to say hello to the object of desire and then run an ad in the *Village Voice*'s "Missed Connections" column.

Art was being flown in from Europe or carted up from downtown basement studios. It was being made by men, women, minorities, and majorities, all with equal access. Whether it was any good or not, the sheer amount of it—to the dismay of cranky critics—was redefining what art could be. Since the 1970s, art schools had shied away from teaching skills and concentrated on teaching thought. Yet this was the first time in conventional art history where no single movement dominated, no manifesto declared its superiority, and diversity bounced around like spilled marbles on concrete.

If the history of humor could be charted, visual art of this period might be seen as its next frontier. Stand-ups were still doing stand-up, but Jeff Koons made a forty-foot-high sculpture of a puppy built out of twenty-five tons of flowers and soil in pots, and Maurizio Cattelan made a life-size sculpture of the pope flattened by a meteor that had just fallen through a skylight. This piece was made only a year before he convinced his gallery director to walk around for a month dressed as a bright pink penis.

We were about to leave when there was a stir by the entrance. A small coterie of people moved toward another group standing mid-gallery, and there was a moment where I thought they were like two

La Nona Ora, Maurizio Cattelan, 1999
Lifesize.

galaxies about to pass through each other. But there was a halt, and the two groups became one. The galaxy metaphor is apt, as this commingling produced two centers. One was a young man we had identified as the artist whose work was on the walls, but the second man seemed to have all the gravity. Lacey looked over, and her first identification in the lineup was a woman: "Oh shit, Tanya Ross." But her second identification was friendlier. "Oh," she said, "Jonah Marsh." She had not seen him in three years, and Jonah had grown from boy to man. His black hair looked uncombed, but the truth was probably a meticulous opposite. Lacey led the way toward the group, and Tanya Ross turned first.

"Hi, Lacey," she said stiffly.

Lacey introduced me, and fixated as I was on Tanya's screen-test beauty, she seemed not to notice me. Tanya reluctantly introduced

Lacey and me to a few more people by their first name only, then she turned to Jonah Marsh and said, "And this is Pilot Mouse."

Lacey cocked her head and uttered a long, slow, "Hey..." It was the first time I had seen her unsettled. Then she recovered, saying, "I owe you a phone call; I've been out of the country." It was as though she had backed into someone at a high-rise and accidentally bumped him out the window but hoped no one had noticed. Unwanted by Tanya, Lacey shouldered her way into the troupe like a boxer muscling her opponent back against the ropes. Lacey's uptown moves, high-style reserve with a playful edge, had been perfected, but she hadn't used her downtown moves—fearless sexuality with a flapping fringe of pluck and wit—in a long time. There was an instant breeze from her, and she was the new alternate center of this group of stars. When she spoke to the young artist whose show it was and whom she had just displaced, she didn't betray herself by flattering him but instead asked vibrant questions about his intent. And after his unparsable response, including a passage where he said he was "blurring the boundaries between a thing and thought," she said, "Thank you, I get lost sometimes," while laying two fingers on his folded arm.

We walked around Chelsea for a while. I was trying to make headway with Tanya Ross, who was clearly friends with Jonah Marsh, and Lacey, not knowing to what degree Tanya was a friend, was staying in Jonah's sight, crossing his field of vision whenever Tanya got his attention. Then there was a discussion of food and drinks. Lacey declined, peculiarly, saying, "No, I'm meeting a friend." The group mentioned Cia, a sushi bar around the corner. "Oh, jeez," said Lacey, lying, "that's where I'm meeting him."

I was relieved that the evening wasn't over, because I wasn't ready to give up on Tanya Ross. It was obvious to me that Tanya was not Pilot Mouse's date, because she had clearly warmed to me and she didn't seem duplicitous, unlike Lacey. She asked what I did, and when I told her I was a freelance art writer, there was no ho-hum blankness that overcame her. Instead she responded with, "Oh, how interesting!" No one had ever said that to me since birth. She even had the courtesy not to ask if I was published, so I volunteered that I wrote regularly for *ARTnews*, and for gallery catalogs. And when I told her I wrote an essay about the rare bird Arthur Dove for the Whitney show, her face brightened and she said, "I read that. I think."

At the restaurant, there was a seating war that appeared casual but if diagrammed would have looked like an Andy Warhol dance-step painting. With me across from Tanya, Lacey positioned herself so that every time Jonah looked at her, he was forcibly looking away from Tanya. With the seating chart done, Lacey excused herself from the table and walked toward the phone with a small swing of her hips.

Patrice Claire sat in his Carlyle paradise, which had so quickly turned itself into hell. There was nothing with which to uplift himself; the repair was out of his control and completely in Lacey's. He had canceled Le Bernardin, but this was not an act of power, it was one of grief. Lacey had said she would call. Did she mean tonight? He had ordered room service to keep him close to the phone. When it rang, he felt a surge of hope that he resented in himself. It was Lacey.

"I'm *so* sorry. I wasn't sure if you meant tonight. We never set a time... I'm downtown at Cia. I ran into an old friend. He's great. Come down. I need to see you."

"I'll find it," said Patrice.

Patrice was used to the steadfast responses of paintings, not the unpredictable responses of people. A discussion of a picture was a conversation of ultimate complexity and intrigue, irresolvable and ongoing. A conversation with Lacey was the same, except the picture did not strike out at him. He fantasized that he and Lacey would have a lifelong conversation—also irresolvable and ongoing—because their common subject would be a route to each other. He was stable and sane, an avid art enthusiast with the same mutant gene as the stamp collector, the coin collector, or the model train freak—except that there were glorious buildings erected solely to house and protect his objects of interest, objects that commanded the attention of scholars, historians, and news bureaus, giving undeniable proof that they were worthy of devotion. But because the objects of his adoration were inert, he was unaccustomed to mood swings. Especially volcanic ones that took place over a few seconds. He was angry that Lacey had canceled, unhappy that he would be seeing her in a group, disturbed that her old friend was male—yet he was eager to see her.

Instead of the serenity and anticipation with which he would have arrived at Le Bernardin, he arrived at Cia with anxiety and vulnerability. He was too old for this place. It was a different crowd, with different slang and different references, a crowd ignorant of the nomenclature of the uptown art world. He did, however, understand sushi.

He passed through the bar, and thankfully, it was an art bar and not a sports bar, so he wasn't the shortest male in the gauntlet. He looked around the darkened restaurant when he heard Lacey shouting from the murk, "Patrice!"

From my seat, I watched as Lacey ran up to Patrice, delivering an affectionate hug that seemed to me exaggerated. She took him to the group and introduced everyone, at least everyone she knew, and except for me and Tanya, whom he knew, there were lackluster hellos.

Lacey squeezed back into her slot across from Pilot Mouse, with Patrice having to turn sideways to sit down. She seemed genuinely in love with Patrice, and genuinely trying to rekindle Jonah's fleeting interest of three years ago. Looking back, I think that both behaviors were valid. To her this was natural, to Patrice it was unsettling, to me it was bewildering, and to Tanya Ross, who had matured normally, it was creepy. Tanya occasionally looked at me with an expressionless stare that I knew signified disgust. Although it seemed that Jonah Marsh was with Tanya tonight, I did notice his eyes glancing over to Lacey with metronomic regularity.

As I reached over to refill her sake glass, Tanya looked at me oddly and said, "Have we met?"

"I would have remembered," I flirted.

"You look familiar," she insisted, and she sat in silence for a minute, trying to work it out.

The party broke up, and Lacey hugged Pilot Mouse good-bye, her actions maintaining that they were just old friends, while Patrice stood by, correctly assuming that Pilot had already fucked her, or was about to again, which made him queasy. They took a taxi to her apartment, and Patrice came up for a few minutes, but this was not the end that he wanted for the night. So he made, enthusiastically, a date for the next night, but he knew Le Bernardin would be impossible on a Friday and he would be settling for a restaurant less major, less symbolic.

He had been knocked backward, but a previously untouched part of his heart kept driving him forward, fueled by fresh emotions emerging from the wound, unknown and uncontrollable. Lacey gave him a ravishing kiss good night, then he walked east to Central Park, where he flagged down a cab. On the way back to the Carlyle, his mental reenactment of their last kiss told him, yes, she loves me, and he once again saw Lacey as an illuminating white light, forgetting that white is composed of disparate streaks of color, each as powerful as the whole.

When Patrice called that afternoon, telling her the restaurant was Nello on Madison, walking distance from the Carlyle, Lacey said, "Can I shower at your apartment? I brought a change." The idea of Lacey showering and changing at his apartment made his heart leap. This was a special gesture of ease, of closeness. Where he had been thrown down last night, he was now proportionately uplifted. This evening was suddenly more than a date; the details bore the assumption of attachment.

Patrice opened the door after Lacey's light rap. "Hello, lover," she said, hitting at least three separate musical notes. Patrice, with comic timing, turned to look behind him. She kissed him hello, strutted into the apartment, and threw herself down on the sofa with a sigh of homecoming. The red lights from last night were turning to green. The bag on her arm slid off onto the carpet beside her. She pulled her knees up, draping her skirt between them as her fingers combed through her hair, spreading it out on the pillow like a peacock's tail. Patrice sat and enjoyed the show.

"Can you see my place from here?" said Lacey.

"I don't know," said Patrice, "I haven't tried."

"Liar."

"I'm an adult."

"I can see the Carlyle from the park, but I couldn't tell which apartment was yours," said Lacey.

"Twenty-first floor. Can't count to twenty-one?"

"I can't see the street level, smart guy. There's no place to start counting."

Patrice looked at Lacey and wanted her right then, but he knew that immediate sofa sex would be an intense but short engagement, and he preferred the promise of a long entwinement between the perfumed sheets of the Carlyle's king-size bed.

After a shared glass of wine taken from Patrice's personally stocked minifridge, Lacey took over the bathroom while he sat in the living room and listened to the sounds coming from behind the door. When he first heard the hard rain of the shower, the image of her naked, with her hands slipping over herself, rose and stayed in his mind. He visualized every move she might make with a washcloth, until finally he pictured her standing motionless under the rich flow of water, taking in the enveloping steam that cumulated around her like summer clouds.

The jet-engine volume of the hair dryer went on for about ten minutes, then it stopped, and there was another ten minutes of intermittent jangling. He saw a quick flash of her, nude, as she dashed across the hallway to the bedroom, where she had hung up her change of clothes. A few minutes later, she came out dressed, still pulling her hair with a brush. "When are we supposed to be there?"

"We are supposed to be there when we get there," he said.

"Yes," she said, "but for normal people what time are we supposed to be there?"

"Eight o'clock." Patrice liked what he saw in this snapshot. She looked sophisticated and confident. He liked that she still had a sense of the normal, and she was treating him as if they were living together. When she finally presented herself, she was wearing the amber necklace he had given her in St. Petersburg.

She leaned against the wall and snaked the amber around her finger. "Remember this? You gave it to me on the night we *got hot*."

Madison Avenue was just beginning to flicker on. They walked down the street, sometimes arm in arm, sometimes with Lacey breaking away to physically exaggerate a point, walking backward, then slue-footing around to take his hand or slip her arm through the crook of his elbow. Her strut appropriately modified, her girlishness tempered and grown up for the richest shopping promenade in Manhattan, Lacey had artfully tailored her downtown vibrancy to an acceptable uptown chic.

Nello was filling up quickly, but Patrice had clout. After being greeted with a genuine smile and handshake from the maître d', they were taken to a small, intimate table that was prime Nello real estate. They had a broad view of the restaurant and its select clientele, who were not the same habitués from even a few blocks down the street.

Lacey scanned the room, able to take in all the faces because of a narrow strip of mirror that ran around the entire diameter of the restaurant.

"No art dealers," she said. "What are you going to do?"

"Art dealers don't have dinners. They have lunches."

"Let's have a prosecco." Lacey laid her calf over Patrice's ankle.

A couple next to them was speaking French. Patrice turned and said in stern French, "You should mind your own business."

"What was that about?" asked Lacey.

"It was about rude snobs who think that nobody in America can understand it when they are insulted."

"You don't look French anymore, Patrice."

"Because of you."

"No more skinny pin-striped suits with pinched waists in your Paris closet?"

"No more cuff links, either."

"And Patrice, no more tanning."

"I shouldn't tan?"

"No," said Lacey, "no more tanning no matter how you're getting it." Then there was a pause while they waited for a new subject to appear.

"What's on your walls?" Lacey asked him.

"Of my apartment? I will give you the virtual tour. Close your eyes."

"I *will* give you the virtual tour, not *wheel* give you the tour. *Will*... *ill*... not *wheel*."

"I *will* give you the tour...," Patrice struggled to say. "Now close your eyes."

"I *wheel* after the prosecco arrives."

She stared at him, unwavering, until the waiter placed the fizzy glass in front of her. Then she shut her eyes. "First," she said, "what's out the window?"

"The Seine," said Patrice.

"Okay, I'm situated," said Lacey.

"On the first wall you see a Miró *Constellation* gouache. You know what that is?"

"Expensive."

"To the right is a matched pair. A Cubist Braque and a Cubist Picasso. To tell which is which is a game only fools play. Over the sofa— and yes, it matches the fabric—is a Cortès."

"Okay, I'm stumped. Who is Cortès?"

"Cortès is a terrible French street scene painter."

"How can you hang it next to the Picasso?"

"It's the best picture Cortès ever painted." At Lacey's look, he continued, "Look, if you want to be strict, there are only six twentieth-century artists: Picasso, Matisse, Giacometti, Pollock, de Kooning, and Warhol. But I don't want to be strict, which is my downfall. I like sentimental Pre-Raphaelites and dumb Bouguereaus, insipid Aivazovskys, and dogs playing poker. As long as they're good, relatively good, I just can't help myself."

"Everyone you collect is dead."

"They're much easier to negotiate with."

"Wouldn't you rather talk art with an artist than a dealer?"

"Oh please, no! Have you ever heard an artist talk about their art? It's Chinese! What they describe in their work is absolutely *not there*. And it's guaranteed that what you think is their worst picture, they think is their best picture."

Patrice was the funniest unfunny person Lacey had ever met. She liked him, yes, and when they got back to his apartment, she told him so without ever saying it. She treated him as though he were the first and last object of her passion, and their ardor was pitched precisely between lust and romance. Eventually, when it was all over, sitting pegged on him with her knees brought up by his waist, their fingers interlaced palm to palm and her hair falling forward over her face, she looked at him with an expression of immutable love.

43.

THE NEXT DAY she went to work, dug out a phone number from the back of her drawer, and booked lunch with Jonah Marsh. The gallery was closing early for summer hours, and Barton Talley had already gone off to the Hamptons. She was to rendezvous with Patrice later, so she went home, wrenched her bicycle from its vertical slot in her closet, and rode down the West Side bicycle path to Chelsea. It was now the glory days of biking, which began in May and sometimes ended not until late October. She could go in shorts and halter tops and let her hair fly free, and she imagined every metallic rattle behind her was an accident caused by the male bikers who swiveled their heads to get a look at her going away.

She got off the path at 26th Street and slowed to a walk as she gazed into the buildings that had stacks of gallery names listed outside. Here was the kind of activity that separated contemporary art from the sticky pace of the modern masters. She was never going to sleep with Chagall, but she had already slept with Pilot Mouse. There were no exciting studio visits to see Mondrian's strict output, but south of 26th Street there were iron staircases that led to grungy spaces still fresh with the smell of paint, or fiberglass, or horse manure, or *whatever*, and occupied by struggling artists who were morosely fucking each other. Lacey could imagine her name headlining a storefront, Yeager Gallery, or perhaps Parrish Gallery, a pseudonym in honor of her first introduction to art. Parrish had a nice sound to it, she thought.

She met Jonah Marsh—Pilot Mouse—at the Empire Diner, and they sat inside rather than join the cattle line for outside. Jonah introduced Carey, his buddy, his buddy with paint splattered on his jeans, and Lacey thought these two cute guys must have their own kind of waiting list.

"I'd heard you worked at Talley. So I called to catch up."

"Well, I caught up last night. Pilot Mouse. Where did you come up with that name?"

"The night we did X. And thus I am born."

Lacey laughed. "Oh, my God. And Carey, where did you get your weird name?"

Carey laughed, catching the joke, and said, "When I took aspirin."

Jonah Marsh had really called Lacey because he was not finished. Their dissolution had been so abrupt, he felt as though he had been left teetering on a precipice and not quite fallen, his arms still circling for balance. I don't think Jonah was in love with Lacey anymore, but he still wanted to sleep with her; he felt she owed him that. Jonah had interpreted their drug-driven intimacy as genuine, and the enhanced sex that accompanied it stayed in his memory as something that was unique to them, and he believed, correctly, that Lacey wouldn't mind the occasional experiment.

It was to Lacey's advantage to keep Jonah interested. It was to her advantage to keep the newly discovered Carey interested—maybe he was a sellable artist. It was to her advantage to keep everyone interested.

44.

THROUGHOUT THE SUMMER, Lacey continued with Patrice Claire. There were parties and introductions, there was a trip to Paris to see his apartment and be shown off to friends. When the dinners were in English, Lacey charmed; when conversations would drift into French, she sat and waited, a pretty young thing. Her high school French was no help when the speakers sped through words and sentences, leaving nothing for her ear to latch on to.

Patrice's travel kept the relationship from becoming routine, but it also kept him from advancing it. They were still in the romantic phase, extended because of their discontinuous time together, which meant that every two weeks there was an exciting renewal. Lacey's indiscriminate joie de vivre, her openness to adventure, never let Patrice feel he was on solid ground. Though he had tacit commitment, he waited for actual commitment. He also believed their relationship deserved a phone call a day, but sometimes she would not return a Wednesday call until Saturday. Once, he decided to punish her by not calling or returning her calls for four days. It was torture for Patrice. He felt cruel, and his imagination pictured Lacey worrying about him. But this behavior would have been better left to expert manipulators. When he finally called, ninety-six hours after they last spoke, which Patrice had timed exactly, he was twittering with nervous energy. She answered her cell phone with party noise in the background.

"Hey," she said, "I'm at a party downtown. All art people. Are you coming in?"

Absent from Lacey's conversation was the simple inquiry that Patrice had expected and had suffered to obtain, which was, "Where have you been? I missed you so much." She was certainly not in mourning; it seemed she had barely noticed he was missing. Patrice's plan had been a trick on himself, one that left him hurting and alone in the City of Light.

The next day, Lacey called Patrice in Paris as though nothing had happened—because to Lacey, nothing had happened—saying, Come in, we'll go to Shakespeare in the Park. Patrice humbly packed his bags, unable to resist the command. But he didn't take the Concorde, as a personal sign of civil disobedience.

Lacey's display of excitement at seeing him compensated for all her misdemeanors of the past month, and she gave her all in bed that night, which brought him back to the mountaintop. While making love to her, he was also watching her. Yes, this was real passion, centered on him, focused and indivisible. He felt he was taking her to a place no man had taken her, that she had given herself over to him entirely. But afterward, when she rested beside him and he watched her sink into her own thoughts, he could feel the communion slip away, and he knew that she was not his.

Patrice was still unable to give up his fantasy of perfect love and a changed life, even with the surprise blows of reality that Lacey delivered. He could distort her shortcomings and make them his own: it was he, he thought, who was not vital enough to make her fully his.

His week with her extended over Labor Day, and they went to Larry Gagosian's house in the Hamptons for an all-day party. Barton Talley was not invited, being a rival dealer, but Hinton Alberg was there and he greeted Lacey warmly. The ovoid Hinton didn't register a blip on Patrice's jealousy sonar, and he felt almost fine the whole day. As they drove back late in the evening by limousine, Lacey fell asleep against his shoulder. He felt that if he moved, she might be displeased with him, so he stayed stiffly in place the entire two hours.

45.

TOWARD THE NEW MILLENNIUM, Lacey began to throw accurate strikes for the Talley gallery. At the end of 1998, she sold a small Léger for over a million dollars (to a French couple Patrice Claire had directed her way), and early in 1999, she negotiated a sale of little-known Warhol black-and-white photographs to Elton John, whose Atlanta-based collection of photography had grown into a treasury. Large numbers were beginning to be easier to say. She had had an initial reticence about saying "one point two" instead of "one million two hundred thousand." It seemed as though "one point two" should be said by people partying on a yacht, not a twenty-nine-year-old woman who still felt like a downtown girl. It remained hard for her to say "three" when there could be a confusion as to whether she meant three million or three hundred thousand. When Talley said "three," the client always understood its meaning.

As comfortable as Lacey was becoming with prices that would have stuck in her throat a year earlier, she was working on salary rather than commission, except for the occasional generous gratuity from Talley, meaning that she was not participating in the newly inflated profits the art market was starting to generate. She continued to imagine a gallery with her name out front. She could likely afford a new gallery that showed younger artists, while she couldn't fund even the frames required to show modern masters, despite her windfall from a few years ago.

To further enhance the viability of downtown galleries, a new category of art was being created. Already in place were "old masters," "Postimpressionists," "postwar," and "contemporary." When collectors said, "We collect contemporary," their scope and interest—and their prestige—could be fairly understood. But when the rubric of "young artists" surfaced, a whole new class of collectors had a label. Saying, "We collect young artists," had extraordinary cachet. It meant that they were in the forefront, ferreting out genius, risking money and reputation.

It was impossible to know if this new art was good, because, mostly, good art had been defined by its endurance over time. But even though this new art had not yet faced that jury, collectively it had a significant effect: it made art of Talley's generation seem old and stodgy. It was similar to what happened to crooners when Elvis came along: they were instantly musty. A living room full of Picassos identified the collectors as a certain kind of old money. But a roomful of unprecedented objects, historically rootless, was lively and game, and the collectors who amassed them were big-game hunters.

The nature of collecting changed, too. Formerly, dealers tried to win the respect of their collectors. Now collectors were trying to win the respect of their dealers. A new social constellation had been created linking New York to London, San Francisco, Chicago, and Los Angeles. Collector stars were once again being created on rumors of buying binges and hearsay about private galleries being planned to house their vast acquisitions.

An art renaissance was under way. Unlike the Italian Renaissance, fueled by science and art nibbling away at a strict anti-intellectual environment, the new renaissance was fueled by an abundance of affordable art that was, in most cases, made by sincere and talented artists flocking to New York, its cultural center. Cortés and Sir Francis Drake were on the prowl, not for land, but for competent artists with an idea.

In 1999, the full potency of young artists was not yet known. Lacey's embryonic notion of starting a gallery had begun before objects that were barely two years old would achieve million-dollar prices.

46.

WHEN AUGUST FALLS on Manhattan, the galleries go quiet, with some of them shuttering until the season opens again in September. Lacey became the gallery sitter while Barton took his Hamptons vacation. By the time the workday ended, she still had hours of sunlight left to Rollerblade around Central Park. Lacey liked the summer heat and the stripping away of sullen winter clothing to near nudity or athletic wear that emphasized the bas-relief of her anatomical landscape. The sky was still dusky when she set out for open ground, the bars and restaurants of young Manhattan.

Patrice Claire still courted Lacey, and Lacey courted him back. But while he was forthright, she was tricky and unreliable. As much as Patrice's every thought was about Lacey, whenever he was wheels up at JFK and heading for Paris, there was an accompanying release of tension, as he no longer felt the need to be constantly interesting or to artificially represent himself to her and her friends as a ceaselessly dynamic person. He made many transatlantic flights that summer, because he knew not to stay too long in New York, not to crowd Lacey with his presence, and not to appear that he was exclusively hers. However, Lacey already knew he was exclusively hers, if she wanted him. As long as Patrice didn't embarrass himself by proclaiming undying love, she was fine remaining involved but uncommitted.

One August night, Patrice landed in New York against a burnt orange sunset and headed for a spontaneously arranged dinner with Cornelia and Hinton Alberg. Unable to call her from Paris without it being a three a.m. wake-up, he phoned Lacey upon hitting the tarmac, and she answered.

"Lacey, tell me you're okay for dinner. Meeting Hinton and Cornelia at Boulud."

"Rats, give a girl a little warning. I've got to be downtown, I don't know how long. Can I come if I can get out of this?"

"Of course. Just come if you can, love to see you."

"Don't wait for me, just start," she said.

Patrice was so polite. "Just come if you can" was not what he meant. He meant "Come. Do it. Show up." But "Just come if you can" made him feel less desperate, more confident. And now he was left with a lacerating curiosity about what she was doing instead of being with him.

Boulud, adjacent to the Carlyle, was the restaurant where upscale dealers took their clients, often to celebrate a sale or to position themselves as matchmaker between an important collector and a museum director. The collectors liked to meet museum people because one approving word from them about a single painting in a hallway could, by liberal extrapolation, validate an entire collection. Directors liked to meet collectors because maybe they would soon be dead and their collection would come to their museum.

But Patrice's dinner with the Albergs was not about business. Hinton could, and would, talk art with anyone, anywhere, and at any time. Patrice and the Albergs liked each other, and Cornelia enjoyed listening to his dating woes and giving him advice and counsel. So when Patrice phoned her to say that Lacey might be joining them and would it be all right, she regarded the request not only as a politeness, but as information about Patrice's heart.

"Lacey Yeager, oh yes, we like her," said Cornelia into her cell phone moments before walking into Boulud.

She and Hinton were seated at a corner table while Patrice's taxi jangled down Park Avenue, heading for 76th Street. There was a moment of repose as they waited. Hinton fit beautifully into the restaurant and its clientele; it was as though he were sitting on an easy chair at home. And Cornelia's frankness made her welcome in an art world so filled with reserve. In came Acquavella with his wife and grown children, clearly not here on business, and Hinton wondered about the practicality of hosting one's family at a restaurant that *Zagat*'s rated as $$$$.

Patrice arrived and took the seat with the best view of the entrance.

"Patrice, you look well. Doesn't he look well, honey?"

"Darlin', don't you know I can't look people in the eye?" said Hinton. "That's why I have pictures. I can look over people's shoulders and land on something so forthcoming."

"But Hinton, there's nothing on the walls here, you might as well look at me," said Patrice, coaxing a laugh from him. "Lacey's going to try and come," he continued, "she's got work downtown."

"When did this start?" said Cornelia.

Patrice smiled at her. "Start? I'm not sure it has. She said to go ahead without her."

Patrice always laughed with the Albergs. Cornelia's curiosity about the forceful personalities that populated their collectors' world and Hinton's lack of interest in anything that moved except by art courier made them lively, made them yin and yang, and Patrice could bounce along over the entire spectrum of conversation. But tonight, as their chatter crisscrossed the table, Cornelia noticed something in Patrice: his eyes shifting from the table to the restaurant entrance. Sometimes a glimmer would come to his face as he spotted the tip of a skirt or a sweater-covered arm that edged inside the front door, and occasionally the anticipatory brightening of his face would turn Cornelia toward the door, too, to see nothing, a mistake, not Lacey.

During the dinner, Acquavella dropped by and jousted with Hinton.

"When are you going to get rid of that stuff and get some real paintings?"

"Well, when are you going to offer me something great?"

"Oh, I've just got Van Goghs and Monets, nothing any good."

"I'll come by tomorrow, Bill."

"Okay, I'll dig something out for you; get you into some quality merchandise. All right, see you later, buddy."

Cornelia was amused by Bill, but she again noted Patrice's distraction from the table and attention to the door. They covered no topic that wasn't attended by this little punctuation. By dessert, Lacey had not shown up, and one last time Patrice gave a now mournful head twist toward the entrance. Cornelia looked at him, squinted her eyes with displeasure, and said, "Women can be so stupid."

PART

III

47.

LACEY, NOW AN UPTOWN WOMAN, felt an increasing tug toward Chelsea. She was like a cat sensing the first vibrations of the oncoming earthquake that was about to rumble through the art market. There were plenty of small signs to be successfully interpreted. Years earlier, SoHo, the former New York gallery center, had proven too successful. Rising rents killed all but the strongest galleries. So the smaller galleries moved leftward to Chelsea, stranding and branding the ones that remained in SoHo as unhip. New galleries sprouted in Chelsea overnight, lacking only fungi domes.

Lacey was aware of an unwieldy rhetorical shift that took place between the Upper East Side and the lower West Side. Art on the Upper East Side was referred to as beautiful, exceptional, serene, exquisite, and *important*. Art below 26th Street was described in the "language of relational aesthetics" or something like that, an argot with a semantic shelf life of about six months. Now artworks "related to spatial, representational, and material functions in contexts defined by movement and transition." An artist who painted a face was now "playing with the idea of a portraiture," or "exploring push-pull aesthetics," or toying with contradictions like "menacing–slash–playful," but he or she was never, ever, simply painting a face.

Patrice Claire, who had chased Lacey into the twenty-first century like a horse chasing a train, and who had allowed humiliations to collect unacknowledged in his psyche, was invited to dinner with Lacey's good friend, me, at Jack's Luxury Oyster Bar. "Oh, you must spend time with Daniel," I could hear her saying, "we're so close."

Jack's Luxury Oyster Bar was a vertical restaurant squeezed between town houses. Quaint and charming, it had silver salt and pepper chicks on the tables and tiny dining rooms trimmed in mother's lace curtains and red-and-white-checkered wallpaper. The rooms were connected by narrow stairs that necessitated an excellent grip on the handrail to avoid a deadly, headlong tumble after a round of cocktails. All this atmosphere was reflected in the bill, which soared into triple digits even for single diners. So when Patrice showed up for dinner with Lacey, it would have been romantic, had it not been for me.

I could see his taxi pull up, and Patrice emerged looking windblown, even though there was no wind. Dressed in a dark suit with a white shirt and no tie, he could have been a fashion model who had been directed to get out of the car as though he were carefree, wealthy, and masculine. My theory of his insecurity about me vanished, replaced by my own insecurity about looks, accomplishment, and money, everything that Patrice effortlessly possessed.

But Patrice was generous toward me, asking questions about my writing, about the art world and the way I saw it. I think he liked that I was not cynical about it, this insular collective that is so vulnerable to barbs from the outside ("Three million dollars for *that*?"), a world that can shield itself from criticism by the implication that its detractors are rubes. So Patrice and I hit it off, and Lacey was in top form, funny and caustic. And naughty:

"Oh, Patrice," she said midconversation, "you like Balthus because you like underpants."

Patrice included me in his response: "Could anyone but Lacey make the word *underpants* sound like a nasty verb?"

"Well, you are a horn dog," said Lacey.

Patrice smiled while he tried to parse "horn dog," concluding it was both funny and accurate, and looked over at me. "What am I going to do with this creature?"

I don't know if the next question Patrice asked me came because he was now satisfied that I was not a threat, hence a few personal questions were okay, or if he was still trying to figure out my status with Lacey:

"Do you have a girlfriend, Daniel?"

"I am currently between girlfriends," I said.

"You wish," said Lacey.

Then I stupidly told them my dating stories, which I realized were all nonstories when I saw their eyes glaze over and stare into their drinks.

"There must be hundreds of women in the art world," said Patrice.

"Yes," I said. "They like artists, not so much art writers. We seem to be on the fringe. Plus, I'm benign. Benign is not a trait women go for."

"But Daniel," said Lacey, "you are in the most desirable category of all for women of our age, the employed, handsome dork."

We all laughed, and I secretly thought, Could I have finally entered into a desirable category?

Precisely after the appetizers, when the last dish was cleared, as though she were waiting for elbow room, Lacey said, "I took a lease on a space in Chelsea."

"A gallery?" I said.

"Yeager Arts," she said. "I've got connections uptown and downtown."

Patrice said, "You're tired of working for the man."

Lacey shriveled. "Oh, Patrice, we don't say 'the man.'"

He looked over at me to check; I agreed with a sympathetic nod.

"Where?" he asked.

"It's at 525 West Twenty-fifth Street. Fifth floor. There are lots of small galleries moving in. I grabbed a space."

"Commercial or conceptual?" I said.

This seemed to stump her. The Chelsea galleries were carefully and willfully defining themselves, breaking away from the more established galleries by presenting art that was "difficult," backing it up with the academic grad school rhetoric. This was art that maintained the irony that began in the sixties, and irony provided an escape valve in case the visuals became too pretty. It was as if a pitcher had decided it was gauche to throw fastballs but still threw fastballs in a mockery of throwing fastballs. These were the conceptual galleries, which garnered respect by defiance and distance, which went *young*, which made you feel that they possessed the cabalistic code that unlocked the inner secrets of art.

I had more trouble explaining commercial galleries because the word implies saccharine merchandise headed for the space above the living room sofa. But Cy Twombly, Richard Serra, Agnes Martin, and Robert Ryman are not saccharine, they are simply *known*. Commercial galleries dealt in artists, famous or not, whose work was in the tradition of something before it and therefore was, in some way, understood.

Lacey got it, Patrice got it, but neither cared. Lacey was opening a gallery, and she needed to find artists, conceptual or commercial, and she was excited.

"Why not both?" she said in answer to my question. "It should be ready in nine months."

"How come so long?" I said.

"Because you're painting it and I know you're slow," said Lacey.

We laughed. But Patrice was drifting out of the conversation. With Lacey's adventure would come new men, and he knew she was careless.

He took Lacey to her home that night and slept with her. Afterward, still between sheets, with a drink beside him, he said to a distracted Lacey, "Do you need money for your gallery? I'll be happy to help out."

"What would I be if I didn't do it myself?" she said. "Besides, I have money."

As noble as Lacey's self-sufficiency was to Patrice, he knew that her refusal kept him out, kept her free of him.

There was a long silence, which, if made audible, would have sounded with the jangle and clatter of Patrice's racing mind and the singular drone of Lacey's will. Finally, hoping for a reprieve from her increasing remoteness, Patrice said to her, probing for conversation, "What are you thinking?"

She lowered her voice to a comic gravel to cut the harshness of her response. "You don't want to know," she said. Patrice suddenly felt very tired.

48.

IN THE SPRING of 2001, Lacey took her beloved Warhol *Flowers* and auctioned it at Christie's—she was too uneasy to deal with Sotheby's. When she heard talk on the street—the art street—that a small *Flowers* could bring as much as eighty thousand dollars, a profit to her of perhaps sixty-four thousand, practicality prevailed. Whatever heartache she felt at selling the painting was soothed by the stunning check she received after it brought a warming one hundred and twenty-nine thousand dollars. Warhol was on the move, and so was she. This would cushion her against the hard landings that can occur when one is in business for oneself. Pilot Mouse had promised her two paintings, not to be sold until her gallery opened; and his friend Carey proved to be an interesting painter, and it was decided that he would be her first show. She liked his work because it was essentially inexplicable, and she knew it would keep her gallery from seeming too easy. She was also a regular at the studio of a beautiful African-American girl just out of art school, Latonya Walsh, whose racy and racial images would be her second show. She knew both these attractive artists would show well at their opening night party, both on the wall and as physical specimens.

She stayed at Barton Talley's through the summer running the gallery, and Barton was happy to have her, as it allowed him to have his Hamptons weekends and summer jaunts to Europe. He had no rivalry with her; he was experienced enough to know that gallerists come and go, and he saw her departure not as creating competition, but as developing connections.

Yeager Arts was scheduled to open after Labor Day, when the streets of Chelsea would be teeming, when the festivities would bloom with art openings that included handsome servers bearing plastic flutes of champagne and patrons backing clumsily into paintings as their chat circles grew wider and wider. The hoopla was a month long, because galleries rolled out their events so they didn't all occur on the same night. When Lacey's opening was postponed several weeks for several reasons, she knew there would still be enough excitement to spare for her virgin upstairs space.

49.

ONE MORNING she woke to a late summer day so glorious, she was compelled to take an early bike ride down to Chelsea to sit in the middle of her still-unhung gallery and contemplate the potential of its blank walls. There was one week left before she was to open.

Outside, it was cloudless and already warming at nine a.m. The silken air slipstreamed around her even though she was trying to be as unaerodynamic as possible. She sat erect, steering the bike with one hand while her other arm swung free. Though now, at thirty-one years of age, she was more respectful of helmets and sunscreen, today she was unhampered by safety apparatus, letting the wind blow through her hair as she turned her face toward the morning sun. This was a free day; Barton Talley was in, and she was attending to the impractical side of her business, allowing creative daydreams to overrule the duty call of daily business.

The sounds of New York were lighter today; fewer cars along the highway made the journey more pleasant, and the whir of Rollerbladers reminded her of the ball-bearing rumble of her childhood skates on a sidewalk. There was a siren in the distance, which she barely noticed. Colors were stark and crisp: there was the blue of the sky against the green of the grass, and Lacey's sun-yellow shirt against the pure white of her shorts. And of course there was the occasional butthead who streaked by everyone with near-miss intentions. She thought she might tour the entire perimeter of Manhattan, after a religious stop at her new gallery. Another siren.

She neared 54th Street, where the bike path emerged from under the highway trestle and the buildings retreated, giving the feeling that Manhattan was doing its best to have a prairie. She imagined her gallery and its accidental golden rectangle interior that would make hanging pictures a joy; and she visualized its cozy back room that would make any artwork hanging in it seem more special, shown to the important clientele only. A fire truck blared down the highway, annoying her. These sirens are ruining my day, she thought. When another and then another siren blared by, she understood: Oh, something's happening.

She looked ahead—the sirens seemed to be headed south—but she saw nothing. A police action, she suspected. She continued down the path and sensed a disturbance in the mien of people who populated the next few hundred yards of path. Some were stalled, talking in groups, while some continued on as usual. She saw a car ahead, barely parked off the path, and a man sitting motionless inside with his foot holding the door wide open. As she neared, she could hear that he had the radio on. A few people were listening around the speaker in the car door. She slowed to a stop, putting her foot on the ground, leaning the bike against her thigh.

"What's going on?" she said.

A Hispanic man turned his head toward her. "They think a plane flew into the World Trade Center."

She looked downtown but could see only one of the giant buildings, as they lined up almost perfectly. There was a stream of black smoke starting to billow from a window-size puncture. She imagined that a stray Piper Cub, guided by a Sunday pilot, had misjudged a banking turn over the Hudson and couldn't pull out in time. She ventured farther downtown, and still nothing changed much. People kept biking, jogging, walking. She stopped again when she saw a small group of people who seemed to be aware of the news, and again she said, "What's going on?"

"They think a plane crashed into the tower."

"A Cessna or something?"

"A jet," someone said.

She believed this report would be corrected, thinking the small plane scenario more logical, and she biked another mile down. Within minutes, she could see flames spewing from a high floor of the building like spitfire, and she paused, thinking how two-dimensional, how flat, it looked. She had to remind herself that as surreal an image as it was, it was also real. Horror was going on inside, and her distance from the site meant that the screams inside were falling silent before they reached her ears.

Decency told her she should not press forward, but her awareness that this moment was unique and probably historical drove her farther downtown. But the previously sparse crowds had turned thick. People were now moving en masse uptown along the bike path, talking unperturbedly, a migration of people away from the towers. Lacey could no longer cycle forward. She turned around, pedaled uptown, veered off onto 83rd Street, carried her bike upstairs, turned on the TV, and stared.

She looked at the towers, believing the camera angle was from her bike path point of view, seeing only one. Unaware that the north tower had fallen, she went to the kitchen for a bottle of water, returning in time to see a replay of the second tower imploding into rubble. She figured out that both towers had fallen, one while her back was turned to the south, cycling home, and one while she stood at her refrigerator. She looked out her window. She could see a slow movement of people heading north, walking safely down the center of West End Avenue, as all car traffic had stopped. The silence brought on by terror struck

Lacey as perversely serene, and it took her a while to notice that all air traffic had stopped, too, reducing Manhattan's constant din to what it must have been like one hundred years earlier.

She went alone to Isabella's for lunch and found it a busy restaurant, with patrons talking, laughing, ordering with puzzled looks while pointing at the menu. It wasn't that life was going on as usual, it was that what had happened was not yet fully known. Over the next twenty-four hours, there would be a dampening in people's gestures, activity, and volume.

Lacey stopped at a market, wondering if there would be a run on food; but there wasn't. She bought enough for a few days and returned home. She sank into her sofa, transfixed by the television, her cell phone and landline jammed by traffic. She didn't move until night came, eventually sitting in darkness, having forgotten to turn on even a lamp. The room was illuminated only by the blue glow of the TV news, while banners of text streamed under the newscasters, amid reports of a Pentagon attack, a delinquent president, a crash in the Pennsylvania woods. The nation grew still, an anesthetized giant waiting to figure out what was happening to it. That night in bed, she revisited the searing image of the tower shooting flames. It reminded her of something—which seemed impossible to her—but she didn't know what.

She woke in the early morning and checked her phones: still dead. The TV was alive, however. She sat again watching while news tumbled over itself, and again she sat until ten p.m., never turning on a light in her apartment, because the TV was all she wanted and all that she needed. She assumed her parents were concerned for her, but there was no way to communicate, so she could only wait. She worried for her downtown friends, but the area was closed tight. The bridges and tunnels remained closed, stranding people where they were at the moment of penetration. She sat and watched.

Wednesday came and went. Thursday morning the phones were still dead. Her cell phone had bars, but service was jammed. She walked outside a bit and wondered if New York had been this silent, ever. Even twenty minutes away from the television created an unease that something worse had happened, which required her to focus harder on the news and its flowing ticker tape of rumors and facts in order to catch up. For another day, she remained motionless in front of the TV, hours passing, night creeping over the city.

It was around nine p.m. when the door buzzer rang. She rose, her legs stiff from the last three days of cave dwelling, and spoke into her intercom.

"Hello?"

"It's Carey. You okay?"

She buzzed him in; he climbed the stairs.

"I thought I'd check in. Nobody can reach anybody," he said when she opened the door.

"How'd you get here?"

"I walked," said Carey.

"Sixty blocks?"

"Yeah." His head gestured toward the TV. "Anything?" he asked.

"All the same," she said.

They were now in the dark, all connections to the outside frozen, all considerations for the outside in suspension. Whatever was about to happen was excusable, was necessary to confirm humanity. As carnal as their night was about to be, they would be visited by a simulacrum of emotion that loomed briefly and moved on. They would be reminded of love without feeling love, reminded of deep human contact without having it.

It was now Friday morning after the awful Tuesday. Carey and Lacey watched the morning news, then walked funereally to Riverside Park, where they stood and looked where the towers once were. It was shocking that there was no trace of them, no afterimage left in the sky, no outline traced around their perimeter.

Lacey said, "I know what I was reminded of yesterday."

"When?" said Carey.

"When I first saw the tower burning. The Ruscha."

"What Ruscha?"

"Los Angeles County Museum on Fire."

When Carey left, they agreed to postpone his opening until a more practical date. This was the first time Lacey thought of her business, a demonstration of the numbing power of shock. Their sexual encounter was never mentioned again.

There was still an art world, but there was no art market. Stocks tumbled; who but the crazy would buy pictures when it was unknown if anything would have value, when our main preoccupation was anticipation of further terror? Lacey mourned for her gallery and her dream of self-governorship, but she knew that rage was useless, that this was an act of God, or godlessness, and that she could do nothing until the world righted itself.

Her gallery finally opened in December, a slow time in the art world, when buyers were about to disappear for the holidays and not straggle back until the second week in January. She sold two paintings by Carey Harden, but they were to his relatives at deep discounts, and the opening party was a fizzle. Patrice Claire was in Paris; he was weaning himself away from her, so he and his dazzling friends never came. She waited for the gallery to fill up, to resemble a crowded first night, but it never did. She felt like another hopeful tucked into the warrens of the building, running a gallery that needed a flashlight and compass to be found, and the long, empty days meant that business, real and imagined, was conducted mostly on the phone.

When Christmas came, she went home to her parents in Atlanta and pretended that everything was fine. But now, away from New York, the idea of selling art after the apocalypse seemed frivolous.

50.

ART MAGAZINES SURVIVED—I guess subscription canceling is the last thing to think about after a disaster. My income stayed at parity, and my savings stayed intact, topped off occasionally by my intuitive parents, who had miraculously timed the sale of a dozen prime acres near Stockbridge. New York still moved, mostly on inertia, like a car coasting downhill after it had run out of gas. It turned out there was nothing to do but go on as usual, with a revival of old-fashioned love-it-or-leave-it patriotism coating everything, and the public eventually caught on that the nascent TV phrase *breaking news* could mean a traffic tie-up in Queens.

I made a lunch date with Tanya Ross. I was attracted to her, and we both spoke art, which meant the conversation never ran dry: we could talk about artists, shows, openings, museums, prices, collectors, Europe, the Prado, uptown, downtown, gossip, theory, Bilbao, the Guggenheim, little-known works at the Met, the Frick, Isabella Stuart Gardner, Chuck Close, Florine Stettheimer, and sales. I met her at the restaurant at Barneys on Madison, and she insisted that we split the check. I tried, but she insisted. I couldn't interpret if this was a good or a bad sign. Splitting the check indicates it's not a date but also shows respect for the other person, especially since she suggested the restaurant. There was nothing datelike about our lunch, but once, she touched my hand as she made a point, and at the end of it, she invited me to a lecture sponsored by Sotheby's. I couldn't tell if the invite was social or professional.

"Oh, John Richardson's talking about his new book on Friday. Would you like to come?"

"John Richardson?" I said. "My superhero, my god, and if it were possible, my Halloween costume."

Tanya laughed and looked into my eyes, pleased.

"I'd love to come," I said. "What's the book? A new one?"

"*Sacred Monsters, Sacred Munsters*, something," she said. "It's at five and there are drinks afterwards."

"Drinks afterwards" made me think that Tanya was putting her toe in the water with me, and it turned out she was. She was Lacey's opposite. She didn't leap in ablaze. She was a tortoise to Lacey's hare, perhaps not as effective, but her goals were less grand than Lacey's, and a modest presence can eventually catch the eye in a powerful way.

The lecture took place at Boulud, which Sotheby's had bought out at tea time for the event. I felt this was the way the art world was supposed to be: sophisticated, dressed, with a British accent and raconteur's tongue. Richardson, a real scholar with a bright pen, was a renowned biographer of Picasso; he had already completed two massive volumes of a projected four. He had escaped from the astringent clutches of Savile Row and didn't wear the English gentleman's uniform of a blue-and-white-striped dress shirt with a white collar, pinched gray suit, and pink tie. Instead, he looked sharp but frazzled: in other words, like an author. He enjoyed humor, especially wicked humor, and at age seventy-seven, he seemed keener and more magnetic than any person in the room. His talk, a form of worldly gossip about the fabulously interesting, was too brief, and I wanted more: I didn't know that the Art Deco designer Jean-Michel Frank was a close relation of Anne Frank, the doomed child from Amsterdam.

Afterward, pools of admirers collected in the dining room. I bought his book—it was actually titled *Sacred Monsters, Sacred Masters*—and he signed it. I of course tried to impress him by quoting back his own lines to him, but what I really wanted was for him to simply tell me his writing secret. Unfortunately, I already knew it: brilliance. Perhaps I should work on that. Then Tanya brought Richardson a six p.m. Scotch, and we all were thrilled by his further stories of the naughty elite.

I walked Tanya down Madison, asked her if she wanted to sit for a while. Yes. We stopped at Le Charlot, an authentic French bistro that made me feel authentically inferior. The waiters sped by us, curiously, since the place was nearly empty. The drinks made us loose, and we got only one-third the way through our art world, and world, topics before it was time to leave. She grabbed a cab, and I took the subway home. I thought about her a lot. There was talk of war, it was cold, but our afternoon spent in peace comforted me, and I think it comforted Tanya, too.

51.

IN FEBRUARY 2002, Chelsea was about to be hit with five hundred tons of steel. The Gagosian Gallery was opening a space on 24th Street, which, considering the timing, seemed like a misstep, inspiring glee in Larry's detractors. And he was bringing in the colossal work of Richard Serra, whose favorite medium was difficulty. Fifteen-foot-high walls of rusted Corten steel had to be moved into an old paint factory, and the old paint factory had to look like a slick gallery in a matter of months. The opening was delayed because the cranes that were necessary to move the leviathan works were all occupied at Ground Zero and couldn't be diverted for something as frivolous as an art show. But eventually, the massive leaves of corroded steel were balanced in the Gagosian Gallery like sheets of paper standing on end, and walking among them produced in the viewer equal measures of awe and nervousness.

Lacey timed her second opening to coincide with Serra's. She installed Latonya Walsh's jumpy, jazzy works, and when a thousand art lovers showed up for Serra's opening, giving Chelsea an unexpected kick start, her place hummed along with the spillover. Pictures sold, and sold to collectors, not friends. The idea of a war in Afghanistan and luxury art purchases running along the sidewalk hand in hand struck everyone as mysterious. The war was away, far over there. Here, we were being encouraged to act normally and to understand that this conflict would affect us not at all, a fly to be brushed away. An unprecedented

Betwixt the Torus and the Sphere, Richard Serra, 2001
142 × 450 × 319 in.

and feverish upswing in the art market was about to occur, one that reached beyond the insiders and the knowledgeable, which would draw the attention of stock investors and financial operators, making them turn their heads toward Chelsea.

This was the opening night Lacey had imagined, not the setback of several months earlier, where Carey Harden's work languished. Lacey put herself forth with charm and confidence, and she pushed the equally compelling Latonya Walsh forward as an intellectual, which she was, steering her into collectors' memories as well as their sight lines.

Patrice Claire was there for this one but guarded by a few friends, and Carey Harden was there, too. I was sorry their secret was invisible to Patrice, because at least this would have been a fact he could have digested, acted on, and used as an escape from whatever airy tethers kept him hopeful. In fact, it disturbed me that their one-nighter was so acutely unnoticeable; what did it mean for my larger world? Was every transgression capable of being so well hid? It suggested that one could connect the dots between any two people in any room and perhaps stumble onto an unknown relationship.

Patrice left, suggesting Lacey join him for a drink later. But she never called, and he didn't expect her to. After that night, he never saw her again.

52.

DURING THE NEXT FOUR YEARS, auction catalogs would swell with glamour. A reader could now see his face reflected in their glossy pages. Color foldouts heralded important paintings or tried to make unimportant paintings seem grander than they actually were. All artists, whether they deserved it or not, were, in bold letters on the page, referred to by their last names only. This made sense if the last name was Cézanne, but when contemporary catalogs announced "Jones," the effect was silly. Somewhere, in the dark heart of the houses, it was decided that the catalogs should not just *present*, but should *promote*. A catalog could no longer be flipped through; it should demand time to spread out and absorb these sexy centerfolds. The catalog entries now had lengthy analytical essays and illuminating reproductions of other pictures, whether they related or not: a minimalist Agnes Martin might be accompanied by an illustration of the *Mona Lisa*, whose best connection to the picture in question might come under a TV game show category, "things that are rectangular." The catalogs' weight increased, and weary postmen in expensive zip codes must have hated it when auction season came around.

These catalogs became like a semiannual stock report. Collectors scoured the estimates, then assessed the sales figures and reinsured their pictures, feeling proud that they had gotten in early. Insurance required appraisals, and Sotheby's and Christie's could provide them, thus gaining entrance to hitherto closed collections and coincidentally finding out where all the loot was. They started to make bold guarantees for paintings, bold enough to pry them off even the most sincere collector's walls. It was unclear why all this market heft was occurring, but money was flowing in from Europe, Asia, the Middle East, and Russia. There was, clearly, a surfeit of cash. New billionaires were being created from apparently nothing. They just suddenly *were*. Ten million spent here and there, even foolishly, didn't matter.

Because established artists were achieving out-of-reach prices, collectors turned to contemporary, and New York responded. Uptown galleries, unable to find goods at profitable prices, watched as Chelsea exploded. One could imagine the classy East Side dealers racing downtown, shedding their ties and tossing their papers of provenance into the wind, trying not only to cash in on art whose only cost was materials, but also to stay relevant.

Lacey's business soared. Over the past year, her gallery, quite accidentally, had become known for female artists. Besides Latonya Walsh, she had taken on Amy Arras, who produced exquisitely detailed drawings in colored pencil of warring soldiers that were remarkable both technically and conceptually.

One Saturday, two major collectors, Ben and Belinda Boggs, wandered in and bought two pieces by Pansy Berks, who made small, glowing portraits of her drugged-out friends. They invited Lacey to attend a celebratory dinner that night, and she was not only thrilled, but obligated to attend. She taxied over to Pastis, the new in-spot.

Belinda's hair was golden and high, sweeping back over her forehead and held in place with lacquer and enamel red headband. The look was of a wave about to crash backward over her head. Ben had a fence of white porcelain for teeth, and his hair was styled just like Belinda's. Their hair color matched almost exactly, which raised questions of duplicate bottle use. His skin was mottled red, sanded to a shine by one too many chemical peels.

Lacey started to take a drink of water, but Belinda held up an open palm, indicating "halt." She signaled the waiter, who brought over an open bottle of champagne and poured three glasses. Belinda passed Lacey a flute, toasted to her and then to her nodding husband, and said, "Congratulations, Lacey. You sold us our one thousandth painting."

They drank to it, and Lacey said, "Well, I wish I had met you earlier. I would have preferred to sell you your first two hundred." Though Ben and Belinda couldn't make jokes, they were able to sense them in the same way a blind man sensed the curb after thwacking it with his cane—they couldn't see it, but they knew it was there—so they laughed exactly on cue.

"We like Pansy Berks's work because we can figure it out," said Belinda. "That's what makes a work appealing; I like figuring them out. Berks paints her friends when they're high, but with colors that are unreal, too bright for the room, so she's saying that she's too bright for this room. And that she should change her friends. Right?"

"Wow," said Lacey, "right." She cringed inside.

"We bought a painting from Yasper," said Belinda, "and Yasper said there was no way we could figure this one out."

Ben jumped in. "We had always figured out Yasper's pictures before, but this one he said we never would. It's one of his paradox paintings."

Lacey figured out, in time, that they were talking about Jasper, Jasper Johns. "Did you figure it out?"

"No! That's what's so amazing. He said we couldn't figure it out and then we couldn't," said Belinda.

"I thought it was a hat; I was convinced it was a hat. But he said no," said Ben.

"It's not a hat," Belinda said.

"It's not a chicken, either," accused Ben.

Felt Suit, Joseph Beuys, 1970
66.9 × 23.6 in.

"I said it was a chicken and Yasper said it wasn't," said Belinda.

"Do you know Joseph Beuys?" Ben said. "We bought one of his felt suits."

Lacey knew. Her days at Talley's always paid off somehow. Beuys made the suits in an edition of one hundred in 1970. They were meant to hang on a wall on a coat hanger, with the pant legs hanging long, almost as though inhabited by an invisible person.

"I love this story," said Belinda.

"We were having a sit-down dinner at our opening of the collection at our gallery," said Ben. "When was this, honey?"

"In the early nineties," she said. "That's when we opened our gallery." The Boggses had a private gallery on their property in Connecticut.

"Big, gala opening," said Belinda.

"I'm in a tuxedo, and let's just say a tuxedo, white frosted cake, and a clumsy waiter don't go well together."

"Oh God, this is so hilarious," said Belinda, who did her hand thing to Ben, stopping him. "So what does he do? He takes the suit off the wall, goes into the men's room, and changes into it. He comes out in the felt suit and there's applause!"

"Most of the people there weren't art people, mostly financial, so I was lucky. The story's a legend now, though."

Lacey laughed, but she knew that Beuys was an emotional artist and that the felt suit was a serious work, probably stemming from his post-war days in Germany, days of guilt and regret.

"The suit got wrinkled, so we bought another one. But it was worth it," said Ben.

"We donated the wrinkled one to a museum in Tulsa. They were happy to get it, after we explained what it was," said Belinda. "We didn't tell them Ben had worn it. We had it steamed."

Midway through dinner, Lacey could see that Ben was drunk. His head would swivel and fall toward Belinda while she ran on, and Lacey could see him try to focus. Lacey worried that someone might think that these were her parents. She excused herself to the restroom, then met them on the sidewalk. When Ben asked if she wanted a lift home in their chauffeured car, she declined, worried that his drunkenness might somehow infect the driver.

53.

WITH THE NATION AT WAR, I went to an art fair. Financed by *ARTnews*, for whom I was writing an article, I landed in Miami for the big mutha expo of galleries from all over the world, or at least countries that participated in the art market. Lacey, as a new gallery, was offered a small auxiliary space, and she took it.

This visit was perfect for me in at least two ways. One, I got to go where the latest and greatest were gathered, sparing myself thousands of miles of travel that neither I nor the magazine could have afforded. Two, Tanya Ross and I were now going out on a date most weeks, and I was glad to have something self-important to say to her: "I'm flying to Miami for the fair." This credited me, in my view, with special involvement and stature: I was the one *ARTnews* was sending. I would, by the way, have asked her out every night of the week, but I could tell she was slower-paced than I, and with each date she leaned my way a slight degree more. And she always seemed happy to see me.

I stayed at a fabulously shabby Art Deco hotel that was walking distance from the humongous convention center, with its seventeen entrances, vast plains of space to fill, and the worst Miami-ugly facade of bleached white stucco. Inside, though, the expo teemed with galleries, some of them so upscale that their booths were covered in brown velvet and had paneled ceilings, and some so slapdash that they could have been selling tattoos and moonshine. There were Picassos near the front of the expo, and as you moved toward the rear, name values diminished to pinpoints. I've heard of museums so large that they're easy to get lost in, but I never did. However, I did get lost in this labyrinth, and I was so befuddled for a few anxious minutes that if I had been five instead of thirty-two, I would have cried.

Lacey had taken a small space at a satellite fair, which by virtue of being labeled a satellite gave the art that was shown there extra cachet. But it put her far from the action. Spots inside the main fair had to be earned.

I walked and took notes, which gave me away as a journalist and not a buyer, but I was still welcomed as I scratched on a notepad while staring at whatever, and I would exchange smiles with the assistant or owner when I left. A few smiles were returned warmly, or perhaps provocatively, but I'm not a pickup artist. Like Tanya Ross, I prefer to talk for months.

The art fair was designed to appeal to almost any type of collector, and there were throngs of people to maneuver through. There was no way to go from start to finish without doubling back, which created an ongoing loop of déjà vu, and I was surprised to see a painting for the second time yet have no recollection of the other pictures around it. It became impossible to evaluate the artworks but easy to enjoy them; they were like a steady parade of beauty queen contestants where you find yourself saying after the fiftieth lovely one, "Next."

Around two p.m., I felt a quiver in my legs and realized I was fatigued and famished. I went to the center of the arena, where wrapped sandwiches were served after a twenty-minute wait in line. Coffee, illogically, was at another line, infuriating me. There was impractical seating, a dozen ottomans strewn around the sandwich bar. I found a tiny corner on one and perched on it, the sandwich balanced on my knee and the coffee set on the floor. As dense as this place was with art world heavyweights, lightweights, and underweights, I realized just how few people I actually knew. Artists weren't likely to show up here, and Lacey was in the hinterlands.

My cell phone rang. The caller ID said Alisa Lightborn, my editor at *ARTnews*. She was pretty, too, and pretty married.

"Where are you?" she said.

"I feel like I'm in Calcutta."

"Me too!" she said.

"I'm at the sandwich bar."

"Oh, jeez..." The woman in front of me turned around. It was Alisa. We laughed and both closed our phones.

"Are you coming tonight?"

"Coming to what?" I said.

"Ah, I was right: you didn't get it. *ARTnews* is hosting a dinner at Joe's Stone Crab, at least a dozen people. We have the glitterati, you could be the literati. And you could take notes."

"Would that be okay with them?"

"When a magazine hosts a dinner, everyone knows it's on the record."

I wasn't so sure they did, but I was chuffed to have a dinner invite at one of the most desirable restaurants in Miami.

I trudged through the rest of the fair and its satellites, and even revisited standout displays. These second visits were valuable; what had charmed me on first glance often bored me on the second. I said hello to Lacey, whose booth was a standout because of both the art and her dress. But I didn't tell her about the *ARTnews* dinner because I figured she'd invite herself, and I didn't want her there. I knew that she could turn an evening upside down and somehow make it about her. Still, when I left her booth, she said, "Have fun at that dinner tonight."

I was glad I had brought a suit and tie. I clean up well. Joe's was an easy taxi ride from my Deco splendor, but I walked in the warming night, glad to be out of New York during a particularly blustery

December. I neared the restaurant, which was as much high-end tourist spot as it was a chow-down family restaurant. Crowds waited in an expansive lobby for a table, and although Joe's ostensibly didn't take reservations, the maître d' dealt with people like a shrink, eagle-eyeing the famous and connected and treating the RV-touring family with equal respect and facility.

I asked for the *ARTnews* table and was guided through a vast dining room where robust waiters with pins on their lapels indicating twenty, thirty, or forty years of service cheerfully entertained while taking and delivering orders. This was not an art world restaurant, even during the busy Miami Basel week. There were families, and there were businessmen sporting lobster bibs. There wasn't a solo diner to be seen; the place was too much fun for that. I was taken to a private dining room with paneled walls and a wagon wheel chandelier looming over an empty table for fifteen. I guessed I was the odd man. The din from the main dining area reverberated in this small room, so things still felt active.

Alisa was there—it was her job to be there first—and there was a well-dressed Englishman already holding champagne. I debated abstaining since I was, in fact, working, but as I might be a poor reporter if I didn't blend in, I took a glass. The Englishman was Kip Stringer, who was in the vanguard of the coming vogue: curator as artist. It was he, he decided, who determined that he could use artists' works to make *his* point, not theirs. He took the artists' right to be obscure and turned it into a curator's right. This resulted in a show in Milan where artists were forced together as though in a hadron collider. Pollock and Monet were hung in the same room under the premise that the heading "Material/Memory" or "Object/Distance/Fragility" clarified everything.

I joined Kip and Alisa just in time to hear him bemoaning the fair, saying that the auxiliary shows that sprang up to capitalize on the influx of art enthusiasts into Miami were much better than the shows in the main room, but he did like that Pace Gallery had hung an Agnes Martin opposite a Robert Ryman so that they were "in dialogue" with each other. "In dialogue" was a new phrase that art writers could no longer live without. It meant that hanging two works next to or opposite each other produced a third thing, a dialogue, and that we were now all the better for it. I suppose the old phrase would have been "an art show," but now we were listening. It also hilariously implied that when the room was empty of viewers, the two works were still chatting. I was tolerant when he said "in dialogue" because I can get it, but when he said "line-space matrix," I wanted to puke.

The air was cleansed when Hinton and Cornelia Alberg entered, Hinton emitting a big laugh for no reason except to greet everyone. Next came another idol of mine, Peter Schjeldahl, the great art critic for *The New Yorker*, and his wife, Brooke, who gave off such a vibe of fun that I knew it was she I would try to sit next to.

A quorum was struck when the Mexican collector Eduardo Flores and a young man entered, along with Gayle Smiley, his default dealer, who stuck to Eduardo like a barnacle, lest he be spirited away by the ghost of Larry Gagosian. The Nathansons, Saul and Estelle, were next, and I started to wonder how *ARTnews* could draw such a diverse crowd. When the actor Stirling Quince and Blanca entered, I thought maybe they were the main attraction, but it didn't seem likely. But soon, a woman ninety-one years of age but a dyslexic nineteen years of age in her soul, entered the room, and everything made sense. It was Dorothea Tanning, a painter whose career had slid into being when this Illinois born woman found herself in Paris married to Max Ernst and aligned with a slew of Surrealists and other "ists," including, in her words, "Yves Tanguy, Marcel Duchamp, Joan Miró, René Magritte, Salvador Dali, Pablo Picasso, Max Ernst, and Max Ernst." After a decade of accomplishment in Surrealist painting, she climbed aboard *The New Yorker* magazine and became a poetry contributor, active into

Eine Kleine Nachtmusik, Dorothea Tanning, 1943
16 × 24 in.

her eighties. An upcoming retrospective at the Metropolitan made her not only hot stuff, but enduring stuff, and her painting, *A Little Night Music,* executed in 1943, made her unassailable, and *ARTnews* had the story. She charmed us with her greeting: "I apologize for being alive."

I wondered how Lacey could have managed to miss a dinner attended by so many of her acquaintances, which in turn made me wonder if perhaps this dinner had missed her.

I knew I was at the position on the totem pole that got chipped by the lawn mower, so I stayed away from Ms. Tanning except to say I admired her work, which I do. With her at one end of the long table, I planted myself at the other, more gossipy end. I was delighted because all I could have done with Ms. Tanning was compliment her, but here in the panhandle I could hope for some loose lips. The conversation started when thespian Stirling Quince stopped everyone with, "How about this war?" referring to the born-again Iraq war, but before we could even nod sadly, he added, "Nobody's makin' any movies!" After the silence and a poor attempt at commiseration, talk of the art fair nicely combusted.

"What do you think of the fair, Mr. Nathanson?" I asked. I remembered him from Lacey's Milton Avery story years earlier.

"Well, things are different. What happened to paintings? Nobody's painting. We found a little Nadelman drawing, but they wanted too much. We went back a few hours later and someone had bought it."

Hinton Alberg broke in. "You gotta snatch! These things aren't lasting. You pause, you missed it."

"Did you see the Gober?" asked Eduardo Flores.

"Too much," said Hinton. "Too much. A million two or something. Even so, I went back. It was sold."

"I bought it," said Eduardo. Fortunato, his young friend, sat prettily next to him.

When he said, "I bought it," Gayle Smiley went white. When, she must have thought, did he leave my sight?

Schjeldahl was uninterested in money talk, so he sat mute. But his wife, Brooke, was forthright and funny, which made Brooke and Cornelia instant friends.

"What was the Gober like?" Brooke asked.

"It's a kitchen sink," said Hinton.

"A what?" said Saul Nathanson.

"It's like a kitchen sink that hangs on a wall, but with an elongated back," Flores told him. "Plaster and wood; it's an amazing piece."

Kip Stringer couldn't resist: "The sink is evocative of cleaning, but the fact it is on a wall, without plumbing, not functioning, creates cognitive dissonance. It embars the viewer from the action it implies."

Schjeldahl, whose art criticism goes down like good wine, said, "Huh?"

"Sort of like a locked door," said Saul. Saul Nathanson did not mock art, so his response was probing rather than cynical.

"Well," said Kip, "Gober actually did install a locked door in the wall of a gallery."

"I would only pay a million for that," said Brooke.

"Not if I'm there first!" said Hinton.

Kip tried to laugh but couldn't.

"No kidding. Hinton would buy paint in a bucket," said Cornelia.

"Is he a bad boy?" said Brooke.

"You would think each gallery had a pole dancer," Cornelia said with a grin, "but honestly, art has enriched us. With things, with thought, with conversation, with people. Don't you think so, Hinton?"

"Art has de-riched me, honey. You know what I thought when we bought the house in Montauk? Walls! More walls! You know what I think when I buy a car? No walls. No goddamn walls."

Nathanson jumped in. "I find it strange that when we have people over for dinner, no one, not one, mentions or ever looks at the paintings. We have all these beautiful works, and it's as though they don't exist. And if we give them a tour, I can feel their struggle to enjoy it, but really they don't care."

"They will notice my sink on the wall," said Flores, now on his third vodka.

"And if they don't, they're not invited back," toadied Gayle.

"I find the fair very hard to navigate," said Saul. "As I wander around, I don't know what anyone *is*."

"There is tremendous diversity," said Kip.

"Look," said Hinton, "up to the seventies, art proceeded in movements. Cubism, Surrealism, Abstract Expressionism, Pop, Minimalism, so everyone, including me, was on the lookout for the next movement. But instead, art in the eighties was at an evolutionary moment where it split into chimps, birds, fish, plants, and cephalopods all at once. Saul, artists can make a living now as a *bad painter*. I'm not kidding. You ask them what they make and they'll say 'bad art.' And they can put the implied quotes around it, too, with just their voice. And you know what? It's bad, but not that bad."

"Do you have any?" said Brooke.

"We've got a roomful of it," said Cornelia.

Hinton went on, "We sure do, and sometimes the bad stuff can make the so-called good stuff seem boring and stiff."

Kip Stringer didn't go for this kind of plain speaking. "The artist has fractured the iconicity," he said.

"Exaaacctlly...," said Brooke, looking over at me with her mouth agape.

"There are a hundred categories," said Hinton, now getting revved up. "There's 'pale art,' faint things with not much going on in them. There's 'high-craft OCD,' you know, those guys who take a thousand pinheads and paint a picture of their grandmother on every one. There's 'low-craft ironic,' a fancy name for wink-wink nudge-nudge."

I dared to speak. "What about 'animated interiors'?"

"Good one," said Hinton. "Apocalyptic scenes of stuff flying around a room. And don't forget 'angry pussy'!"

"Hinton!" said Cornelia.

"Oh, do go on," said Brooke.

"Oh, you know. Stuff made with menstrual blood."

"I'm *so glad* I asked," said Brooke.

"How can we forget 'junk on the floor'? You walk into a gallery and there's stuff strewn everywhere. I've got three of those. Wanna buy one, Eduardo?"

"So if you think it's silly, why do you stay involved?" I asked, reporter style.

"I don't see it as silly. But outsiders do. What was that guy today, honey? Oh yeah, there's an artist who's documenting his own peeing. Photos, videos, he's...

237

"The artist is making us question the act of urination," said Kip.

"Right. Now, that line should never be quoted or they're going to use it against us at our *trials*."

"How would you defend yourself?" I asked.

"Well, let's see... Hey, what was that piece that won the Turner Prize last year?"

"The Lights Going On and Off," said Kip.

"Right. So the Tate buys it for twenty thousand pounds, and it's an empty room, with a lightbulb going on and off. This hit the news so fast...two-inch headlines. They tried to make the art world look stupid. But, you know, I saw the thing and liked it. So at my trial I'd start to say, 'Twenty thousand pounds really isn't that much,' but I'd stop myself because I wouldn't want to be executed right off.

"But then I'd face the jury: 'Let's say you're going to buy a puppy. You're going to buy a yellow Lab. A cuddly yellow Lab. So you read that you should go to a breeder, because you don't want to get one that's going to go sick on you. Now you get to the breeder and you find out there's English Labs and American Labs. American Labs are good for hunting because they're kind of lithe. But you don't want to hunt him, so you go for an English Lab, more stocky. Then you're told that the real prize of the Labrador breed is one with a big head. So you wait and wait, and finally you get one with a big head. Now you take it home and proudly show your big-headed puppy to a friend. You're thinking, I've got this great show dog, an English Lab with a big head, and your friend is thinking, What an ugly puppy."

By now the other end of the table was tuned in, Tanning enjoying Hinton. He turned to her and said, "Excuse me, Miss Tanning, I'm orating."

"Please, go on." She smiled.

Hinton smiled back. "I would rather hear what you have to say."

Tanning paused thoughtfully. "I believe the last twenty years has been the most desperate search for artistic identity in the history of the arts. Don't you think so, Peter?"

Schjeldahl, now that the conversation had turned to art and not money, finally spoke: "All the cocksure movements of the last century have collapsed into a bewildering, trackless here and now."

The table went silent, then the chatter resumed at the same tempo as after a distant gunshot.

When we left the restaurant, I saw Lacey canoodling at a corner table with a known Russian collector, also known as a playboy, also known as very rich. Now I knew why she'd missed this dinner. Cornelia saw it, too, and she did not like it.

54.

BY THE END OF 2003, Lacey had solidified her business. She had several employees and was making a profit. I dropped by the gallery, meeting her for lunch; she was on the phone, and I could hear her voice from the back office as she closed a deal:

"You know it's a good picture... Still, you know it's a good picture. And your Basquiat, how much did you overpay for that at the time? And now it's worth whatever... Okay, sorry, millions... Look, you know you love this piece. You should buy it because you need it... No, you're right, nobody needs art. Nobody except for you. You need it. You know I'm right... Okay, then, I'll take it off hold... No, I'm going to take it off hold. I'm taking it off hold in thirty seconds."

Then I heard her laughing. "I'm telling you, off hold in twenty-four seconds."

She laughed some more, and I could intuit that the person she was speaking to was laughing, too.

"I've got another buyer on my speed dialer. Twenty seconds..." Then she said, "Smart move. I'll have it delivered. When's a good time?"

I took her to lunch, which began with her saying, "I'm dating a vibrator. I think I love it... him... whatever." I laughed. "And it never cheats on me."

"Have you been cheated on, Lacey?"

"Never. I always strike first."

"Where's Patrice these days?"

"Nowhere. He was a bit too interested, wouldn't you say?"

"I don't know him that well."

"Plus, I'm thirty-three, he's forty-five. And when I'm thirty-three, he'll be fifty-five, and when I'm thirty-three, he'll be sixty-three."

I laughed. "You don't plan on aging?"

"Why would I?"

We both had news, and we both waited until the entrées to report it.

"I'm moving into a new space," said Lacey. "Around the corner, window to the street, a real gallery. Like Andrea Rosen and Matthew Marks...well, not that big, but it'll have clout. Daniel," she said, "it's ten thousand a month. I'm going from seven hundred to ten thousand a month."

"Jeez."

"But I've been making ten thousand a month, or I'm starting to. I figure the added square footage will pay for itself and attract more artists. I'm doing resale, like at Talley's. Nobody down here is doing secondary market stuff, nobody. It's like they never think about it."

Secondary market is what all the uptown galleries are, what Sotheby's and Christie's do—they resell previously owned works. Lacey was right: the contemporary market had little outlet for private sales of this nature.

"I do it in the back room, on the phone."

"Do people want to buy such a recent picture? Don't they wonder why it's being sold?"

"I say divorce, distress, and people love it. Somehow it makes the piece more desirable. And these pictures are going nowhere but up, so no one's afraid."

"But ten thousand a month."

"Plus I have to remodel. With a fancy architect. Look, the only money

I need is lunch money. I put everything back in. So I'm not strapped. Clothes cost, though. They're like a car for a Realtor. They've got to be all class. Lots of evenings out. And you, what's new with you?"

"Are you sitting down?"

"I could sit on the floor, I guess."

"Remember Tanya Ross?"

"Lovely girl, nice person," she said with a tinge of color.

"I'm dating her. Exclusively."

"What happened to what's-her-name?"

"Lacey, that was so long ago."

"But what happened?"

"No fireworks."

"And there are fireworks with Tanya Ross?"

"Well, she's not a fireworks person; she's a different kind of person."

"So, no fireworks."

"I'm not looking for fireworks with her. I'm enchanted, maybe in love, with the idea that she's someone who would always do the right thing. It's taken a while to get through to her, but I think she's bending."

"Over?"

"Lacey."

"Have you kissed her?"

"Lacey."

"Sorry. She probably wants to punch me. Tell her she can, and invite her down to the gallery. After the new one's open. I can make peace; I have that in me."

55.

I CONTINUED TO SEE Tanya that winter, twice a week, then three times a week, ending with an all-out-effort dinner at Del Posto, paid for by one paycheck for five reviews from *ARTnews*. She dressed up for it and so did I, and she looked so beautiful that I thought I didn't belong with her. But my best behavior makes me look better: I stand up straighter, and I'm more polished, the way I've seen other men be.

She had one glass of wine to my three, but mine were spread out over two and a half hours, so I was never tipsy, just loosened, and she was constant and forthcoming by choice, not alcohol. This night, so memorable, seemed like the last step before unspoken commitment. And when I kissed her good night, it seemed as though little animated larks circled around our heads. She reminded me of a song... what was it? And when she said, smiling broadly, "I think I love you," she put her hand over her face and smiled into it. I felt as though I were Fred Astaire, my top hat and tails magically appearing, and I sang to her, making up the lyrics, which made her laugh on the dark stoop. Then we paused and looked at each other. She said, "Come up."

So I was surprised, three days later, when I called her to confirm a dinner date and she said, "I could see you for lunch."

I can't think of anything that unnerved me so quickly. My response was so shaky, it meant I had been walking on air, not solid ground. I assured myself that nothing, nothing could have happened between our flawless night spent together and this phone call. But Tanya, I knew, does not mislead. So the bliss of the good-night kiss and the frost of our latest exchange were both true. This state of unease could properly be called "disease," because I felt sick. But at least disease has the courtesy to develop over time; this infection was abrupt and arrived all at once. By the time the receiver was replaced on the hook, I was fully in it. I had an elevator-drop loss of appetite and found it difficult to stand: my legs were shivering like a tuning fork. Had she met someone? Impossible.

The two events I am about to describe did not happen simultaneously, but I will present them as though they did, because they are so intertwined by cause and effect that they may as well be connected in time.

I met Tanya for lunch, not at one of our romanticized regular spots, but at the place of one of our first, pre-romantic, all-business lunches. Tanya picked it. On 68th Street, a short distance from Madison Avenue, the restaurant was detached from our previous dating life and empty enough that we could have a conversation without being overheard. I arrived first, my timing sped up by anxiety, and when she arrived, each of her steps toward me was freeze-framed in my mind while I analyzed each inflection of her body language. I perceived nothing, except that she was withholding what I was searching for, intimacy, and that for several minutes there was a faking of normalcy.

"How's work?" I said.

"Oh, that," she said. "Just going on. We have a beautiful early Picasso coming up; lots of talk about that."

"Which one?"

"*Garçon à la Pipe.*"

"Wow, important picture."

"It's going to bring a lot."

Then the conversation withered like a dehydrating prune on the science channel. I requested menus, not wanting to start anything with this sudden stranger until we got our first course.

244

While Tanya and I diverted into art small talk, two men walked up the seven flights of metal stairs of 525 West 25th Street and spent minutes turning a guide map this way and that before they found Lacey's gallery. The Chelsea galleries always look closed and unwelcoming, and they swung her door open a few inches to make sure the lights were on and the place was operating. They went into the gallery and stood at its center, and Lacey, having heard the shuffle of feet and low voices, appeared from the office doorway. These men were familiar. It wasn't so much their faces that jarred her memory as their clothes—plain suits, dark fabric, beige trench coats that were too thin for the cold outside—and the short army hair.

These were the two men she had seen at Talley's on her first day in the gallery. They were also the men who had approached her in Boston, covertly handed her an envelope, then faded back into the alleyways.

"Miss Yeager?"

"I probably am," she said.

"We're with the FBI."

"Show me your stinkin' badges. Or don't you need them?"

The two men looked at each other, confused. "I'm kidding," she said.

They tried to smile. "Could we talk with you?"

"Sure," she said, and they entered her office, knocking about like Rosencrantz and Guildenstern.

The salads arrived, and I finally began to speak with Tanya. I had no appetite. I suppose I ordered food so I would have a plate to look down

245

into, some reason to look away from her if the conversation turned uncomfortable, which it already had.

"Something's up," I said.

"Yes." She nodded.

"I'm so curious. And a bit worried."

"Do you remember the first night we met?"

"At the opening."

"Yes, and do you remember I said you looked familiar?"

"Yes."

"Well," she said, "I remembered where I saw you. On the video. Do you know we tape all our auctions?"

———

Lacey did not sit behind her desk; she sat in a chair across from the two men and deliberately crossed her legs in front of them.

"I'm Agent Parks and this is Agent Crane."

"Yes, with the Isabella Stuart Gardner case."

"Well, that case is dead, at least for now. We investigate art issues, and with nothing happening on that front, we had time to take a look at some other unclear activities."

Agent Crane then spoke. His eyes kept shifting involuntarily to her crossed legs. "The statute of limitations on fraud is six years, so we asked around the auction houses about questionable events at the furthest end of that time frame and came up with a bothersome issue."

———

Tanya was a bit nervous. "You know Lacey, right?"

"A long time."

"Is she trouble?" asked Tanya.

"I think some people would call her trouble."

"We tape all our auctions, mostly so the auctioneer can check his performance, but also to confirm bids, just for records. About six years ago, there was an American sale. Lacey is standing by a phone desk, holding a folder with some papers, near the auctioneer. Her arms are crossed around it. There are a few people bidding on a Parrish."

"And one of them is me," I said.

"Yes, one of them is you. That's unlikely, isn't it? That you would be bidding on a six-hundred-thousand-dollar Parrish?"

I looked at her, unable to answer. I felt a surge of adrenaline's opposite.

"Anyway, it comes down to you and one other phone bidder. And just before the six-hundred-thousand-dollar bid, the last bid, Lacey unfolds her arms and leans forward. And when she unfolds her arms and leans forward, you stop bidding."

Agent Parks rose and walked over to a window. "So we recently reviewed this tape... a tape that was the reason you were dismissed from Sotheby's, isn't it?"

"Unfairly dismissed," said Lacey. "They never accused me of anything. I could have made a fuss, but I had a place to go. We all parted friends."

"Don't you find it odd that exactly when you leaned forward, a bidder, who you evidently know, stopped bidding?"

"No. People stop bidding."

"We think it's pretty clear that this was a signal of some kind."

"Well, you can amuse yourselves with that thought," she said.

"Why would you want someone to stop bidding?" they asked her.

My heart was racing as Tanya paused. "We checked out the Parrish sale," she said. "The painting was represented by a lawyer, so we really don't know who sold it. But I can't figure why you were bidding. Something's wrong. Can you explain it?"

"I was asked to bid for a friend. I didn't really know it was wrong."

"Have you ever owned a painting by Parrish Maxfield?" said Agent Crane.

"You mean Maxfield Parrish," said Lacey.

"Oh yes, Maxfield Parrish."

"I own a print. I inherited it from my grandmother and I still have it. It's on my wall in my apartment if you want to see it."

"I might like to see it," replied Parks. "You can give me your contact information."

"We looked at the tape recently," Tanya said. "It's a definite move. It's clear. And it's clear you're cooperating. It's clear, Daniel. It's clear." Then she looked down at her plate before I could. Her eyes moistened, and she stayed bowed.

"I checked your paddle number: 286 was registered to Neal Walker. How did you get a paddle?"

"The paddle was arranged."

"I know how rigorous we are. Arranged how?"

"Tanya, I thought it wasn't much. Afterwards, I found out it was worse than I thought."

"Tell me."

I told her what I knew: "I was told to stop bidding when Lacey leaned forward."

This information made her face go slack. She got up and left the restaurant, but unfortunately she wasn't angry. She was finished with me.

56.

AGENT PARKS came to Lacey's apartment around seven p.m., in the middle of New York's deep winter darkness. He came alone, without Crane, which was fine with Lacey because she knew this was both an investigation and a date. She guessed he was an all-American boy with a dirty side, and she guessed that an affair with him would put a legal end to this annoying stumble. Someone investigating her seduced her? It certainly could be implied that the seducer would have a conflict of interest, though of course it would be Lacey who would be in charge of the seducing. All this did cross her mind, in fact, but here is the fine point on Lacey's sexual conduct: She never did it for gain, only for excitement. The *promise* of sex was what she did for gain.

She took Agent Parks into the bedroom to show him the Parrish print. She told him the story of its acquisition.

"How long has it been in the family?" he asked.

"Eighty, eighty-five years."

He looked at it; she could tell he did not know how to look at a print. He might be on the art squad, but he was not an art person. He left the bedroom after glancing around, and Lacey followed him into the living room.

"Sit?" he said.

"Sure."

"So what do you think of all this leaning forward stuff, Miss Yeager?"

"If you call me by my first name, I'll call you by your first name."

"Bob."

"Lacey." Then she said, "Take a look at that tape. I'll bet at the same moment there are people coughing, scratching their ears, tapping their chests."

"Who's the guy? Bidder 286. Neal Walker."

"I'm supposed to know bidders; it was my job. But I don't know Neal Walker. Would you like a cocktail?"

57.

I WILL TAKE YOU back six years:

"When I lean forward, you stop bidding."

That's what Lacey told me to do. It seemed like a crime in the negative. It seemed untraceable, not provable. We sat in a restaurant, drinking Kirs, and she was all but hanging out of her dress, which reminded me of when I slept with her. But that was so long ago, and even though I was unattached at the moment, I still maintained to myself that she was an object of human, not sexual, interest.

"I will be giving out the paddles; you come up to me, tell me your name: Neal Walker. I'll check the list and give you one. You might not even have to bid at all; there could easily be other bidders. As soon as the action starts, I'll move to the podiums in front to be a spotter. When I'm standing, you bid. When I lean forward, you stop."

"What if I get stuck with the picture?"

"You won't."

This seemed to me like an art world game, a mystery of sorts, and Lacey was convincing and fun. So I went to the auction and Lacey gave me a paddle. I sat through the auction for about forty-five minutes. Finally, the Parrish came up. And when Lacey leaned forward, I stopped bidding. She had never once looked at me.

After the sale, there was a phone message waiting: "Call me." I did. "Come over," she said. She was jubilant. "Let's take X."

"Not for me, Lacey."

"Come over anyway, we'll celebrate."

"Celebrate what?"

I walked up the steps of her 12th Street apartment. "It's open," she shouted when I knocked. I came in and she locked the door behind me. She handed me a check for one thousand dollars.

"What's this for?" I said.

"For helping," she said.

"Did I break the law?"

"No, darlin', you helped an old friend. There's no law against that." I kept the check because I needed it.

Then she opened her fist and revealed two small pills with pentagrams etched in them. "This could be so much fun," she said.

"Lacey, I'm spooked by drugs. You take it. I'll watch the floor show."

I didn't know much about the effects of the drug, its duration, its downside. But Lacey made me promise not to leave without her okay. She opened a bottle of wine, but she took none. She poured me a glass of red, then picked up the tiny pill between her fingers, clinked my glass with it, and swallowed it down. She pulled the sheers closed, darkening the room by half, and threw a towel over the lamp, darkening the room further. Then the winter sun dropped so fast that the room went blue.

Lacey walked the two steps to the kitchen. "Do you want a sandwich?"

"Yes," I said, and she quickly prepared a deli-worthy pile of ingredients, including tomato and mozzarella, that looked as good as a food section photograph. While she worked, I asked, "So what happened today?"

She turned to me, exaggerated a shrug, and spoke in the voice of Minnie Mouse: "I dunno, Mickey." As she put the last slice of brown bread on the stack, she paused and said, "Oh," her movements slowing down perceptibly. She took a breath and walked the plate over to me, handing it off. Standing in place, she closed her eyes, raising her right arm and moving it through the air as though she were hearing and conducting a Satie étude.

Then she walked over to her bed and lay down, staring out through the sheers of the window, not saying a word. Sometimes she would sigh deeply, shift, or feel her face. I sat in her only upholstered chair and watched as she drifted through an internal space. I thought of the Warhol movie *Sleep*, in which he filmed someone sleeping for eight hours. I saw it as a gung ho college student and remembered how the slightest movement of the sleeping man had the same impact as a plot twist in *The Maltese Falcon*. When Lacey moved, I was fascinated.

The drug began to affect me, too. It was as though it seeped through Lacey's skin and emanated into the local ether. I, too, was happy not to move, and eventually I realized that an hour had passed since Lacey had lain down.

She began to make an occasional noise, like someone reacting to a dream. I could tell she was watching an internal drama, sometimes speaking to the characters, saying, "no," or, "I didn't." Her eyes opened and she looked at the ceiling, blinked once or twice, and then closed them again. She was seeing something or reliving something. Then she turned her head and looked at me.

"You are such a good friend," she said.

"You are, too," I said. Though I know now that the statement was incorrect, at the moment it seemed like an eternal truth.

"Come over..." And she made room on the bed for me. The invitation was delivered with a love that was neither romantic nor sisterly, but some other kind of love discovered in the moment, one of the least complicated invocations of caring I had ever witnessed. I walked to the bed and lay down next to her. She snuggled into me, holding my arm the way a child holds a teddy, burying her face between my shoulder and the bed.

"My grandmother will die soon. She will die."

I said nothing. It seemed to me that she was speaking to herself.

"So beautiful. When she was eighteen, he made paintings of her. He painted her like she was; I'm sure of it. I think I look like her."

She turned on her side again, toward me, and put her hand on my stomach. She began to rub me, lifting my shirt, touching my flesh. She would lower her hand across my jeans, gliding around, moving back up to my stomach. Each visit to my penis got a little longer, but it was absentminded motion, and my dick got absentmindedly hard. She treated it like a curiosity that was third or fourth on her to-do list. I was glad when she just as casually stopped, which meant I had no decisions to make. Then she turned toward the window, and for the next thirty minutes she either slept or dreamed.

It had been two hours since she'd ingested the drug, and she was beginning to stir. She sat partially up, opening her eyes and looking around, as if trying to determine where she was. She looked at me, hugged my arm again, said, "I'm sorry you didn't take any." She got up and found her legs, stretching long, the high starting to recede and the drug's amphetamine base starting to take over. She opened the refrigerator, poured from a pitcher of ice water, and drank it down, pausing between gulps as if it were a hard Scotch.

She sliced some fruit onto a plate. We sat at the small kitchen table. "Daniel, I have money now."

I thought she would stop talking if I seemed too interested, so I tempered everything I said. "Because of today?"

"Yes. Today."

"Oh," I said.

"I can't see the wrong in it."

"In what?"

"The Parrish print. A couple of years ago I visited my grandmother, who was very sick. Remember? I told you."

"Yes."

"I've worked at Sotheby's for years; I've seen a million pictures. I'm used to looking at things close, trying not to be tricked. I went into my grandmother's room, we spoke a bit, and I took the Parrish print over for her to look at. It was a sunny day. If not, I might have missed the whole thing. I took the print back to put it on the wall. I used my coat to clean dust from the glass. But something wasn't right with the print."

"How?"

"The surface was odd. There were textural changes. The surface of a Parrish print would be uniform, except for the blacks. The prints were extremely well done, very easy to distinguish copies from the real thing, because their surface is so remarkable. I went into an empty bedroom and closed the door. The frame hadn't been touched in decades. There were rusted metal points holding in the glass, pressing against a wooden back. I got a nail file and moved them aside. I turned the frame upside down on the bed, and the picture and glass fell out. I took away the wooden back and saw another panel, with an old sticker on the back, 'Maxfield Parrish Studio.' I picked it up, expecting the print to be underneath. It wasn't. I turned over the board, and there was the image. Maybe they glued the print to the studio board. I looked; I looked closely. I looked at the edges. There was no paper trim. No, they hadn't. I looked at the surface. This was not a print. It was a painting. Parrish had given my grandmother the painting of herself. She had assumed it was a print."

"How could she not know it was a painting?"

"Parrish used his own framer. And his prints were often framed close in like paintings. He must have given it to her framed, and she assumed it was a print. She had said he gave it to her in his studio and there was a stack of prints nearby. We've always assumed it was a print because that's what she told us."

"What did you do?"

"I reassembled it and put it back on the wall. And I didn't tell my grandmother or my mother."

"And today?"

"I thought about the painting, how valuable it was. Circumstances got worse for me. I could not fail. I could not be driven out of New York by a simple lack of money. And my taste was improving. I needed better things.

"I went to New Hampshire where Parrish lived and found a dealer. I told him the print I wanted, and a few months later, he found one and I bought it. It was the print of the painting. I paid two hundred fifty dollars for it. The image had advertising around it, for Fisk Tires, but otherwise the image was the same size as the painting. I trimmed away the margins that included the advertising. I went to a framer and had them glue the print to an antique artist's board. My next trip to Atlanta, I took out the painting and replaced it with the print. It was an incredible match. The Parrish print surfaces are remarkable, exactly like his paintings. I wrapped it in a towel and put it in my suitcase.

"I put it at auction through a lawyer."

"And me?"

"I knew there was a bidder hot for the piece. He was going to leave a maximum bid, but I didn't know what that bid would be until just before the sale. I wasn't going to let him get it for four hundred thousand if I knew he would go to six hundred. Just before the sale, I made sure I glimpsed the auctioneer's cheat sheet, and beside the lot number for the Parrish was written, 600k. So I had you stop bidding at five eighty. There was no bidder on the phone; it was a Sotheby's rep, bidding for the absent client."

I was a beginning art writer, just starting to make my way in New York, and now I was a participant in a newsworthy fraud.

"You will never tell."

"No," I said, "I will never tell."

58.

IF YOU EVER get lost heading for Chelsea, use your X-ray vision to find a truck bearing hundreds of gallons of white paint; it will lead you to where you want to go. White became the default color for modern gallery walls as early as the 1920s, when Bauhaus rigor dictated it. White feigned neutrality, but it was loaded with meaning. It was the severe reaction to Victorian darkness, to the painted walls of Art Nouveau and the elegant wood panels of Art Deco. A painting looked good against it: there was only it to look at.

Even older pictures took on an air of modernity when surrounded with white paint. Chelsea was awash in it, and so were collectors' homes and museums. The only things that didn't look good against it were people. Light was coming from everywhere, windows, ceilings, and walls, illuminating every makeup smear, skin flaw, and case of thinning hair, no matter what efforts were made to disguise them. Collectors' homes, now high-ceilinged, spare, rugless, and chromed, became echo chambers.

The theoretically ideal space for showing pictures was deemed a windowless white cube, an idea that was cumulative rather than birthed, and a gallery called White Cube opened in London in 1993, further solidifying the concept. Frames were dispensed with, as much for reasons of economy as taste.

Lacey's new gallery, drenched in white though not quite a cube, was located on the north side of 22nd Street, between the ultracool 303 Gallery and the architecturally oriented Max Protetch Gallery. Her gallery was flooded with sunlight, and only the gray concrete floors diluted the glare. When Lacey wore yellow, which meant that she was blond from head to toe, she stood out against the bleached walls like the Sun King.

But during the few months it took to relocate, there was a slow desertion of Lacey's friends and acquaintances. Hinton Alberg never visited the gallery because of Cornelia's disapproval of the way Lacey had treated Patrice Claire, whose life went on fine without her, though he still felt shivers at the mention of her name. Pilot Mouse had been collected by celebrities and major dealers and didn't need Chelsea or Lacey. He had delivered on his promise to get her two paintings to sell, but his new girlfriend made sure he stayed away from her. Carey Harden was never given another show and resented her for it, and he spread around the art world a weak, self-serving ill-will toward Lacey and her gallery. Sharon, her formerly impetuous cohort, had gotten married and settled into life with her new baby, and Angela had moved out of state to work as a writer's assistant.

After my breakdown with Tanya Ross, I, too, bore a grudge against Lacey, and it kept me at an angry distance from her. I hoped that Tanya might view my rejection of Lacey, if she ever heard about it, as remorse, and the memory of our romance might settle on top of and obliterate the stink of the nasty event at Sotheby's that had taken place now seven years ago. But I also knew she would always think of me as a crook, something that was beyond her nature to forget.

I had tried to repair my relationship with her, but my calls were not returned, and intermediaries I enlisted did not succeed in even framing a tea time with her. Eventually, I heard she was taking dates with a financier, which made me ill. I wanted to write her a letter explaining that a financier was more likely to engage in misadventure than an art writer, but wisely, I didn't. I could not imagine that Tanya was any less sad than I was; we had both said I love you—something neither of us would have said frivolously. We had moved easily as a couple through the art world waters. I found her attractive; I felt she reflected my own good taste in a mate. But I knew now that I would never reflect her own good taste in a mate, even though the case against Lacey and me was never pursued. I was now cast down with the sleazeball hustlers who inhabit the back alleys of the art world, whom the legitimate folk can smell coming.

I had heard that Agent Parks was a gallery visitor who was allowed inside Lacey's inner sanctum office at odd hours. And it could only be ironic that I had turned down requests to review Lacey's shows in *ARTnews* because of my "integrity."

The missing people in her life, however, were replaced by an influx of new collectors and personalities, raging, competing, socializing. There were dinners and openings, invitations to fund-raisers, and a fluctuating, dynamic mix of people that transformed her impetuous youthful charm into professional adult ease. Lacey poured her profits back into the business, taking out full-page ads in art magazines, funding promotions, delivering guarantees to her hot artists, and financing better-than-average catalogs for her shows. She was living well, if only breaking even, and her gallery, it appeared, was prospering.

59.

IT IS EASY to think that the hot young art stars who were dwarfing prices for old masters at auction were newborn arrivals reaping the rewards of fashion. But most of the celebrated artists only looked like new arrivals. Koons, Hirst, and Gober had all been working since the eighties. Basquiat was achieving sensational prices but at least had the courtesy to be dead. Warhol led the pack, though it was unlikely he would ever have been in a footrace.

Arab money. Asian money. Russian money. The auction houses were seeing most of it, but there was a nice trickle-down from Wall Street collectors, who heard about their clients' investments in art and decided to get in on the action by frequenting Chelsea. Artists flooded Manhattan, then all the boroughs of New York City, and it became inexplicable why one artist would be swept up by a dealer while others of apparently equal talent would be ignored.

But what could be a better mix than action and aesthetics? Everyone was alive. Each auction price was tallied and measured. Art reviews were either neutral or unfathomable. Collectors pretended to care about criticism, and artists pretended not to care about success, making them interlock like Velcro. Fund-raisers tripled, and MoMA, Dia, the Hammer, and the Guggenheim had benefactors lined up to get in. If you think this description is negative, I will remind you and myself of the particular ether that pervaded the contemporary art world's

261

reach: vitality. This secular renaissance, this abundant artistic output, made news. It brought people to the arts, engendered thought, analysis, swagger, winners, and losers, and created a cache of art, whether on display or in storage, that will probably supply the cultural world with aesthetic grist for the next five hundred years.

60.

BARTON TALLEY, in an effort to get a piece of the booming market, made a lighthouse search around the globe for new artists, until his beam finally landed on China. China, whose artistic output for thousands of years relied on a tradition of calligraphy and flat perspective, seemed the unlikeliest place from which to emerge painting that would catch the attention of a western hemisphere art scene where the avant-garde was the norm.

But Chinese art was hot. Yue Minjun, who sold the painting *Execution* in 1995 for five thousand dollars, must have been flattered and frustrated when it sold in 2007 for 5.9 million dollars. The surprise in all this activity was that the Chinese painters were reviving a dormant subject matter: political commentary, which had not piqued collectors' interest for years. The message was, of course, diffused through the intangible glaze of artistic interpretation, making the artists somewhat safe from retribution by glaring Communist overlords.

Barton Talley had asked Lacey several times to accompany him on reconnaissance missions to China to uncover artists who might have star power, but she turned him down, unwilling to leave her gallery even for a week during its crucial early days. She regretted her decisions as she watched even an uptown gallery with a reputation for conservatism have a successful sale of a middling Chinese artist.

Proceeding parallel to the art boom was a real estate boom, inspired by crafty lenders who assured easy profits in home ownership, no money down. These weak paper promises to pay were sold off to investors in every corner of the world, and Wall Street saw a glut of money. Wads of cash fell off the money truck as it trundled through Chelsea, across 49th Street for a stop at Christie's, and onward to Madison Avenue and Sotheby's.

The publicity that convinced broke home owners that they could make nice profits flipping their houses was the same as that which motivated moneyed art collectors to go further into the market than was practical. The lure in art collecting and its financial rewards, not counting for a moment its aesthetic, cultural, and intellectual rewards, is like the trust in paper money: it makes no sense when you really think about it. New artistic images are so vulnerable to opinion that it wouldn't take much more than a whim for a small group of collectors to decide that a contemporary artist was not so wonderful anymore, was *so* last year. In the ebb and flow of artists' desirability, some collectors wondered how a beautiful painting, once it had fallen from favor, could turn ugly so quickly.

Lacey knew the contemporary market did not have the buoyancy of the modern art she had sold at Talley's. Even the lamest Picasso could coax a bid from someone, but work by an unknown artist was valueless until someone decided to buy it. This was rather like doing business from a cloud, but it was the business she was in, and she decided that if she didn't believe in it, neither would her customers. So in 2004, when Talley called her again, asking if she wanted to invest in a batch of pictures straight out of the studio by Feng Zhenj-Jie, a Chinese artist working in Beijing who painted Day-Glo images of glamour girls and was rumored to be sought after by several galleries, she listened.

She would need a million five, said Talley, a sum to be matched by him, to purchase a half-share of thirty paintings at approximately one hundred thousand dollars each. Talley believed that the pictures could be sold for a quarter of a million each, plus or minus depending on size. Lacey didn't really like Feng Zhenj-Jie's work; it seemed to belong to the school of *Playboy* more than anything else. But the images were strong. Talley said, "You can spot a painting by Feng Zhenj-Jie across a room and never quite forget it."

"Is that so good?" asked Lacey. "If you can remember it completely, there's nothing there when you go back."

"Lacey," said Talley, "we're talking about a moment. You buy the moment. There's no way to know if the moment will last. I think the moment is coming for Feng Zhenj-Jie. There's too much momentum. Everybody's talking Chinese."

"Problem," said Lacey. "I don't have a million five. I've got about five hundred thousand, but I operate on it. It's a cash pool I dip into, and it's absolutely necessary. Ever had a client want to sell a painting that you sold them and you have to act like it's the most desirable thing in the world so you give them their money back plus?"

"Of course."

"That's why I need that cash." Lacey declined the offer.

"You shouldn't be afraid of these deals, Lacey, my advice to you."

"Odd, isn't it?" she said. "You sell the conservative paintings and are risky in business, and I sell the risky paintings and I'm conservative in business."

One year later, Feng Zhenj-Jie set an auction record of three hundred fifty thousand dollars. He became an auction regular with consistent prices while Lacey sat by.

She did, however, sell her uptown apartment for a nice profit and buy a loft in SoHo on margin. The new place was better suited to the display of her artists and better suited for the occasional art parties she threw—all promotional and therefore all deductible. Decorative sparseness was a practical aesthetic, requiring less expenditure on furniture and fixtures while still keeping up with the Joneses, whose imagined apartment was also bare.

61.

LACEY WAS NOW THIRTY-FIVE. If her inner light had softened, her ambition had not. But in New York, one's sense of competition had to be practical: there was always someone doing better than you, always. Tanya Ross had acceded to department head, but Lacey still figured she had outdone Tanya simply because her name was in lights. There were rival dealers she couldn't quite topple, like Andrea Rosen and Marianne Boesky—both dealers operating within blocks of her and with nicer galleries. And of course there was Gagosian, who could, it seemed, like a quantum particle, be in two places at once, emerging from the back room of either his uptown or his downtown gallery whenever an important client strolled in. There was no place within Lacey that could properly couch her envy. She just burned up inside and that was that.

Agent Parks became a physical comfort for Lacey; there was evening activity between them that could be categorized as convenient, though there was a humor gap that Lacey could see and he could not. She never took him out to the art parties, and he never wanted to go out to the art parties. After all, he was an investigator of the very people he might meet, and he liked the surreptitiousness that guided their hours together. His business was clandestine encounters; why not have the same in his personal life, too?

He was one year younger than Lacey, with a tight, wiry body that was fun for her to explore. He kept himself in shape as part of his job, though the art world seldom required him to climb over chain-link fences or race along rooftops. Lacey liked to say to him, "Fuck me, Agent Parks," and when it was all over there was no awkward silence, because Agent Parks was not trying to make Lacey his girlfriend. He was not swooning over her, or worrying if he was saying the right thing, or going out of his way to be nice. Out of professional responsibility, he even kept secrets from her that were about people she knew, no matter how much she prodded him. He was a jock with a lust for Lacey and a job situated squarely in the art world, a trifecta of qualities that could never be printed in the personals section of *The New York Review of Books* but was nonetheless desirable in this combination.

In January 2006, Agent Parks went to Lacey's gallery, showed his badge to the receptionist, and asked if Miss Yeager was in. Lacey emerged from her office, and Parks held up a manila envelope. "I'd like to discuss an issue in private with you," he said.

Lacey took him in the office and closed the door. He whispered, "Shhhh." Agent Parks bent her over the desk, made a few clothing adjustments—he left his overcoat on—and quickly inserted himself into her. This visit had happened only a few times in their two-year-long relationship, and what appealed to Lacey about it was that Parks didn't seem to care whether she was in the mood or not. It was just urgent, and he needed it done. With her palms on the desk and her hair grazing its surface, Lacey's eyes were positioned directly over a pile of unopened mail. The pieces tended to move around as she raised and lowered her body on the desk, and one time, as she arched her back slightly, her blouse buttons brushed aside a few envelopes, revealing something unusual in this pile of announcements and bills: a corner of an envelope, handwritten. She used the momentum that was pushing her from behind to shift the envelopes that covered it and read who'd sent it. "Claire," it said, then above it in engraved letters: "The Carlyle Hotel." She grabbed it in her fist, not because of its sender, but because she had to grab on to something when Agent Parks intensified from behind.

She had not heard from Patrice Claire in years. She had heard about him, and no doubt he had heard about her, but there had been no direct communication. She was not curious about this letter. In fact, it bothered her. Inside, she guessed, was something quasi-romantic, something thought-out and carefully written, with probably either a request for an explanation, which she didn't have, or a request to meet, which she knew would be excruciating. Then Agent Parks came inside the condom that was inside Lacey and let her know it by stopping mid-stroke and squeezing her waist with both hands.

On his way out, the receptionist said to him, in complete ignorance, "That was quick. " He smiled, touched the brim of his fedora between his first finger and thumb, and left.

Lacey knew that at some point she would have to open the letter, so she picked it up, along with a few art magazines, and took it home. She dressed to go out, pausing first to vibrate herself in order to release the head of steam that Agent Parks had built up in her. She walked several blocks in a freezing wind before she found a taxi to take her to an artist's studio. She spent a half hour looking at work she instantly knew she hated, but she had to invest the time since she and the artist had a mutual friend.

Back home, she poured herself a glass of white wine and sat at the kitchen table in front of the day's mail from the gallery. Patrice's letter was on top, and she was still loath to read it because she knew that whatever was in it would mean more work for her, another ego to soothe. But with the wineglass on her right, easily grasped, she pared back the flap of the envelope and slid out a solitary card. In Patrice's handwriting, it read, "Dear Lacey, You should know that your Aivazovsky is worth much more than you paid for it, Patrice."

She turned the card over: nothing. She smelled it and wasn't sure if it carried Patrice's aroma. She put it back in the envelope, then took a sip from her glass. She got up from her chair and thought, Where is that painting?

She went to a hall closet, where a dozen framed things, wrapped in cardboard and tied with string, were filed as rejects. She searched through them and finally came across the picture. She had wrapped it for the move and never unwrapped it. She had meant to get to it, to sell it, but it was too much trouble, and she was always so preoccupied. She snipped the twine with scissors, took the picture back to her bedroom, and hung it in place of a small Amy Arras across from her bed. It looked better than she remembered, especially now that it was in a spot that had been professionally lit. Lacey figured it might now be worth double or triple what she had paid for it.

She called the Carlyle and asked for Patrice Claire, even though it was past ten p.m. The operator said, "Just a minute," and a full minute later, she came back on and said, "He's not in, can I take a message?" She left her name, but Patrice never called back.

Unlike the glory and wonder of the Warhol, there was no sentimental attachment to the Aivazovsky, but Lacey still waited a few days before pursuing the sale of the picture. She thought it would be more likely to find an enthusiastic customer in Europe, so she found a house in Sweden, the Stockholms Auktionsverk. She had her gallery photographer come to the loft and photograph the picture, then she e-mailed the image and information about where she got it—Patrice Claire's name gave it good provenance—and waited.

The picture hung in its spot across from the bed, in limbo, an ugly puppy about to be sold. But one night Agent Parks (she just couldn't call him Bob), after a wrestling bout in the clean linens of her bed, observed the picture. "What's that?" he said. "That's new, right?"

"Not really, it was put away."

"What is it?"

"It's Russian. Nineteenth century. Artist's name unpronounceable."

He walked up to it. "He's painting like Rembrandt. You know the one that was stolen? *The Storm on the Sea of Galilee*? With the ship? This has the same surface."

"You know the surface of the Rembrandt?"

"Yeah. I've seen so many photos, transparencies. Plus I saw it, quickly, in a locker at the train station. It was a bargaining chip, but I couldn't tell if it was the real thing. They called the wrong dude. They thought I was a reporter. They wanted to give the pictures back in trade for no prosecution. But how can the government agree to that? They can't say it's fine to steal a bunch of pictures as long as they are returned. Then the Rembrandt went underground again. Too bad. I've begun to feel for those pictures.

"The Rembrandt *Galilee* has a layer of varnish over it," he continued, "like you're looking at it through amber, but I don't think it's the varnish that gives you that feeling. It's somehow in the paint. This has it, too." He moved in close to the picture, moving his head from side to side to avoid the shadows from the overhead spotlight.

"You know about varnish?"

"Yeah. I had a quickie course when I started in this department."

"Who teaches art courses at the FBI?"

"We had someone from Sotheby's. Ross somebody?"

"Tanya?"

"Miss Ross, is all I know."

"So you didn't fuck her."

"How do you figure that?"

"Well, you called her Miss Ross."

"You call me Agent Parks. But no, I didn't. I didn't even think about it. Not my type, I guess. Too sane." He smiled at her.

"I'm selling it," she said.

"Really? I like it."

"Tell me why you like it."

"Well, it's pretty. Kind of lonely looking. And it's symbolic, don't you think?"

"Symbolic?"

"That's where something in the picture stands for something else. Like truth or something."

"Thank you. So what's symbolic about it?"

"Remember, this is not my best subject."

"I'll remember."

"Well, the water, to me, represents the earth and all the things that happen on the earth, reality. And the moonlight represents our dreams and our minds."

"And..."

"And the reflection...well, I guess the reflection represents art. It's what lies between our dreams and reality."

62.

THE NEXT DAY, Lacey received an e-mail from the Stockholms Auktionsverk saying they could give an estimate on the picture at somewhere between one hundred fifty thousand and two hundred fifty thousand dollars, and that the wide range could be adjusted after they saw the picture.

None of Lacey's huge returns in the art market had been based on wise investing: one had been bought to show off, one was bought out of her surprising response to it, and a third was essentially stolen. But in an exploding market, it was hard to make a mistake. The Russians had come in the way they came into Poland, and while raiding the modern masters, paying huge sums for Lucian Freud and Francis Bacon, they eventually looked to their own nineteenth-century artists, whose prices rose with every fall of the gavel. Aivazovsky was one of the three or four nineteenth-century Russian artists who qualified as collectable. Except for one gigantic spike for the rarest bird of all, Kazimir Malevich, who sold at sixty million dollars, the Russians' own great modern movements of suprematism and constructivism attracted little attention because the market was flooded with homegrown fakes.

Too late for the fall sales, the Aivazovsky would be sold in the spring of 2007, almost eight months away. Lacey called the art movers, and the work was sent off to Sweden.

Ben and Belinda Boggs continued to befriend Lacey, which she sometimes viewed as her punishment for leaving Barton Talley, for moving downtown, for opening a gallery, for having ambition. They also bought pictures from her and gave her pictures to sell. There was a monthly train ride to Connecticut for an art dinner at their home, with guests numbering about forty. Dinner was inevitably accompanied by tours of the house, gallery, and sculpture garden, which she had memorized, and each repetitive tour was excruciating. She was running out of things to say, and she did not, absolutely did not, want to climb the stairs one more time and see their horse photos. The only light for her was the occasional presence of Barton Talley himself, who was often her dinner partner. Whenever Belinda started a soliloquy, Lacey would turn to him with a neutral stare that was code for an expression of disgust.

At one of these dinners, Belinda started in: "Oh, oh, stop me if I told you this. We were hosting a big gala event and we were showing our collection and we had the Beuys felt suit...well, Ben had a new tuxedo..."

Lacey turned to Talley with the blank stare and he gave the blank stare back. But this time, Lacey whispered, "Can we stop her with a gun?" and Talley snickered. Fortunately, there were ten seats between them and the hostess.

Belinda went on, soon to be interrupted by Ben: "Honey, you left out the part..." Finally, Talley turned to Lacey.

"Lacey, you know the artist Hon See?"

"Yet another Chinese," said Lacey. "The one who does large paintings of news stories."

"Yes, up-and-coming. Another opportunity. A collector in Singapore has thirty works. We could buy all of them and dole them out, a few yearly. An annuity."

Lacey remembered the missed opportunity with Feng Zhenj-Jie and viewed Talley as a dealer who never made mistakes. "Oh God, Barton,

I just can't do it. I'm in the same situation. I exist on the cash I have. How much do I need?"

"A million should do it. I'm putting in a million, and Stephen Bravo's putting in a million."

The difference between Bravo and Talley putting in a million and her putting in a million was that her cash was all she had and theirs was tip money.

"I can't. I just can't."

"...we steamed the suit and gave it to a gallery in Tulsa," said Belinda, eliciting courteous smiles from those who had heard the story before, which was nearly everybody.

After dinner, valet parkers pulled cars around, and Talley offered her a ride back to the city, liberating her from returning in the minivan that had ferried her and a few of the other lesser lights to the dinner.

In the car, Talley and Lacey reminisced. "You've done well, Lacey."

"The truth is, I've done just well enough," she said.

"It's a tough business."

"I miss the old pictures. Picasso drawings. Klees. Remember that small Corot landscape you had? So beautiful."

"Sold to the Met," he said.

"Thank you for hiring me."

"You were an asset."

"I might not have come to you highly recommended."

"You mean because of the Sotheby's thing?"

"What did they tell you?"

"Not much. They said you were bright and fast. And that there might have been a bidding issue, but they didn't know. Just that they had to let you go."

"That's what they said?"

"Yes. Was there a bidding issue?"

"I helped a friend."

"Was the friend you helped yourself?"

Lacey didn't answer, but Talley didn't care. He went on:

"When you start in the art business, you can see that there are ways to illegitimately cut corners. And because you're so desperate to make a sale, you do. Then you come to a crossroads and you decide the type of dealer you're going to be. I cut a few corners early on, then I realized being straightforward was so much easier. So whatever you did, I hope you moved on."

"That's what I learned from you," said Lacey, "and yes, I moved on."

There was silence in the car for several miles. Then:

"And oh, remember that FBI guy?" said Lacey. "On the Gardner thing you got me into?"

"I think so."

"I'm dating him."

"You never throw anything away, do you, Lacey?"

"All the time," she said.

63.

IT WAS FIVE PM one April day in 2007, and Lacey was sitting at her desk, fretting that she could not, or best not, participate in Talley's Hon See deal, worrying that the outlay could put her in jeopardy, and hating that she had to miss this big league opportunity that would put her in Talley and Bravo's world. Then the phone rang. It was Stockholms Auktionverks calling, the voice said.

"Is this Miss Yeager?" The accent was difficult and the connection worse.

"Yes."

"We have your auction results for today's sale. Lot 363, the Aivazovsky, sold for five million ten thousand Swedish kronor."

Her heart leapt when she heard "five million," but then she came to her senses.

"How much is a krona?"

"How much is a krona?" the voice responded.

"How much is a krona in dollars?"

"Ah, I see. Let me calculate that for you." And then: "That would be approximately seven hundred thousand U.S. dollars."

Lacey hung up the phone and thought that there were still a few surprises left in the art market: with the sale of one painting, she had paid for her entire gallery and its inventory. She called Barton Talley's cell and caught him in an elevator.

"Is the Hon See deal still open?"

"I'm meeting with Stephen Bravo now, to finalize."

"Is it still open?"

"We bought part of it, but we could buy the whole thing if you want in."

"Let's take the whole thing."

"Can you be at Bravo's at six? This will take some rejiggering."

"I'll be there."

Lacey didn't let Bravo's private elevator or the three hundred feet of art reference library in his Manhattan office intimidate her. She entered as Talley was listening to the Los Angeles art dealer on the phone. Bravo signaled her to sit down.

"We'll confirm it tomorrow," he said. "Yes, it's a done deal, but we'll confirm it tomorrow...How much more done could it be? Because we've got a third party and we've got to talk at least once. It's not done, but it's done."

Where would the pictures go? Half stored at Bravo's and half at Talley's gallery. They would wait until the fall 2007 auctions were over: there was a sensational Hon See coming up that would likely set a record, since everything was setting records. It was decided that the show would be split between Talley, uptown, and Lacey, downtown. This hadn't often been done before and would indicate that Hon See was a master in either milieu. Stephen Bravo would sell the pictures to select clients out of his back room in Los Angeles. The first show, they decided, would open in late September 2008, perfect for the fall gallery openings and in plenty of time to massage the market into a Hon See frame of mind.

64.

LACEY'S BUSINESS CONTINUED strong through 2007 and 2008, strong enough that she did not wish she could dip into her now invested, and therefore impossible to retrieve, backup fund. The fall sale saw a Hon See bring one hundred fifty thousand, and in the spring of 2008, a Hon See again brought one hundred thirty thousand dollars. Though it was less than the previous season, the price was solid, making the pictures worth at least what had been paid for them.

During the summer, Lacey prepared for her opening show, now set for September 18. She had tiny reproductions of the Hon See pictures made and paid an architecture student to render a two-foot-square model of her gallery. She could move the small images around and design the best layout for the show. Some of the pictures were floor to ceiling, while the smallest was thirty-six inches square, and Lacey thought the show was going to look handsome.

She ordered champagne and sent out pre-invitations saying, "Save the date," followed up by a formal and more exquisite foldout that made the night seem extraordinarily special. Talley did the same, and both their addresses were on the invitation, a coup for Lacey, as she was now linked with one of the most prestigious galleries in Manhattan. Ben and Belinda were invited, of course, and had accepted. Hundreds of others, too, had told Lacey they were going to both openings, uptown and down, and the evening, intended to flush art sales from the distant bushes, was turning into a soiree. Already there were holds on three pictures, at two hundred fifty per, minus a ten percent courtesy discount, and with two holds at Talley's end, she was at least one-third out of her investment.

On the Sunday before the opening, Lacey celebrated with Angela and Sharon, both of whom were coincidentally in Manhattan for the weekend. For this rare girls' night out, she bought dinner, and they seemed happy for her. Sharon, continuing on with a decent man and pregnant with a second baby, and Angela, who was accompanying her famous writer boss on a promotional tour, seemed happy with their lives far away from Manhattan. Lacey went to bed that night with visions of sugar plums dancing in her head.

Monday morning would be a day spent adjusting the show, sprucing up the gallery, and doing touch-ups on the shoe-level scrapes that had inevitably bruised the white walls. The gallery would be officially closed until opening night, and Lacey knew there would be urgent calls made by collectors trying to get an early peek. Monday noon she called Talley, but he was unavailable. "Have him call me," she said. By two there was no call back, so she called again. This time he took the call, but breathlessly.

"Have you been watching the stock market?" he asked.

"I hate the stock market. Why would I watch it?"

"It's down over five hundred points. Lehman Brothers is bankrupt, Merrill Lynch is sold, and AIG is bankrupt."

Lacey didn't quite know what all this meant, but Talley's voice was shaking.

"They're already calling it Black Monday," he said.

The next day, Tuesday, the stock market just quivered, but on Wednesday it fell four hundred fifty points. Investors, meaning not just high-end Wall Street pros but every civilian with a few thousand dollars, pulled their money and bought T-bills and T-bonds, and they certainly didn't buy art. There was no credit, which the U.S. mainstream had relied on for at least thirty years. Only the credit card system was still operating, and with usurious interest rates, those companies had little to worry about. Several were taking three percent of every purchase and eighteen percent on every unpaid debt.

Thursday, the day of Lacey's opening, the stock market gained a bit, and she called Barton Talley.

"Up today," she said.

"Lacey, still not good."

"But it's up."

"Even a dead cat bounces."

Opening night, Lacey swung open her doors to a few students. The only thing missing in Chelsea was tumbleweeds. There were a few stragglers, who looked like scavengers prowling for bodies from which to pluck watches and gold teeth after the big shoot-out.

By eight p.m., Lacey's receptionist was afraid to look at her. Talley called, reporting that there were a few people there, but all they talked about was the collapse. "Lacey," he said, "I've never heard anyone talk about global financial disaster and then say, 'I'll take it.'"

"But there's a market," Lacey insisted. "What about the last Hon See that sold at auction? Just four months ago."

"We bought it. Bravo and I bought to keep the prices up. We were the only bidders."

The last Monday in September, the Dow fell seven hundred seventy-eight points and continued its slide through the week.

Overnight, the Arabs, the Russians, and the Asians left the art market. The holds on the Hon Sees were released, with, "Sorry, can't do it right now," and, "I'm going to wait and see." Lacey's show hung for another month to cobweb silence.

Art as an aesthetic principle was supported by thousands of years of discernment and psychic rewards, but art as a commodity was held up by air. The loss of confidence that affected banks and financial instruments was now affecting cherubs, cupids, and flattened popes. The objects hadn't changed: what was there before was there after. But a vacancy was created when the clamoring crowds deserted and retrenched.

Art magazines and auction catalogs thinned. Darwinism swept through Chelsea, killing off a few species, and only the ones with the long necks that could reach the leaves at the tops of the trees survived. There was still some business, but not for Lacey, and negotiations got tougher and tougher up and down the street as collectors, even the ones unaffected, wanted bargains. Lacey was willing to give bargains, but no one wanted what she had to offer.

She needed an influx of buoyant money, but in her heart, she didn't know if it would be wise to keep the gallery afloat. She might just be incurring more debt by delaying the inevitable. She called Barton Talley. He could meet her at his gallery later that day.

The taxi ride uptown turned into a coincidental Grand Tour of her life in the art world: through Chelsea, past Christie's, and up Madison where all the galleries hid. Upon arriving at Talley's, Lacey pushed the doorbell as she had so long ago. It clicked and she muscled it open. She threw her weight against the inner door when there was a second click, and she saw Donna, older, shopworn, still feigning efficiency, with her thumb pressing on the door buzzer long after Lacey had entered the gallery.

"Hi, Lacey. Can I offer you something to drink?"

"Is there any poison?" said Lacey.

"Sorry?"

"I'm here to see Barton."

"I'll see if he's in."

Then she heard Donna say over the phone, "Are you in for Lacey Yeager?"

Donna looked up at Lacey and said, "Go on up."

The nostalgia continued for Lacey as she recalled her initial ascent of these stairs almost a dozen years ago, where she had encountered Agent Parks, now her boyfriend. She recalled her accidental peek at the Vermeer copy at the wrong end of the hall, and her first entrance into Talley's expert world. Her time in this gallery was the best of it, she thought, and as she walked down the hall, she recalled her footsteps years ago when she headed excitedly toward the window to look for Patrice Claire. Her memory couldn't quite trace what had led to this now funereal march to Talley's office; she just knew she had come, and gone, a long way.

"In here, Lacey," she heard Talley say.

She entered the office. "Well," she said, "I've come full circle."

"I've been through troughs before. They keep the boom times from looking like a Ponzi scheme. You want a drink?"

She said yes, and Talley poured.

"Lacey, I've seen a lot of beginners in the art business. You were the smartest one of all of them. You seemed to know things before you knew them."

"I just paid attention."

"Are you looking for investors?"

"What for? The fever is over, and without the fever..."

"What about dealing privately? No rent, except your apartment. You develop clients who trust you," said Talley.

"I've still got a gallery. I can work harder."

"Can you?"

"No, actually, I can't."

"So why'd you make the trip up here?"

"Oh, I suppose to say thank you, now that I've had a cocktail."

"I liked you, Lacey. You were always fascinating to me. And you brought in a lot of clients. Especially single ones." Talley laughed.

"And some married ones," Lacey said. "But, I'm looking you in the eye and saying thank you."

"It was fun. Fun and business. What's better?"

"I guess I got more out of it than you."

"In what way?"

"I had sex, fun, and business."

Talley laughed again. "Well, maybe I had a little of that, too."

"What's on the walls?" asked Lacey.

"We're low. Nobody wants to sell in down times. We've got a few things," Talley indicated the few drawings on the office wall. Then he pointed behind her. "What do you think of that?"

Lacey turned in her chair and saw against the velvet easel a painting in a gilded frame, overframed, in fact, for its diminutive size. There was a jab of recognition for this old friend in spiffy new duds. It was her grandmother's Maxfield Parrish.

"It was traded by some collectors to another dealer, and I got it in trade. It's a gem, don't you think? The condition is flawless, like it has been under glass."

Lacey got up and walked over to it. It was indeed a gem. She wondered if Talley was feeling her out, but he seemed innocent and she was content to believe he was.

"It is a gem," she agreed.

"The picture's right," said Talley, meaning that it was a genuine Parrish, "but we have provenance issues. We can trace it back to Sotheby's and there's a block. Can't trace it back to the artist. Doesn't really matter. It's real."

"Yes," said Lacey, "it's real."

"You know Parrish's work?"

Lacey turned toward him, taking a sip of her drink. "The girl in the picture. That's my grandmother."

"What?"

His disbelief assured Lacey that this was a coincidence and that Talley was not on FBI detail. "Kitty Owen, that's her, was my grandmother."

"My God. Well, there is a resemblance in the face."

"And ass, just so you know," said Lacey.

"Well, how lucky for you," he said with a smile.

Lacey stared at the picture, got lost in it, in fact.

Talley broke the spell. "They want a million six for it. Won't get it now. But it is a top Parrish."

"Well, let me know who ends up with it. Maybe one day I could buy it back."

"Back?"

"Buy it. Just buy it," she said.

65.

HER CASH POOL DRAINED, Lacey held on through the new year, finally accepting that her lease was worth more than her gallery and its inventory. In June 2009, she sold it at a loss to a restaurateur. The Hon Sees were sold to a speculator for nine hundred thousand dollars, less than one-third the cost, returning three hundred thousand of her million-dollar investment, which she used to the pay the capital gains tax on the Aivazovsky, which she had forgotten about. Her loft was destined for foreclosure.

Months earlier, on the drive home from Connecticut when she confirmed her misstep to Barton Talley, she didn't realize that, as discreet as he was, he still saw Cherry Finch and that pillow talk had leaked the confirmation of Lacey's grift to her, and thus to the world. The moment was so slight that even Talley didn't understand that he had passed along the information. When Lacey announced that she would become an "art adviser," working from home and taking ten percent from every sale advised, this little negative, that she was a bit of a crook, was made clear to clients by her rivals, even if they were crooks themselves.

Ben and Belinda Boggs were among the first to recoil from Lacey, sensing that she was an outcast. They also rehung their entire art collection, placing into deep storage objects that the new, dismal market shouted they had overpaid for, and pulling out more classic objects, including the Beuys felt suit, bought when prices were sensible. They hoped this would peg them as astute collectors.

Lacey's larger secret, that the auctioned Parrish had been purloined from her own grandmother, remained secret, and Lacey remained curiously, disturbingly, guilt-free.

66.

NOT MANY ART world denizens wanted to talk to me after the crash, fearing journalists, fearing would-be novelists, fearing parody and revenge for the free-spending years. I had drinks with Lacey once before I lost contact with her, and I told her of my intent to write this book. I offered to change her name. "How about Alison Ames?" I said.

"If I had to hear the name Alison Ames in my head for three hundred pages, I'd go insane," she said.

"It won't be all flattering," I said.

"I'm not trying to be a good little girl," she said.

Lacey seemed not to care that her life might be mirrored in a book, that she might not be portrayed as a heroine, and that art world readers would certainly deduce that it was about her. She seemed to have the attitude that of course she would be the subject of a book.

"My mother is ill, so I'm going back to Atlanta for a while."

"I'm sorry."

"*You're* sorry? She's so nuts about Jesus that I can hardly speak to her."

This was the mother whom Lacey had maneuvered out of six hundred thousand dollars that was presumably hers.

"Lacey," I said, "you're going to have to do something in Atlanta besides caretake."

"Elton John is disposing of some of his photography collection and I've been asked to help, so I can do two things at once. Help Mom.

Help Elton. And the High Museum there is good; I bet I can worm my way in somehow." On the word *worm*, she twisted her baby finger through the air, but it seemed a tired gesture.

"How'd you get into the Elton John situation?"

"I don't know. They called, saying someone recommended me."

I wondered who that might be, perhaps a sympathetic Barton Talley.

"Are you seeing anyone?" I asked.

"I'm seeing a guy who's got me figured out. He never says I love you."

"That's good?"

"I love him for it."

"Will he go with you to Atlanta?"

"He travels, he's FBI."

"FBI?"

"What did I say?" she said.

"Do you think it will last?"

"Daniel, there's no way it's going to last." Then she paused, staring at me. "Goddamn it, the art world ran out on me."

"You're still in the art world even if you're in Atlanta," I said.

"Paris doesn't qualify as being in the art world, why should Atlanta? I know I'm in purgatory." She sipped her coffee. "I'm going to take the Parrish print back to my mother. She says she'd like to see it."

It wasn't clear to me whether Lacey remembered that while under the influence she had told me about her larceny.

Lacey looked around the walls of the restaurant. "God, I've seen thousands of paintings. High and low. Remember the Avery I told you about? I'd like to see it again. It's like a first love; it might be nice to say hello."

Her energy seemed drained, but I knew it was not a permanent state. She even laughed a bit, saying, "Damn it, why didn't I try to seduce Rauschenberg? He might have given me a silk screen."

"Rauschenberg was gay and near death," I said.

"You don't know my powers," she said.

67.

ART WAS STILL ART whether it was tied to money or not. People continued to attend art fairs, museums, galleries. They thought about it, they chatted about it, they pontificated about it, but the financial race over it had stalled. Most art enthusiasts who resided outside of New York or Los Angeles didn't know or care about the market's collapse. The collectors stood back and tried to remember how to love art the old-fashioned way, and the dealers developed strategies—that finally included discounts—on how to survive the trough. A Pilot Mouse work died at auction. He was a symbol of the bubble, and the bubble had burst.

New York City's Armory Show of 2009 was just barely breathing, and collectors who asked prices always feigned disbelief and shock, trying to indicate lower, lower. There was acting on both sides, with the dealers citing sales and European notice, real or not. Two giant hangars housed the works for sale, connected by a membrane of jerry-built steel stairs, which allowed only ten people on at a time, for fear of another kind of art world collapse. The Modernist galleries were on one side and everything else on the other. Gold frames to the left; no frames to the right. The Nathansons would peer at a Miró gouache, then time-travel—to next door—and be puzzled by the extreme art of the present month.

As a writer—though one now fearing at all times for my reputation—I covered this waterfront, also attending the Miami Basel art fair in the fall. This fair was always a big draw, recession or not, and the gallerygoers included the sandals-and-T-shirt crowd out for an afternoon of eyeballing. I did not see Hinton Alberg there, and the usual party festivities were thinned out. I did see Patrice Claire, affectionate with a woman in her late forties who had streaks of gray in her black hair, and overheard them speaking French. I caught them at the drinks bar and introduced myself, reminding him that we had met before with Lacey Yeager and that I was a writer for *ARTnews*. Would he allow me to interview him, I asked, just to get his take on the fair?

No, he didn't want to comment; forgive him, he said. He was, characteristically, friendly toward me.

"How is Lacey?" he asked.

"Well, she closed her gallery in June, and she's moved to Atlanta."

"I think I heard that," he said.

"Too bad for her," I said. "I can't think of a personality less suited to becoming marginalized."

Patrice drank a sip of afternoon champagne and turned toward the woman with him, speaking as he turned his head back to me, which meant he was addressing the air: "I think Lacey is the kind of person who will always be okay."

68.

TWO MONTHS LATER, my article about Miami was published in *ARTnews*, and I received this handwritten card:

Dear Daniel,

It was so lovely to finally read an essay about art that did not mention money. Congratulations on a refreshing take on things, and I hope you're doing well.

Tanya Ross

I could not tell if this was exactly what it was or something more. I wrote her back a handwritten card saying that it was nice to hear from her and that I had been working on a book, and if she had the time, I would love to get her comments. I couched the request as a favor, saying I could use her expertise to root out factual errors I might have made describing the workings of Sotheby's and, of course, wanting her general reaction. She responded yes and sent me an address, which was the same as when I was seeing her. Which made me have hope that she was still living alone.

My real wish, of course, is to have her read this story and understand that my small crime is now the stuff of novels—which I'm hoping might ameliorate it—and to make it clear that my loss of her is the most damage that has been done in my eighteen years of knowing

Lacey. If her response is not the one hoped for, I have thought of converting the book to nonfiction—which they tell me sells better—and leaving Lacey's name unchanged. But I'm not sure if that would ruin her or make her famous. I will determine which to do at a later point.

I sent Tanya the manuscript, but I have not yet heard from her.

PHOTO CREDITS AND COPYRIGHTS

Page 14. *La Mondaine,* by James Tissot. Photo: Snark/Art Resource, NY.

Page 18. *Daybreak,* by Maxfield Parrish: Copyright © Maxfield Parrish. Licensed by ASaP Worldwide and VAGA, New York, NY. Photo: Christie's Images/The Bridgeman Art Library.

Page 23. *Nude Bathers,* by Milton Avery: Copyright © 2010 Milton Avery Trust /Artists Rights Society (ARS), New York. Photo: Bethany Rouslin.

Page 42. *Mug, Pipe and Book,* by John Frederick Peto. Photo: SuperStock.

Page 43. *Herald,* by William Michael Harnett. Photo: SuperStock.

Page 52. *Watson and the Shark,* by John Singleton Copley. Image courtesy National Gallery of Art, Washington.

Page 54. *Woman I,* by Willem de Kooning: Copyright © 2010 The Willem de Kooning Foundation/Artists Rights Society (ARS), New York. Photo: Copyright © The Museum of Modern Art/Licensed by SCALA/Art Resource, NY.

Page 56. *Los Angeles County Museum on Fire,* by Ed Ruscha: Copyright © Ed Ruscha. Courtesy Gagosian Gallery, New York.

Page 65. *November in Greenland,* by Rockwell Kent appears courtesy of the Plattsburgh State Art Museum, State University of New York, Rockwell Kent Collection. Bequest of Sally Kent Gorton. Photo: Pushkin Museum, Moscow, Russia/The Bridgeman Art Library International.

Page 86. *The Bay of Naples by Moonlight,* by Ivan Aivazovsky: Copyright © Anatoly Sapronenkov/SuperStock.

Page 97. *Still Life with Wine Bottles,* by Giorgio Morandi: Copyright © 2010 Artists Rights Society (ARS), New York/SIAE, Rome. Photo: Gagosian Gallery.

Page 101. *Flowers,* by Andy Warhol: Copyright © 2010 The Andy Warhol Foundation for the Visual Arts, Inc./Artists Rights Society (ARS), New York. Photo: The Andy Warhol Foundation, Inc./Art.

Page 114. *Untitled,* by Tom Friedman. Art and photo are copyright © Tom Friedman. Courtesy Gagosian Gallery.

Page 126. *El Jaleo,* by John Singer Sargent: Copyright © Isabella Stewart Gardner Museum, Boston, MA, USA/The Bridgeman Art Library International.

Page 148. *Woman with Pears,* by Pablo Picasso: Copyright © 2010 Estate of Pablo Picasso/Artists Rights Society (ARS), New York. Photo: Copyright © The Museum of Modern Art/Licensed by SCALA/Art Resource, NY.

Page 149. *Marilyn,* by Andy Warhol: Copyright © 2010 The Andy Warhol Foundation for the Visual Arts, Inc./Artists Rights Society (ARS), New York. Photo: The Andy Warhol Foundation, Inc./Art Resource, NY.

Page 163. *Three Parts of an X,* by Robert Gober. Art and photo are copyright © Robert Gober. Courtesy Matthew Marks Gallery, New York.

Page 166. *Initiation,* by Wilfredo Lam: Copyright © 2010 Artists Rights Society (ARS), New York/ADAGP, Paris. Photo: CNAC/MNAM/ Dist. Réunion des Musées Nationaux/Art Resource, NY.

Page 182. *La Nona Ora,* by Maurizio Cattelan. Courtesy of the artist and Marian Goodman Gallery, New York.

Page 222. *Betwixt the Torus and the Sphere,* by Richard Serra: Copyright © 2010 Richard Serra/Artists Rights Society (ARS), New

York. Photo: Copyright © Richard Serra. Courtesy Gagosian Gallery. Photo by Robert Mckeever.

Page 227. *Felt Suit,* by Joseph Beuys: Copyright © 2010 Artists Rights Society (ARS), New York/VG Bild-Kunst, Bonn. Photo: Tate, London/Art Resource, NY.

Page 234. *Eine Kleine Nachtmusik,* by Dorothea Tanning: Copyright © 2010 Artists Rights Society (ARS), New York/ADAGP. Photo: Tate, London/Art Resource, NY.

All photos of artwork are used by permission.